THROUGH THE EYES OF DARKNESS

ALEXA BOURNE

❦

Decadent Publishing Company
www.decadentpublishing.com

THROUGH THE EYES OF DARKNESS
Copyright 2013 by Alexa Bourne
ISBN: 978-1-61333-456-0
Cover design by Mina Carter and Cribley Designs

Published by Decadent Publishing Company
www.decadentpublishing.com

Printed in the United States of America

"What the Critics are Saying..."

Her Highland Champion

"This is a delightfully charming novel, full of adventure and romance. The characters are deeply developed, and easily readable and understandable. The story flows exceedingly well, and could very easily be a much longer novel. This was a truly enchanting story."
~Night Owl Reviews (www.nightowlreviews.com)

"I knew this was romantic suspense, but I didn't expect the romance to be so . . . hot! If you love Highland Warrior heroes, Alexa Bourne has brought one right into the twenty-first century for us. He's a keeper, ladies - sexy brogue and all." ~Irene Preston, author of *Infamous*

"I wanted something light to read while I was feeling sick. This was perfect. I liked this romantic suspense because the heroine was likable and the hero was sighworthy."
~Colette, A Buckeye Girl Reads Blog
(www.lovesromances.blogspot.com)

Fractured Paradise

"This is a highly sensual, fast-paced romantic suspense with a craggy, grieving hero and a determined yet guilt-ridden heroine. Together, in both wanting and striving for a cottage on small Northumbrian island, they discover love, passion and the strength to move on. Aidan is just the kind of man I would like to spend time with in a cottage on an island! An inspiring, romantic read."
~Lindsay Townsend, historical romance author

"*What a great book! From the beginning, I was hooked... Ms. Bourne's vivid descriptions take me thousands of miles away. Rachel is smart, caring and real. And Aidan... Oh, Aidan! Hot, sweet, strong. And the man has that sexy accent! I swear sometimes I could almost hear him, but I'm sure that's just me :) Yes, I got really involved. I'll definitely be reading more from this author. Well done!*"
~Carmen Falcone, author of *A Vengeful Affair*

"*I absolutely loved this novella! The tight knit community of Sunderland gives the reader an intimate feel for the town, and its residents. Though Rachel was an outsider, despite having childhood ties to the area the townspeople seemed to embrace her presence from the beginning. Well, not everyone! That is where Ms. Bourne cast the line and I was hooked!!...I loved everything about this read!!...The conclusion of this story was wonderful, and I literally had an "Awww" moment when I finished! If you're looking for a quick romantic read that keeps you on the edge of you seat, you'll love Fractured Paradise!!!*" ~Angela Rose, Satin Sheets Romance (www.satinsheetsromance.blogspot.com)

"*A good novella is the equivalent of haute cuisine-fantastic quality that leaves you satisfied yet wanting more. That is how I would describe Fractured Paradise- a well written story, with believable characters that I wanted to get to know even better... The language Alexa Bourne uses is rich and sensual, creating realistic scenes of love and lust, which only added to the story....But Fractured Paradise is not solely a love story but a suspense, which entraps the reader into devouring the whole story in one sitting as I did. My only disappointment was that it finished all too quickly. A very enjoyable read.*"
~Laurey Buckland, author of *A Girl's Guide to Fairy Tales*

Simple Treasures

"*I loved the look Simple Treasures gave us of the Hogmanay celebration and the culture and history of Edinburgh. And I can see definite possibilities for continuing stories revolving around the IPN. I loved Rachel at the home office and...I also loved the fact that the "home office" seemed to be run by woman, a really great switch on a typically male field.*

Simple Treasures also kept the suspense level high, with some interesting twists and unexpected turns. The new Honor Guard Line from Decadent Publishing shows a lot of promise and I look forward to reading more in this series."
~Tamara Hoffa, Sizzling Hot Book Reviews
(www.sizzlinghotbooks.net)

Her Highland Champion

Chapter One

*M*alcolm Fraser's feet pounded against the hard-packed dirt footpath along Loch Finnan. He'd come home to his remote Highland village to clear his head, plan his future. So far nothing had been decided, and the demons chasing him nipped at his heels no matter how fast he moved.

Midday sunlight, a rarity these late September days, reflected off the water. The wind whipped the grass and leaves. The cool air burned inside his lungs and his muscles ached, but he welcomed the discomfort.

He knew his daily activity wouldn't solve his problems, but he could at least push the horrid memories of his last International Protective Network assignment from his mind for a while. Indeed, running had become the only way to hold the guilt at bay. Saving the world was too much of a burden for a man who couldn't trust his instincts. And if he couldn't trust his instincts, he had no business trying to protect anyone.

In the distance, tourists roamed the ruins of Castle Callagham. Malcolm ducked under a wall of trees and descended toward the shore. The path would be more challenging down there, with rough rocks, long grass, and soft sand, but it would be worth it to avoid conversation.

A few feet away, water slurped against the shore in an uneven rhythm. A couple of *meters* away, he corrected himself. He'd spent too much time in America. Up near the stone bridge someone had lost a shoe and a sweater. Why couldn't people pick up their own rubbish?

Malcolm slowed, his breaths coming hard and heavy.

The shoe was attached to a leg. He squinted into the sun and moved closer. The cuff of blue jeans swayed with the waves. He moved closer still and assessed the scene. Long curly hair, jeans, curves. Movement?

"What the devil?" He closed the distance between them, crouched down, and touched the woman's neck. A faint heartbeat pulsed against his fingertips.

He dropped to his knees. Her skin was cold to the touch. How the devil had she survived this long? As gently as he could, he rolled her to her back and set her arms down by her sides. When he leaned down with his ear to her mouth, no breath stirred against his cheek. Straight away he shoved the mass of dark, wet hair away from her face, pressed his lips to hers, and pushed oxygen into her lungs.

Nothing happened.

"Come on." Again he forced air into her body. "You'll not do this to me." Again he breathed into her mouth.

Her body jerked. Water gushed out of her mouth, and she began coughing. Malcolm's shoulders relaxed, and he sighed as he helped her to sit up.

The woman blinked rapidly and struggled to focus. When the coughing subsided, her big, brown eyes settled on him and then flew wide.

"You're all right."

She shoved against his hands. "No!" Her heels splashed in the loch's edge and dug into the sand.

Malcolm grabbed both her wrists in one hand. "Calm yourself, lass. I'll not hurt you."

Her lips trembled. From a chill or fear, he couldn't be sure. Probably a bit of both.

He raised his hand toward her forehead, and she flinched. "It's all right. Can you tell me your name?" He brushed mud from her brow. But some of it wasn't mud. Bruises had formed near her temple and along one cheek.

His innards clenched. Had she gotten the bruises from falling off the bridge or had someone hurt her? Too many years with IPN made him suspicious of everything. "Your name, lass?"

She stared blankly at him, still shivering and clutching the sleeves of his sweatshirt.

Her clothes were soaked through, her lips a troubling shade of blue. She had to have been out here for hours.

"It's all right. We'll get you some help in a bit." Malcolm pulled her against him, yanked his mobile phone from the pocket of his sweatpants, and dialed 999. "I need an ambulance near the old bridge by Castle Callagham. There's a woman...." *In my arms.* "She's been in the water, and she's in danger of hypothermia."

She leaned back against him and closed her eyes.

With his mouth near her ear, he pleaded, "Stay with me, lass. Help is on the way. Keep those beautiful eyes open." And they were beautiful, too, framed by faint bruises he couldn't swipe away.

He should have made an anonymous call to the police and kept to his run. And yet here he was, dragged into a situation thanks to one haunted look.

No, this was only a Good Samaritan deed. Once he gave his statement to the police, he'd walk away. She deserved competent help, not him.

ᗅ

The smell of lemon-scented antiseptic was the first indication she was still alive. That, and the garbled voices rattling off orders over a loudspeaker every few minutes. Something soft but firm cushioned her body, and every inch of her skin was a lot warmer than she last remembered.

She opened her eyes and scanned her surroundings, seeing a rollaway table near her feet, darkness creeping in the lone window in the room, and two metal bars pulled into place, one on each side of her.

A small sigh escaped her lips. She shifted in an attempt to sit up. A vise-like pain sparked across her skull and forced her to lie back down. Damn, that was why she was in a hospital bed.

Wood scraped along the floor. "Take it easy," a low voice called to her.

She turned to the bedside. A man stood there dressed in dark green sweats, with both hands clenched around the silver bedside bar. He was handsome, with light eyes, dark hair cropped close to his head, and a firm jaw. It was his hands, though. They drew her attention. Clean skin, defined knuckles, large fingers. Hands rough from a hard day's physical labor, and yet, she imagined, gentle enough to caress the afternoon's sufferings away.

"It's good to see you awake." He smiled. "You gave us all quite a fright."

Okay, the Scottish accent drew her attention, too. At once, it both melted away some of her fears and sparked a whirlwind of questions.

"Where am I?" Her throat scratched like sandpaper.

"St. Catherine's Hospital."

She swallowed hard. "Where is that?"

"Fort William." He reached for something on the table by her bed and brought back a plastic cup with a straw. "Here."

"Thank you." The warm water coated her sore vocal cords. She handed the cup back to him.

Wait a minute. Fort William? The only Fort William she knew was in Scotland. "I don't understand. How did I get here?" Ignoring the aches in her body, she pressed both palms to the sheets on each side of her and pushed herself up. The blanket fell away from her chest and a new chill surrounded her. "What's going on?"

Her arms shook, and she collapsed back to the bed.

"Relax." The man set his palm on her shoulder, as if to keep her flat against the mattress. The heat of his fingers seeped through her hospital gown and into her skin. "I found you unconscious on the beach in Glenhalish. I called for an ambulance, and they brought you here."

"I was in Glenhalish?"

"Aye, on a three day tour of the Highlands. Do you not remember being there?"

"No." She squinted and studied him. No memories surfaced. "Do I know you?"

He shook his head. "Only from the beach. I'm Malcolm Fraser."

She opened her mouth and then closed it again. Her gaze drifted to her lap as tears burned in the corners of her eyes. Panic swelled in her chest and into her throat.

"What is it, lass?" he asked with such tenderness.

"Can you tell me my name?"

The panic in the woman's voice yanked at Malcolm's heartstrings. If she couldn't remember anything, finding out what truly happened to her would be that much harder. "Aye, lass. According to the identification in your pocket, your name is Heather Winchester. You're an American graduate student at the University of Edinburgh."

All cleaned up, she was a rather attractive woman. Her curls, black as licorice, fell freely over her shoulders, with one dangling over her forehead he desperately wanted to tuck behind her ear. She had a bit more color as well and clear skin with only a hint of black and blue along her cheek. She was a little thing, surely weighing no more than ten stone.

"A graduate student?" She scratched her head. "What am I studying?"

"We're not sure yet. The police are trying to find out more about you. I'm sure they'll share more information when they can."

"How come I can't remember?" She gripped the guardrails, and yet her voice remained steady. "What happened to me?"

"Dinna worry." He lifted his hand over hers and hesitated, but then covered it. "The doctor will explain everything. I'll go get her."

He walked out and scanned the corridor for the doctor.

Aye, he definitely should've kept running this afternoon. She needed someone and already he felt the pull.

While the doctor examined Heather, he wandered toward the waiting area. He spotted Officer Osborne leaning against the nurses' counter, chatting up the cute, new nurse. Osborne waved to him and then pulled himself and his coffee cup away from the woman.

Malcolm stopped by the window and looked over the hospital parking lot. The sky was darkening a bit now, his whole afternoon wasted on the beach, in the ambulance, and at the lass's bedside. Inside, he beat himself up. What had happened to doing his part and then leaving the woman in someone else's hands? Hadn't he learned his lesson while on assignment in Los Angeles?

"Hiya, Fraser." Osborne hoisted his coffee toward him. "I'm surprised you're still here."

"Not for much longer." Malcolm glanced at his watch. If he hurried, he could catch the last train back to Glenhalish.

"I was just on me way to speak to the American," Osborne said. "The nurse says she's awake."

Malcolm nodded. "The doctor's in with her now."

"Did she tell you anything? The lass, I mean."

"No. She has amnesia."

Osborne's eyes widened. "Hhmmm, that will change things." He slurped his coffee and stared past Malcolm. "I've put a call into the university asking for more information."

"What else are you doing to investigate?"

"Well, I've taken your statement. I'll take the lass's, I'll talk to the doctor, and then I'll write up my report."

"That's it? You'll not contact the Edinburgh Police?"

"What for? She's only got a nasty bump on her head. We don't even know yet if there's been a crime. For all we know, the lass could've tripped on the rocks and bumped her head herself."

He gritted his teeth. Osborne hadn't a clue how to investigate anything more than a wee lad stealing sweets off Mrs. Sinclair's windowsill. Of course there had been a crime.

Hadn't there?

Bugger. This was exactly why he had no business being here.

But.... "She has bruises. You have to at least rule out the possibility someone did this to her."

Osborne stiffened. The easy smile disappeared. "I know how to do my job. And you've done yours, getting her here. It's time for you to go."

Malcolm drummed his fingers against his thigh. The opportunity to walk away was oh-so tempting.

But so was Miss Heather Winchester.

No, her *case*.

"Go on." Osborne waved him off. "This isn't one of your fancy jobs."

He curled his fingers. "Aye, you're right. It's your job, not mine." Technically, he had no job. And truthfully, there was no proof anyone had hurt Heather.

So, he walked out of the hospital to go about the rest of his day. Only, as he watched the scenery change on the train ride back to Glenhalish, he couldn't help but go over all the details of Heather's case from a professional point of view. And as he showered and changed, he couldn't help but think about the fear in her eyes when she realized she didn't know who she was. She was all alone in the world.

He wanted to be alone; she had no choice.

And if someone really was after her, at the moment, she only had Osborne to protect her.

Malcolm stood in the center of his bedroom, closed his eyes, and leaned his head back. He had repairs to do round the property, projects he'd been putting off. He owed the woman nothing, but his conscience refused to leave her unprotected. "Bugger."

He descended the wooden stairway in the center of the Kierlain House, his bed and breakfast, his sanctuary. He greeted an elderly couple he'd met the day before, grabbed his coat off the rack by the front door, and stopped.

If he walked out, he'd be making a commitment to help this woman at a time he shouldn't be committing to anyone.

Slowly, he reached to put the coat back on the rack. His mobile phone rang.

Malcolm pulled it from his pocket, glanced at the screen, and answered it. "Hello, Cam," he greeted one of his best friends.

"Only you would walk away from your job and walk straight into saving a damsel in distress."

"How do you know about Heather?" Behind him, Barcleigh's paws clacked against the floor. One of the bairns staying in the house carried on a one-sided conversation with Malcolm's dog as they both slipped past him out the front door.

"Ah, so it's Heather, not Ms. Winchester."

Malcolm bit his tongue. Aye, she was a bonnie lass, but it meant nothing.

"I spoke with Osborne," Cam continued. "That man's a daft

bugger."

Confirmation Malcolm didn't need. "Are you taking over her case?"

"Aye. Since she's a temporary resident of Edinburgh, and Glenhalish doesn't have a very skilled police presence, I'll be the lead inspector on this."

His stomach churned in knots. So his first instinct had been right. Heather needed protection. He reached again for his coat, slid his arms through the sleeves, and walked out the door. "How is she?"

"Physically, she's got a concussion and some scrapes and bruises, but she'll recover within a few days with some rest."

"And the amnesia?"

"She remembers nothing before the beach. She knows the month and year and who her president is, but that's it. The doctor says the lass will get her memory back, but she'll need to feel safe and comfortable before she starts remembering. They're keeping her overnight."

"It's just as well." He pulled his car door open and slid behind the wheel.

"It's good you're the one who found her."

Malcolm drummed his fingers against the wheel. "Why is that, Cam?" he asked, although he was sure he knew the answer already.

"Your background, for one. And you being on holiday at the moment. You can look after her."

"I'm not on holiday. I quit." He'd submitted his resignation after his emotions had made him hesitate, causing disaster for his clients.

Cam chuckled. The bugger. "And from what I hear, your boss has 'misplaced' your resignation. If I know you, you're in your car on your way back to Fort William to make sure she's all right."

Malcolm clenched his fist. Was he really that easy to read? No, Cam just knew him better than almost anyone.

"You're all she has."

Every instinct screamed "no," but he defied his brain's logic. Just like during his last assignment. He started the engine. "Only for tonight. Come tomorrow, you better have this solved or have someone else to watch after the lass."

Cam snorted. "You can always leave her in Osborne's care."

Malcolm twisted in his seat and backed the car out of the drive. "She's been through enough pain already. I'll not subject her to that."

"I'll check in with you tomorrow. If anything happens through the night, give us a call."

"Aye." He hit the end button and tossed his phone onto the passenger seat.

ﾒﾔ

When Malcolm stepped into Heather's hospital room, he knew agreeing to help Cam had been a mistake. His chest constricted. She looked at him with such hope and gratitude swimming in her eyes. How could he live up to that?

"You came back," she said simply.

"Aye." He moved farther into the room and pulled the wooden chair closer to her bed.

A beautiful smile pulled at the corners of her mouth—a mouth made perfectly for kissing, not trembling with worry. "You didn't have to. I've taken enough of your time today."

"I run a guest house in Glenhalish with a staff that's more than capable. They don't need me. Besides, what red-blooded lad would give up the chance to spend time with a bonnie lass?"

Heather rolled her eyes and held her arms out to the sides. "I'm so bonnie with my frizzy hair, my fancy hospital gown, and my bruises."

His gaze drifted over her ever so slowly, catching for an extra moment on the flimsy fabric draped over her full breasts. "Nonsense. You're alive and healthy, except for your temporary memory loss." He reached forward and tucked a strand of her hair behind her ear. "Nothing's more important than that."

"Thank you for saving my life. I should've said that earlier, but I was a little overwhelmed."

"It's understandable." He gripped the guardrail to keep from reaching for her again. "Are you not so worried anymore?"

"Well, like you said, I'm alive. After that, everything else is minor. I'll take one day at a time, one hour at a time if I have to, until everything gets sorted out."

"It's a good attitude to have. Did Officer Osborne talk to you about your case?"

"He said he was working with an inspector in Edinburgh to learn more about me."

"Inspector Cameron. I've spoken with him as well. He's a good friend. We thought it best for someone to stay with you through the night."

"Why? Do you think I'm in danger?" Worry crowded her features, and Malcolm could have kicked himself for putting the panic back into her.

He shook his head. "It's not likely, but we want to be sure."

"Okay." She nipped the corner of her bottom lip. She gripped and released the blanket over her stomach.

"Heather." He waited until her gaze returned to his. Still she tugged on her lip with her teeth. "I promise you are safe here."

"Thanks."

As she smiled up at him again, Malcolm wondered if he wasn't the one in danger. The way she looked at him made him want to set things right for her. He should turn around and walk straight back to the waiting area. Or drag the chair out of the room altogether. He could protect her just as well from the hallway as he could by her bedside. To stay here would encourage a bond he had no intention of pursuing. A bond he couldn't pursue if he wanted to keep her safe. Los Angeles had taught him he wasn't strong enough to care for her and see to her safety.

He tapped his palm against the metal bar at her side. "Get some rest, and I'll be in and out of here throughout the night."

Settling in the chair, he clasped his hands over his stomach and closed his eyes. If all went well, he'd not have to look at the lass again until Cam came for her tomorrow. Miss Heather Winchester would go back to her university life, and Malcolm would return home to where he belonged. Alone.

Then everyone would be safe.

Chapter Two

When Heather awoke the next morning, she had a clearer head. Her body still ached some, but she understood what had gone on over the past twenty-four hours. Her once tangled, wet hair now fell around her shoulders in a frizzled mess. A defiant curl fell at her temple but she let it hang. Her limbs felt frail, but she knew that would change as she regained her strength. And she *would* regain her strength. She might not know all the details of her past, but she would not cower.

She squinted at the clock on the far wall. 6:32 a.m. The sun still hadn't risen, but short streaks of red and orange peeked out over the horizon. Slowly, she shoved off the covers and set her legs over the side of the bed. With a deep breath, she braced her arms and pushed herself into a standing position. Cold from the tile floor seeped through her socks and rushed along her calves. The shiver continued through the rest of her body.

"Will I ever be warm again?" she whispered. She pulled the blasted hospital gown tighter around her and shuffled toward the window.

The breaking of the new day shadowed a large mountain in the distance. Leaves on the trees close by danced in the early morning breeze. Few vehicles shuffled through the roads.

She crossed her arms and harnessed what body heat she could. Today, she would leave the hospital and venture into the streets to reclaim a life she remembered nothing about. Would this be a good day? Would she remember anything on her own? Would the officer be able to tell her why someone had tried to kill her? He and Malcolm had been careful not to mention that fact for whatever reason, but she wasn't a stupid woman. She unfolded her arms and studied the bruises against her skin. Someone had made quite an effort to end her life. Would they make another attempt? With no memory, would she even recognize the danger?

Would they succeed?

All her blood drained from her head with that thought. The room began to twist and turn out of focus. Heather gripped the window frame and locked her knees. She grasped for the wooden chair by her bedside.

Footsteps hurried behind her. "Heather, lass."

Malcolm's smooth-as-caramel voice soothed her like a warm blanket.

He set a Styrofoam coffee cup on her rollaway table and wrapped his strong arm around her waist. "Are you all right?"

The scent of him—warm, strong, male—enveloped her. His gentle but capable hold caressed her frayed nerves. She pressed her palm against his free forearm and glanced up into his worried eyes. "Yeah, thanks." He was taller than she'd thought; close to six feet at least, she was sure. In his arms, she felt…fragile.

He scraped the chair across the floor and swung it beneath her.

She settled into it. "I guess I'm not as strong as I thought yet."

He crouched by her side then rested one arm casually on the chair arm and let the other drift to her knee. "You'll get your strength back. It'll just take a bit of time."

"Honestly, I'm a little nervous about life outside this hospital, too."

"You needn't worry. Inspector Cameron's quite good. I'm sure he'll have your case solved in no time."

"Malcolm, yesterday someone tried to kill me, and today I'm going out into the city where they might try again," she said softly. "I want to be strong, but how can I when I don't even know who I'm fighting or why?"

"You *are* strong. You survived." He grabbed her wrist and threaded their fingers. "I know it's frightening, but you will be well protected, and you will get through this. I have no doubt."

She nodded and gripped his hand tighter. His fingers dwarfed hers. His calloused palm warmed her skin, reminded her she was safe with him around. With all the uncertainties in her world at the moment, she'd hold onto her lifeline for as long as he stayed with her.

But how long would that be? She brushed her thumb over his knuckles. Would he be the one protecting her, or would he turn her over to someone else?

Malcolm pressed his lips together and tugged his hand free.

"I'm sorry." She clasped her fingers in her lap. Heat traveled up her neck and settled in her cheeks. How could she feel so comfortable with this man, this stranger? She'd known him for less than twenty-four hours, and yet he alone had the power to calm her frayed nerves. But he wasn't hers, wasn't a part of her world, and she had no right to put that burden on him. "I didn't mean…." To make him uncomfortable? To offend him?

Thankfully he said nothing. She glanced out the window over the city. "So yesterday you said we were in Fort William."

"Aye." Malcolm shifted, set one knee on the floor, and scanned the skyline. The tip of the sun peaked over the mountain now. "Can you see that ridge over there?"

She followed his finger. "Yeah."

"That's Ben Nevis, the highest peak in Britain."

"The summit is a little over forty-four hundred feet, right?"

"That's right." A smile tugged the corners of his mouth.

Her jaw dropped open. "How did I know that?" Hope bubbled inside her chest.

"I don't know, but it's definitely a good sign."

"Maybe it'll only be a matter of hours before I remember everything."

"Then you'll be one step closer to getting your life back."

The door to her room burst open. Heather inhaled sharply. Malcolm spun around, careful to keep her behind him.

"Who let you in 'ere?" The nurse demanded as she planted her fists on her hips and glared at Malcolm.

"I can go where I like." He rose, shifted to Heather's side, and grabbed his coffee.

"Not while I'm in charge." She motioned him toward the door. "You'll have her soon enough."

Heather looked up and met Malcolm's gaze. Her body tingled with the nurse's double entendre. A flash of desire swept through his eyes for the briefest moment.

Or had she imagined it?

"Out you go. I've got to get your lass ready for discharge."

၄၃

Malcolm paced the length of the waiting area corridor a short distance from Heather's room. What was he doing? Taking Heather under his protection would be disastrous. If he tried to protect her from whoever wanted her dead, who would keep the lass safe…from him?

He already felt a tug toward her he neither needed nor wanted. The last time he'd allowed emotion to crowd his judgment, a woman and child had almost died. He rubbed his knuckles against his forehead.

It didn't matter. Cam would be picking her up today, and not a moment too soon.

Malcolm pulled his mobile out of his pocket and dialed his friend's number.

"Cameron."

"So, do you know who's after the lass yet?"

"Christ, Malcolm, it's the middle of the night!"

"No, the sun's up, and Heather's being discharged shortly. I told you I'd watch her through the night. Now she's your responsibility." That was right. Pawn the lass off on the right man for the job.

There was a long silence before Cam spoke. "Malcolm, list—"

"No. You'll not do this to me." He turned his back on the nurses' station. "I'm not the man for this job." Especially when his thoughts drifted to *having her*.

"Malcolm, she doesn't have anyone else."

"She doesn't have me either. I'm not doing this."

"All right, then. Can you at least give her a room in the Kierlain House until I can get up there to get her?"

Malcolm said nothing and ground his teeth together.

"You said yourself Glenhalish's police weren't capable of looking after her properly, especially if someone is out to kill her."

"How long?"

"I'll get up there as soon as I can."

"Cam."

"Don't make me take time away from investigating who's after the lass to pick her up and take her home to a place where someone might grab her again."

Malcolm huffed. "Fine. I'll keep her with us for one night, but after that if you don't come for her, I'm taking her back to Edinburgh meself."

He stuffed his phone in his pocket and stared down the corridor toward Heather's room.

He could do this. He'd spent many years as a successful professional before disaster had struck. Surely he could rely on old instincts to guide him.

At least he'd be able to pawn her off on Mary, his office manager at the Kierlain House. He could go about his own business, but he'd be available if there was any danger.

The nurse walked out of the room a few minutes later. "You'll have to wait on the doctor's discharge orders, but for now the lass is all yours."

Oh no she wasn't.

Malcolm walked back in. "Right. I've spoken with Inspector Cameron."

He stopped in his tracks. Heather stood next to the bed dressed once again in her own hip-hugging jeans and a hospital top. She'd pulled her hair back into a ponytail and was in the process of slipping a sock over her foot.

She glanced up. "What's wrong?"

Malcolm rubbed his eyes and shook his head. She was a victim, vulnerable, hadn't a clue who she was. He had no business studying her curves or her red-painted toenails. "Nothing. Cam's not picking you up until tomorrow." If he were lucky. "So, as soon as you're released, you'll be leaving with me."

She stood straight. "That's generous, but I can't let you do that."

"I'll do as I like. You're coming home with me and there's no discussion about it." Even as the words left his mouth, his gut coiled.

She needed him, plain and simple, and his bloody conscience would not leave her alone to fight whatever demons wanted her dead. He may not be the best man for the job, but he was the only man at the moment.

Despite his insistence that his time with the IPN was done, he'd make an exception for the bonnie American lass. She stared at him now with such hope and confidence he wanted to be worthy of it.

He only hoped his choice wouldn't come back to bite him on the arse.

Chapter Three

*H*eather relaxed as the streets of Fort William gave way to rolling hills and open spaces. The scenery took her breath away. Grass so green, sky so blue, scattered clouds like cotton balls. Flowers grew wildly in the fields. Malcolm took the Road to the Isles, one of the most scenic routes in all of Scotland. Dark clouds huddled in the distance. Sheep grazed on the land, and there were a few cattle by some of the more remote homes as they drove closer to Glenhalish.

Malcolm groaned.

"What's wrong?"

"We'll have rain shortly."

Heather's smile widened, for even at the darkest point of a miserable afternoon, the Highlands still held a mystical beauty. That much about the country she did remember.

She gasped.

Malcolm turned to her. "What is it?"

"Some more memories coming through, not so much about me but about Scotland, and where we are."

"Any memories are good."

Mist covered much of the horizon as they drove west. The rains held off, however, and by the time they reached the bed and breakfast, the sun was struggling to make another appearance.

Heather stared at the ancient building before her as she stepped from the car. A simple home, he'd said while they waited for the doctor to release her, but his description had not done it justice. The building was a castle and stretched far along the land. A Union Jack flag flew in the breeze at the top of a parapet next to the flag of St. Andrew.

To the right of the front door was a sign in Gaelic, *Ceud Mile Failte*. A hundred thousand welcomes. "Malcolm, this is gorgeous."

"Thanks." He tugged Heather's plastic hospital bag from the back seat and closed his door.

A thin, copper-haired woman with bright eyes and a pleasant smile came down the main stairs with a foot-high Scottish terrier waddling behind. "Hello!" She walked straight to Heather and clasped both her hands. "You must be Heather. I'm Mary. Welcome."

"Thank you. Nice to meet you." Heather glanced at Malcolm. Was Mary his wife? Girlfriend? Maybe she had imagined the chemistry between them.

"Mary's the caretaker of the Kierlain House." Malcolm turned to rub the dark coat of the dog. "And this is Barcleigh, the best friend you could ever have." Barcleigh barked loudly and snapped playfully at their heels.

"He's adorable." She held her hand out for the dog to sniff.

"Mary, Heather will be staying with us tonight." Malcolm got back to his feet.

"Aye, I've already prepared the Flora MacDonald room for her."

He stilled. "The MacDonald room?"

The woman's smile faltered, and she kept her gaze from Malcolm. "Aye."

Tension electrified between them with each beat of silence.

Her gaze drifted between the Scots.

The woman slid her arm through Heather's and turned toward the building. "Are you hungry, dear? I've made some fresh scones, and the kettle's just boiled."

"Sounds great," she said as she let Mary lead her into the house.

CB

Malcolm stared after the women.

Mary had set up the *MacDonald* room. The room two doors down from his room. The only other bedroom on the fourth floor. He'd hoped to put Heather in one of the rooms on a lower floor at the opposite side of the house. Now she'd be close by, a temptation he didn't need.

"Bloody hell."

He followed them into the kitchen. "Heather, I'll take your bag up to your room."

"That's all right, Malcolm. I can do it." She reached for the plastic handles of the bag. Her soft, cool fingers brushed against the back of his hand and sent a surge of lust straight to his groin. What would her fingers feel like running over him?

He released the straps as Heather's inquisitive eyes flickered up to his.

The sooner he got rid of her, the better. He turned to the other woman in the room. "Mary, I'm leaving Heather in your hands this afternoon. I've some work to take care of, all right?"

"Oh, I'm sorry, Malcolm, but I cannit stay. Jamie needs us in the pub." She glanced at her watch as the kettle began to whistle. "In fact, I'm already late." But she still poured Heather a cup of tea and grabbed a clean plate for her.

Heather waved her hand. "Both of you, please go. I can take care of myself." She set the bag down by the table and moved to the counter.

"I'm sorry, lass. You must think me a terrible hostess." Mary scrambled to gather milk and sugar for the tea.

Heather smiled and slipped a few curls behind her ear. "Don't be silly. Besides, I'm not your average guest."

No, she certainly was not. Malcolm had never had this tight of a tug for any of his guests before.

She pulled Mary's hands from the task. "I'll be all right. Go."

"I'll call in when I can." She grabbed her coat and purse, said goodbye, and rushed out the door.

Heather turned to him. "You too, Malcolm. You've spent enough time with me over the last twenty-four hours." She marched to him, planted her hands on his back, and shoved him out of the room. "It's time you take care of yourself."

"Would you like to see your room first? Are you not tired?"

"No, I'm fine."

He grinned as he let her maneuver him toward the center of the lobby. "We've learned something else about you."

"What's that?"

His grin widened. He glanced over his shoulder. "You're a bossy little thing, aren't you?"

"And don't you forget it." She returned his grin and swatted his shoulder. "Now, go." She went back to the kitchen.

For one second, he wanted to pull her back, to hold her close, and kiss her for making him feel like a whole person instead of a broken man.

But she wasn't his woman. Wouldn't be his woman no matter how much his body begged otherwise. She had no past at the moment, and he was desperate to forget his. He snorted. "What a grand couple we'd make," he whispered as he slipped out the front door.

With Malcolm and Mary gone, Heather helped herself to one of the scones set out on the table and several cups of tea. She sat at the wooden kitchen table, glanced out the bay window, across the front yard to the loch, and savored the quiet.

For the first time since she woke up in the hospital, she truly felt relaxed. Someone might still be after her, but what threat could reach her in such a beautiful, magical place as this? And Malcolm might not be by her side, but she was confident he was close by.

Her Highland champion, going about his duties, protecting his keep.

A smile pulled at the corners of her lips. She'd bet Malcolm would look sexy dressed in a Fraser plaid with a claymore clutched in his strong, competent hands.

She shook her head. "Don't be ridiculous," she whispered. It was the twenty-first century, not the eighteenth, and she wasn't the lady of the keep. She was a modern-day woman, confident and competent.

Or so she kept trying to tell herself. It was hard to buy into when she had huge gaps in her memory, and every decision brought on a panic she could barely contain. What if she made a wrong choice, one that put her in more danger? And what about Malcolm? He wasn't a cop. She'd never forgive herself if he was hurt defending her.

She jumped up from the table and deposited her empty scone plate in the sink. There was no use in dwelling on what could happen. At the moment, she was safe.

After making one last cup of tea, Heather did make a decision. She clutched the mug in her hands and wandered through the rooms of the first floor. Behind the kitchen was a formal dining room with two long tables big enough for at least a dozen people each. A crystal chandelier hung from the center of the room, and a cabinet sheltered a host of sterling silver serving trays and dishes.

The common room behind the stairs held several bookshelves. Heather brushed her fingers over the spines and read the titles—tons of useful information about Scotland, past and present. A fireplace with a marble border sat in the back wall. Flames crackled, and Barcleigh lay lazily on the throw rug in front of the fire. A small TV sat catty corner to the left side of the room. Several types of chairs were scattered throughout the room and an oversized couch sat in the center. A simple desk to the right of the door held copies of current magazines and newspapers, and a liquor cabinet rested against the left wall.

Barcleigh pushed himself up and followed Heather out of the room, his nails clicking on the floor.

Across from the kitchen was a formal parlor. With its priceless antiques, art, and beautifully decorated furniture, it was the kind of room she'd avoid as a child, with her shovel and trusty rucksack.

She stilled. Another memory, something else to identify herself.

Huh. The doctor was right. Heather did need to feel relaxed and comfortable before the memories would return. She crouched down, rubbed her hand over the dog's coat, and sighed. "And how can I not be relaxed here, huh, Barcleigh?"

The front door opened. Malcolm stopped in the doorway, his chest heaving, both hands dropped to his sides. "I see you've found a new friend." He peeled off his coat and hung it on the standing coat rack.

"I'm the lucky one." She rested her head on the dog's, and he licked her cheek.

Heather laughed and pulled away. The dog followed with his wet tongue. She plopped down on her butt and tea sloshed over the side of her mug.

Malcolm said, "Barcleigh, down."

Immediately the dog left Heather. Malcolm held his hand out to her. "Let me help you."

She slid her hand in his. The callused skin of a hard-working man warmed her palm, sending a tingle jolting up her arm.

"Thank you."

He stiffened slightly with her words, but only for a second, and then he released her. "To see you with Barcleigh, you must've had pets at some point."

"When I was really young we did."

His eyes widened. "Another memory?"

"Yes. I've been having a few."

"That's grand. You'll have your past back before you know it."

"The memories aren't telling me who is after me, though." She drummed her fingertips against the mug.

He nodded once. "It's a start."

"I suppose." She walked around him and set the empty mug in the kitchen sink. "I'm feeling kind of tired. Can you show me to my room?" She picked up her plastic hospital bag from beside the table.

"Aye, lass." He escorted her up to the fourth floor. Paintings and ancient weapons lined the walls along the stairs. When they stopped in front of a door, she brushed her fingers against the name carved on it. "Flora MacDonald. She was the woman who helped Bonnie Prince Charlie escape from Scotland in 1746, right?"

"That's right. A student of our history, I see." He opened the bedroom door.

Heather stepped into the room. A large window on the northern wall gave her a spectacular view of a small town nestled among the majestic hills. The room held a canopy bed with thick velvet bed curtains on each side, a handcrafted armoire, and a plain writing table. There were flowers in the sill of the picture window, and a basket of feminine toiletries sat on the table. The bedspread was probably MacDonald plaid. Paintings of Flora and the prince decorated the walls.

Malcolm stepped inside the room and shoved his hands into his pockets. "Will this do for you?"

"Yes, thank you. And thank you again for"—*being my lifeline*—"everything." A thick ball of various emotions formed in the middle of her chest.

"Heather, lass, you have to stop." He shook his head. "I'm just a lad who found a bonnie lass and took her to hospital. I'm not that good of a man."

She lifted her hand and placed her palm on the side of his face. His stubble prickled against her skin. "You are to me." Her other hand settled on his chest, his strong heartbeat against her fingertips. The scent of him, of a real man working his own land, tickled her nostrils. Her mouth remained inches from his as she whispered, "Malcolm Fraser, you're my hero." She brushed her lips against his cheek.

Malcolm stiffened beneath her touch. The feel of her soft curves pressed against him stoked a furnace fire inside him hotter than he'd expected. With a simple tilt of his head, his mouth could overtake hers. He could taste the sweet, sultry lips of this sweet, vulnerable woman. His tongue could sweep along hers, dart in and out of her mouth much like another primal act between a man and a woman.

She stepped back and let go of him.

Already his body hummed, missing her touch. He closed his fingers to keep from reaching for her. "You've had a long day. Get some rest, Heather."

"Right." She crossed her arms, holding both her elbows, and lowered her gaze. In her cheeks, a solid shade of red formed. Without another word, she turned to the bed and pushed the curtains back.

Malcolm walked out of the room and closed the door behind him. Gratitude. That's what she was feeling. He'd come across this several times throughout his years of guarding people. The women often grew attached to him or his colleagues. They'd forget it was a job for the men, nothing more.

He glanced back at Heather's door. And yet it felt like more with her with each passing second.

Enough, you daft bugger. He hurried down the stairs and walked straight to the kitchen. From the refrigerator, he grabbed a beer, twisted the cap off, and took a long pull.

He wouldn't think about the woman in his guest room. He wouldn't wonder what she wore to sleep in. He wouldn't imagine how she'd feel wrapped in his arms and quivering beneath him.

Christ. His cock ached.

He leaned against the counter and took another long pull on the beer.

This evening, he'd have another beer. Or two. Tomorrow, he'd go for a run and then convince Cam to come and take Heather off his hands. Despite her insistence, he was not good for her. When he let people in, they got hurt. He'd not subject her to the same fate. She'd already been through enough.

Chapter Four

Heather sank lower in the bathtub. The warm water enveloped her. A sweet Celtic melody played softly from somewhere behind the walls. Its calming effect washed over her, and she gladly gave in to the peace penetrating the very core of her being.

The room's heavy wooden door creaked open. Malcolm stood still in the doorway with his shirt hanging from his hand, his Fraser-colored kilt resting on his hips. The man was magnificent—his skin, as bronze as the sun, his arms corded with muscle. Wisps of light hair covered his chest.

Her fingers itched to trace the contours of his abs, to slip under the kilt, and feel the hard-packed thighs, and the treasure they cradled.

The flicker of hunger in his hazel eyes stirred the flutters in her belly. A need for his touch pulsed in her breasts, between her legs, deep in her heart. Her Highland champion. Had he come to claim payment for rescuing her?

If so, she'd gladly give herself to him. She sat up, rested her cheek against her folded knees, and left her bare back to the ravages of the cool air.

He dropped his shirt where he stood and walked to the tub. "Stand."

"I have no towel."

"You will stand."

Heather gripped the side of the claw-footed tub. Water sloshed as she pushed up. The cool air whirled around her body. Her nipples tightened. The tingling in her stomach pulsed heavier.

He took his time studying her and licked his bottom lip. "I saved you from the enemy. You are mine now." His hands drifted over her belly and up to cup her breasts.

She gasped.

"Are you frightened, lass?" His thumbs brushed over her hardened nipples, his palms caressing the sensitive skin on the underside of her breasts.

"No. I'm ready to please you."

"'Tis I who will do the pleasing." He set his mouth on one nipple. He circled it with his tongue and grazed the sensitive tip with his teeth.

She sighed and arched closer to him.

Malcolm rewarded her with moving to her other breast. He tugged gently with his teeth.

Hundreds of thoughts ran through her mind but none were coherent. All she knew was her body wanted him, her mind wanted him, and she was determined to get what she wanted. She set her hands on his broad shoulders. His skin shimmered in the candlelight.

Malcolm circled an arm around her waist and picked her up. Water sloshed below as her feet left the tub. She wrapped her legs around his waist. His hands fit perfectly against her bottom, shifting her so she could cradle his erection.

"Soon I will claim you as my own."

The feel of him pressing against her sex made her shiver. Oh how she needed him, craved him sliding into her body, stretching her, stroking her, bringing her exquisite torture.

Heather awoke with a start, the sheets clenched in both fists, her legs spread apart with moisture between them. Her body vibrated with the sensations of Malcolm's touch in the dream. She clamped her legs shut and released the fabric as heat soared into her cheeks. The man was her guardian, nothing more.

But if he was anything like that dream....

Her nipples ached with the memory of his mouth.

"Insanity." She didn't even remember her life before yesterday. How could she even be thinking of Malcolm like this? She needed to think about who wanted her dead, not about how sizzling it would feel to make love to him.

Plus, the way he kept balking every time she touched him should be proof enough the man was not interested in her as a lover. "No more touching him."

Sunlight filtered through the bedroom window. She tossed off the covers and disappeared into the bathroom for a quick shower and then dressed in her own jeans. In the night, someone had left her a shirt several sizes too big. But it was clean and warm and held Malcolm's unique scent. Her own sweater had been ripped and tossed out at the hospital.

Another reminder a madman wanted her dead.

After making the bed, she opened the bedroom door and then descended to the first floor. A couple greeted her on the stairs. From the common room, she could hear the laughter of children, and Barcleigh barking. She glanced out the bay window in the kitchen. Sunlight reflected off the loch like shimmering diamonds.

A plate of fresh fruit and scones sat in the center of the table along with a note from Malcolm insisting Heather make herself at home. He was out on the property doing repairs to the fence if she needed him.

She made herself a cup of tea, ate, and perused *The Scotsman* newspaper left on the counter. When she turned the page, she almost choked on her scone. Staring back at her was a wallet-sized photo of herself with a heading that read: American Investigates Our Heritage.

She bolted upright and scanned the article. With each paragraph of information on her and her studies, she gripped the edges of the paper a bit more. Her heart pounded.

Heather jumped out of her chair. She had to find Malcolm.

She hurried to the front door like a kid on Christmas morning. When she pulled the front door open, a gust of chilly wind smacked her in the face. She grabbed a plaid pashmina from the coat rack and stuffed her feet into a pair of too big Union Jack slippers. Barcleigh rushed to catch up to her from the back of the house. "I'm waiting, boy, but hurry up." He bolted past her and danced in circles on the pebbled footpath leading around the house.

As she jogged out back, her gaze scanned the fence for Malcolm until she found him nailing wooden boards back into place. With each swing of the hammer, the muscles in his shoulder strained against his tight gray shirt. He wore blue jeans today drawing her attention to how well they fit his backside.

Thwack, thwack, thwack.

Butterflies stirred in her stomach and heat simmered just beneath her skin as memories of her dream swam in her head. At once, she imagined him a fierce Highland warrior, in nothing but a kilt, slaying enemies with a claymore, muscles rippling, body hard and strong; him working as the vigilant protector, taking care of all her needs.

Thwack, thwack.

Barcleigh snapped at her heels and pulled her out of her reverie. Her too long hair flew wildly behind her. She struggled to pull the plaid shawl around her and still keep the newspaper from flying across the yard. "Malcolm!"

Malcolm lowered the hammer and listened. Behind him, Barcleigh barked. He turned around and Heather rushed toward him.

An easy smile crossed his lips, and he let out a sigh. Her cloak flipped back in the wind, leaving him a perfect view of his navy blue shirt clasping against her skin, molding against her breasts. A surge of lust shot straight to his groin. Her dark curls flew wildly in the wind, her smile wide, her eyes bright.

Aye, her eyes. Look at nothing but her eyes. "What is it?"

She stopped in front of him and pulled strands of her hair out of her mouth. "I'm in the paper!"

"Eh?" Malcolm took the paper from her hands and scanned the article.

"I'm a graduate student at Byrne College in New York. I'm studying for my Ph.D. in Archaeology. I took classes last spring in Edinburgh, and I've been doing research on the Orkney and Shetland Islands." She rubbed her hands together. Her nose took on a delightful shade of pink.

"Do you remember any of this?" He pulled her plaid firmly around her shoulders.

"A little." She studied the paper again.

"That's great."

"You said yesterday Inspector Cameron would be picking me up today. Is that still the plan?"

"As far as I know. I'll call him in a bit to see when we can expect him. Why?"

She turned away from him toward the loch. The ease with which she spoke was lost, and for a second, Malcolm wished he could do something to bring it back.

He reached out and clasped one of her curls between his thumb and finger. "What is it, lass?"

She glanced back up at him with a tender bit of worry in her eyes. "I think I should go back to the beach where you found me." She folded her arms across her chest. "I might be able to remember more." Another gust of wind brought her lavender scent to tease his nostrils.

"I'll take you."

She shook her head. "You've done so much for me already."

"I'll do as I please. I'll finish the fence, and then we'll go."

Her tongue moved up to the edge of her front teeth. She was surely going to thank him.

Not if he could help it.

Malcolm pressed his finger against her lips. "Don't say it. It's not for you. It's for Cam, one less thing for him to do." Her soft lips spurred warmth along the pad of his finger and visions of her mouth moving over other parts of him. His cock twitched with hope.

Bloody hell. You'd think he was a schoolboy all over again. He yanked his finger back and moved to the next section of the fence.

"Is there anything I can do to help?" she asked.

Aye. Walk away. "No, I have it." He tugged on the rotted board, once, twice.

She pressed her delicate fingers against his shoulder blade. "Are you sure? I don't mind a little work."

He closed his eyes for a moment. He'd subdued some of the most dangerous men in the world. Surely he could stand a bit more time with a wee lass. "All right." He picked up one of the wooden boards and

37

held it out to her. "Hold this steady while I nail it in."

They worked together in silence through a few more sections of the fence. Heather turned out to be an excellent assistant.

"Did you replace all the boards on the fence up to this point?" she asked.

"Aye, but at different times, depending on my assignments." He stilled for a fraction of a second. She believed him to be just a guest house owner, nothing else. Bringing up IPN would subject him to a load of questions he needn't answer since she'd be gone by tea time.

Heather stared toward the house. "I imagine there's a lot of work to do running a bed and breakfast as big as this."

"It can be overwhelming." He nailed the next board in place.

She moved back to the pile of boards and picked up another. "It's a shame you don't have someone to share it with."

"It's better this way." Having someone else in his life would make him weak, and weak bodyguards didn't have jobs for long.

"Better to be alone?" She lifted the board and set it in place.

Malcolm bit his tongue before responding. She spoke from desperation, a need to feel she belonged somewhere, to someone. Nothing more.

Didn't she?

He shrugged. "I'm hardly alone." With the hammer, he pointed to the house. "You've seen how alone you can be in there."

"That's not what I mean."

Of course it wasn't.

Malcolm considered his words carefully as he drove a nail in the board. "Heather lass, with the type of man I am, it's the way it needs to be."

She propped her elbow on the fence. "Why?" she asked simply, as if the answer could be folded neatly into one short sentence.

He gripped the top of the board and kept his gaze on the grooves in the wood. "It's complicated."

"As are most things worth exploring." She squeezed his arm and returned for the next board.

His chest began to ache with the pressure of a fist squeezing tight around his sternum in an attempt to break it off. Part of him wanted to pull her close, to hold her in his arms, to show her how very grateful he was for her not pushing the issue. She saw him as her hero. He'd not ruin that image with the twisted truth, because at this moment, no matter how wrong she was, he wanted to be worthy of her faith.

The other part of him wanted to shove her far away. Exploring this attraction between them would feel good at the time, but Malcolm had no intention of toying with Heather's already mixed emotions. She deserved a man who could take care of her in every sense of the words. He was not that man.

She deserved better.

Oh, but she did tempt him.

They'd finish the last few sections of the fence, he'd take her back to the beach, and soon after, Cam would come for her. Then Malcolm's job would be done. He'd hand her over and celebrate with a pint or two at the pub.

🆑

Heather followed behind Malcolm as he walked toward the shore. He climbed over the rocks, turned back, and held out his hand for her. She accepted his help and moved down to the smooth sand. In the distance, she watched a tour bus unload its passengers at some ancient ruins.

"This is where I found you." Malcolm halted by a clump of boulders and shrubs a few feet from a stone bridge. "You were lying here face down. I pulled you out and rang for an ambulance."

Heather stared at the spot, willing her brain to work at 100 percent capacity. She closed her eyes and listened to the waves swish against the shore as Malcolm continued recounting how he'd found her two days earlier.

In only a few moments, she could remember the cold shivers of her body. The wet sand clogged her nose and squished between her fingers. Breathing became difficult again, and then she saw *him*, a sinister smile on his lips, his body shaking with laughter she was too far away to hear. He stared down at her, presuming she was already dead. "Up on the bridge. He's watching me."

Her heartbeat sped up, grew louder in her ears. She went further back in her memories. In a flash, she saw a small light burning. A mass moved toward her, and she saw his face again. The images were not very clear; dark shadows haunted her eyes. She started to fall, and the man with a vacant face reached down to grab her.

She gasped as she stumbled back to reality. Her knees buckled, her eyes flew open, and her vision tunneled.

"Heather!" Malcolm stepped up to her and used his body to brace her. One of his hands slid along her arm to grasp her fingers. The other circled her waist and held her up.

She sagged against him, her fingertips splayed across his chest. Beneath her palm, his heartbeat pulsed strong and steady. Her protector. "I'm okay." She nodded.

"You need to sit down," Malcolm chided gently as he led her to a boulder.

She peeked behind at the bridge a few yards away. "But I need to check—"

"Sit," he ordered.

Heather shot him a vicious glance as she sat.

"You can glare at me all you like, but you can't trust your legs at the moment." He settled next to her on the boulder, his body twisted just enough to cradle hers again. Whether he meant to offer her comfort or not, Heather took it. A chill ran up her spine, and with apprehension on the heels of her memory, she needed to feel safe. She folded her arms and moved closer to him.

"You mentioned a man on the bridge. Did you get a look at him?" Malcolm asked.

"A few details."

"Even a few details will help with the investigation." He gave her a light squeeze.

"But they're not fast enough. I guess patience is not one of my virtues." Her fingers drifted over his chest, smoothing out the fabric of his shirt, stroking the hardened wall of muscle beneath her fingertips. "I just hate being weak."

Laughter rumbled through his chest. "You've come back here, a place that clearly frightens you, to uncover whatever you can. That takes courage most people don't have."

"Yeah, right. Lots of courage."

He set his fingers under her chin and forced her gaze back to his. "You are a beautiful, intelligent, *brave* woman."

Warmth coiled in her belly. He held her gently, staring at her with such tenderness, Heather wanted to lose herself in him. Her gaze flickered to his lips, so very tempting and close to hers she could feel his warm breath on her cheeks. The scent of him surrounded her, making her dizzy all over again but for a very different reason.

She pressed one hand on his thigh for leverage and pushed herself up.

The muscle contracted beneath her touch. Malcolm sucked in a breath. He didn't move except for his hazel eyes. They studied her every movement.

Heather shifted her weight to the hand on his thigh, leaned up, and pressed her mouth against his. Her tongue dipped against his lips, begging for his participation.

He stilled but only for a moment, and then the gentleman in him disappeared. At long last, he surrendered to her and kissed her back. He opened his mouth and met her tongue with his. He tasted like coffee and heaven and sin all rolled into one. His hand drifted to her side, to hover next to her breast. She could feel the movement of his thumb, as if he wanted to brush against her nipple but was afraid to for some reason.

She shuddered with his touch, with the possibilities, with the memory of her dream. As her tongue continued its dance with his, she pushed her body closer to him, for him. She dragged her fingernails along his jeans, closer to the treasure between his legs. The backs of her knuckles brushed his already hardening cock.

Malcolm pulled his head back and sucked in air through his gritted teeth. He grabbed her wrist with firm pressure against her bones.

Heather looked up into his face, expecting censure. Instead, was that…regret?

"Dinna play with fire, lass." His accent grew thicker.

The warmth inside her shot rumbles of desire to every nerve ending in her body. "I'm sorry." She lowered her gaze and moved away from him. Immediately, her body revolted with shivers and prickling skin, lost without his touch. She crossed her arms and glanced out over the loch. What had happened to keeping her hands to herself? "I didn't mean to offend you."

"The only offense would be if I followed through as I want while you still have a hazy memory."

Her eyes widened. Did she hear him right?

"Aye, I do want you, Heather Winchester. Make no mistake about it." He brushed his knuckle along the side of her face. "But I'm not the man for you," he said with more than a hint of sorrow.

"Why not?" She dared to ask.

"You don't know who you are. You don't know who I truly am."

"I know enough."

"These feelings you think you're having are a result of your fears, of all you've been through."

"Don't use me as your excuse. Talk to me."

"I'm a broken man, Heather."

Him? Broken? That was insane. "What are you talking about? You're kind and gentle and proud, and you have a big heart. Nothing's more important than that."

He smiled but said nothing. He stared across the loch, a thousand miles away from her.

Thunder crackled above them. Dark clouds gathered, as if to reinforce Malcolm's declaration that they could never be an *us*.

She wanted to wring his neck.

Malcolm looked up into the sky. "We'd better go. We'll get soaked through if we sit here much longer." He pushed himself up from the rock.

Heather stared after him. His chivalry was just a ruse to keep her from getting too close. She was smart enough to understand that. But why? What was he afraid of?

The man was as much a mystery to her as her own past, but Heather had every intention of uncovering the truth if for no other reason than to prove to him how wonderful a man he was. She owed him that much.

Chapter Five

$\mathcal{A}$s they drove from the southern side of Loch Finnan, they left the rain clouds behind. The mountains came alive with every color of a painter's palette. The clouds hugged the hills like an old friend and settled shadows over the sun-filled landscape. Glenhalish came into view over the horizon.

Heather's heart leapt. It was bigger than she had first imagined. The Cuan MacDougall Pub, the post office, and a general store stood in plain view. She could see the rows of houses down the side of the hill. One main road ran through the town like a racetrack. A church sat at the far end of town with an ancient tower looming protectively over all of Glenhalish.

Malcolm parked the car in the lot beside the pub. As they walked toward the entrance, he explained, "Mary's husband, Jamie, runs this place. Actually, it's a family-run pub. Mary divides her time between here and the Kierlain House. When I'm away, she takes on more at the B and B."

They could hear loud cheers filtering through the walls.

"Sounds lively."

Malcolm opened the door. "There's a football match on."

"Ah." She nodded. The smell of fried food and free-flowing beer grabbed her the moment she stepped inside. The pub held lots of tables and artifacts and hardly any empty seats. A large video screen at the back of the open room showed the soccer game.

"Well, look who's joined us for the game!" a booming voice announced from behind the bar. "Oh, and what a lovely lass he's brought us."

Mary swatted the big man. "Hush, Jamie. Dinna embarrass the lass." She rounded the bar and disappeared into the crowd with a wet rag and an empty tray.

"Hi." Heather stripped off her jacket.

Malcolm grabbed it and motioned her toward the last empty stool at the bar. "Go on. I'll set these on the rack."

When Malcolm returned to the bar, Jamie set a pint in front of him and then turned to Heather. "What can I get you, love?" He stood taller than anyone else she'd met here, with hair like fire, a beard to match, and a twinkle of mischief in his eyes.

She pointed to the beer. "I'll have what he's having."

Jamie poured her drink, grabbed a soda for himself, and made a toast in Gaelic. When he turned to give Heather a translation, she beat him to it. "May I find peace and contentment in Glenhalish, and may my soul be blessed while on Scottish soil."

The men's eyes widened. "Bonnie and smart!" Jamie beamed. "Oh, this one's a keeper."

She turned to Malcolm, smiled, and took her first sip.

He, of course, focused his attention on the screen and took a hefty swig from his pint. "How does our team look?"

Heather tuned out Jamie's recap of the first half hour of the game and drank her dark beer. She glanced around the pub, catching sight of a dartboard on one side of the room, and a hefty claymore sword mounted above the doorway toward the bathrooms.

Mary returned to the bar and set a hand on Heather's forearm. "How have you been today?"

"Good. I've had more memories, and hopefully, some of them will help the police find whoever's after me."

"And the MacDonald room. Is it all right for you?"

She nodded. "It's great. Thank you for the flowers and the basket. They made me feel welcome."

"I wanted it to be nice for you. It's not often that Malcolm brings a lass home."

Her eyebrows shot up. "Really?" With his looks, his quiet confidence, she'd imagined he'd have women lined up out the door.

Immediately Mary's face blanched. "Oh, I dinna mean it like that. I only mean he's a private man, and when he's here, he'd often rather be alone."

And yet, he'd spent much of the last forty-eight hours with Heather.

Interesting. Further proof, perhaps, he didn't want to be as alone as he claimed.

Mary closed her eyes for a moment. "I mean to say you must be important to him if he's brought you home."

"I don't know how important I am. He's just giving me a place to stay until the police can find where I'm meant to be."

"Well, however long you're here, it's good to have you." She smiled again, squeezed Heather's hand, and then continued to the kitchen with her tray full of dirty glasses.

Heather turned back to the men. Malcolm stood beside her, his arm brushing hers, texting on his phone. "I'm trying to get Cam to call me back. I've left him two messages today, and I'm texting him about our trip to the beach."

Jamie touched her forearm. "There's a table free over there. Go and sit and I'll send over some food. Fancy a bit of haggis, lass?"

"Oh, Jamie, you'll not." Malcolm stuffed his phone back in his pocket.

"I'm probably one of the few Americans who actually likes haggis." She slid off the stool and picked up her drink. "So bring it on, Jamie MacDougall."

Jamie's hearty laugh brought about a few stares. He leaned his elbow on the bar and pointed to her. "I like you."

"Thank you. You're not so bad yourself." She winked at him.

Malcolm set his hand on the small of her back. "Let's get that table before someone else does."

Heather knew her time here in the Highlands was limited, but at this moment, in this place, she wondered what it would be like to be Malcolm's woman and to live in this community.

But little girl fantasies needed to remain in childhood. She was a grown woman, with a life somewhere else, with friends of her own and possibly a family, too. Even with the feelings rumbling through her, she couldn't lose sight of the truth—she was temporary.

Still, a few more hours living this fantasy couldn't hurt, could it? Soon enough she'd be forced to unravel the rest of the mysteries of her past...alone.

Ω

Malcolm slept little through the night. Instead, Heather occupied his every thought. He remembered the feel of her hand on his thigh at the beach, the look of want reflected in her brilliant eyes, the confusion he'd wrestled with in his own mind. It had taken every ounce of restraint to keep from pulling her into his lap. Even now his cock grew hard as he imagined what it would feel like to have her dark curls spread out over his pillow, her body his for the taking. And he would take her in every sense of the word, in every way possible. He'd roll her underneath him and slide into her tight heat. He'd keep his eyes on her to watch how her body responded to his every touch.

Bloody hell. He bolted upright in the bed. This would not do.

Malcolm Fraser didn't become attached. He had no right considering any kind of relationship between them, physical or otherwise.

He changed and went for a run.

When he returned, he'd solved his current problem. He grabbed his mobile from the desk in the study and pulled his sweatshirt off as he listened to the phone ring on Cam's end. The sun had barely risen. Of course Cam wouldn't pick up, but Malcolm left one message he was sure his friend would return.

"Cam, since you keep avoiding me, I'm taking steps of me own. Heather and I will be back in Edinburgh before noon. I'll be leaving her there. Whether in her own flat or with you, I don't care, but she'll not return to Glenhalish with me."

One way or another he'd have his peace again.

After his shower, he sat in the kitchen and waited for Heather to get up. The front door opened and in walked Meggie MacDougall, Jamie's younger sister and Glenhalish's town gossip. "Morning, Malcolm."

"Meggie." The lass's wild red hair was pulled into some kind of contraption at the back of her head. She helped herself to a cup of tea and plopped down across from him at the table. "So, where's your lass?"

"I don't have a lass."

"That's not the word around the village this morning." She sipped her tea and winked at him.

"The village is mistaken."

"Come on, Malcolm. It's the first time we've seen you obsessed with a woman in ages."

That was all he needed circling round Glenhalish. Further proof he needed to pass Heather off to Cam. "Heather's nothing more than an assignment. She needed help, and I was forced into giving it. Truth be told, she's more of a nuisance than anything."

Meggie's eyes drifted over his shoulder. Her grin disappeared.

Bugger. Malcolm closed his eyes.

"Morning," Meggie said before she stood and slurped her tea. "I'll just go and find Mary to bother." As quickly as she'd come in, the Glenhalish tornado rushed passed Heather and left him to clean up the debris.

Malcolm turned around. "Heather."

The long, drawn look on her face and the pain in her eyes confirmed he'd been a horse's arse, and she'd heard every word. Deep inside his chest, his heart clenched tight. Yes, he'd wanted to get rid of her, but no, he hadn't meant to hurt her in the process. "Heather lass, it's not what you think."

She held up her palm. "It's okay. You don't owe me any explanation, and you're right. It's time I started taking control of my own safety and case." She tossed her curls over her shoulders. "If you have a copy of the train schedule, I'll go see about getting a ticket."

"I'll take you back to Edinburgh." Because a three-and-a-half-hour ride with her beside him was just the punishment he deserved.

"Malcolm, you've done more than enough. Besides, it was my memory I lost, not my mind. I can get back to Edinburgh on my own." She reached for the train schedule tacked up to the corkboard by the phone.

He grabbed her wrist, stilled her hand. "You'll not."

She didn't look at him.

"Look, Meggie has a big mouth. If I didn't say something to discourage her, the whole village would be planning our wedding inside of four hours."

She did glance up then. "Well, that's ridiculous. Like you said, we barely know each other."

"Aye, but it is the way of a small community. I'm sorry if I hurt you, but it wasn't my intention." No, he'd meant to protect her...and himself.

"Whether you mean that or not, thank you."

"Heather, you're not to use those two words for me anymore. You'll give me a champion's complex I don't deserve."

"Well then, stop being so good to me, and it won't happen again." She smiled, bumped his hip, and went about making them both a cup of tea and a breakfast plate.

The woman was amazing. When most lasses would be crying out after his sharp denial of the obvious chemistry between them, she accepted his harsh words and moved on. Despite her own physical ailments, she still worked to care for those around her. Indeed, she had the heart of a champion herself.

As she wandered through the kitchen, Malcolm let his mind wander to what it would be like to have her in his life day after day, for him, not because she needed his protection. A better lass he'd surely never find.

And not for the first time in the last few days, he found himself wishing he could be good enough for her.

Cʒ

Cam returned Malcolm's call during the drive back to Edinburgh. "He said to call him when we get there, and he'll come by to give us— you, an update." Aye, Malcolm had to stop thinking in terms of *us* and *we*. Heather was about to be on her own, and his complete focus could turn to the Kierlain House and all the projects he'd neglected while traveling around the world to keep people safe. "He also said to tell you he's arranging for extra patrols in your neighborhood and someone to check in with you daily."

Heather wrung her fingers in her lap. "That's good."

A dull ache formed in his insides. This was the best decision. "You'll be all right." And so would he.

"I know," she said, and yet she glanced at him with as much worry as the first day she awoke in the hospital.

Malcolm turned back to the road and flexed his fingers around the steering wheel. "You're strong and intelligent. You'll take precautions, and before you know it, Cam will be calling to tell you they've arrested the man who hurt you."

"Right." She nodded.

But was he trying to convince her or himself?

ﾟ

When Malcolm pulled into the only parking spot in front of her building, Heather studied their surroundings. Bits and pieces looked familiar, like the newsagent's on the street corner where she remembered often running down for a Mars bar during study sessions. But that was about it.

The apartment was as much a mystery to Heather as it must have been to Malcolm. She wandered around the living room randomly touching furniture and knickknacks. There were several framed pictures spread out on various flat surfaces, some of her alone at different sites throughout Scotland, some at what she guessed was her home in New York, and some with various friends.

Malcolm stood in the center of the room with his hands in the pockets of his long, gray coat. "Anything?"

"No." She picked up a replica of Hadrian's Wall from on top of the television and then set it down carefully. "It's weird knowing these things are mine, but not being able to tell you the history behind them."

"You can tell a lot about someone from their home."

"How?"

He pointed across the room. "Your desk, for example. Your

research is in neat piles and easily accessible. You take pride in your work. You have a small television so you can't be concerned with sitting in front of it all day."

"Maybe I couldn't afford a bigger television." Her fingers drifted over a row of books on a hardwood bookshelf.

"You could probably afford anything you wanted." He fingered a flowered vase on another bookshelf. "In this part of Edinburgh, you're likely to be paying at least a thousand pounds for rent."

In her head, she did the currency conversion. Heather's eyes widened. "You're kidding!"

Malcolm glanced at the rest of the room, as if mentally taking inventory.

"I guess I have some money, huh?"

He nodded. "More than likely that has something to do with someone being after you."

Right. Someone wanted her dead. She couldn't lose sight of that fact. She crossed her arms.

"We should check the other rooms." Malcolm disappeared down the short hallway and slipped into what she assumed was her bedroom.

The handle on the front door rattled.

Heather froze.

The door opened, and a tall, dark haired man rushed into her living room. His eyes widened when he saw her, and the cigarette he held between his lips threatened to fall to the floor when his jaw dropped. The scent of his cigarette drew out her memories.

It was him! The man from the beach memory. "Malcolm!" She turned to run.

The man grabbed her jacket, yanked her to him. He slid his arm around her throat.

Chapter Six

*H*eather punched. Pushed. Kicked. The glass candy jar toppled off the coffee table and crashed into pieces on the floor.

Rancid breath drifted over her shoulder. "Just in time to give me what I want," he whispered in her ear. His grip around her throat tightened.

Her breath disappeared. Blood pounded in her ears. Panic surged through her. She yanked on his arm, but he was too strong.

Just as her vision began to blur, the man's grip loosened. He knocked her to the floor.

Heather sucked in air and scrambled toward the wall. Her limbs shook.

"Heather, get out!" Malcolm yelled in between blocking blows from the intruder.

In the center of her living room, he fought the man punch for punch. The intruder flipped Malcolm and dropped him back first on the coffee table. The wood splintered under the human weight.

"Malcolm!" Heather called, but her bruised vocal cords made it nothing more than a raspy whisper. She scanned the room. 999…999. Where the hell did she keep the phone?

Another crash of furniture and…silence.

Her heart constricted. She gasped and whipped around to see which man still stood. *Please, don't let Malcolm be hurt.*

He stood over the slumped, motionless body of the intruder, breathing heavily, and flexing his fingers into fists.

Heather dropped from her knees to her bottom, propping herself up on her fists. She let out a long breath as she stared at the body and then at Malcolm. Had he killed the man? She watched the lump on her floor, almost willing it to move with easy breaths so she knew her Highland hero wasn't a killer.

"Heather."

She yanked her gaze to him.

"Next time you do as I say." He pulled a gun apart like an expert.

The intruder had had a gun? Her stomach roiled. Or did Malcolm carry one?

"Is he dead?" She still hadn't seen any movement from her intruder.

Malcolm pointed to her spot on the floor. "Stay right there until I tell you to move." With his back to her, he pulled his phone free and dialed.

"It's me." He spouted off some kind of code, took a picture of his victim, and sent it to someone. "Right. I'll call in later." He hung up from the call, made another, and left a message. "Cam, you need to get to Heather's flat as soon as possible. There's been an incident."

Damn right there had been an incident.

Malcolm reached out to the coat rack and yanked a plaid scarf free. He knelt next to the body and tied the man's wrists behind his back.

Once that was done, he turned to her.

Every muscle in her body froze. What had happened to the kind and gentle man she had come to trust? He'd subdued the man with lethal moves no bed and breakfast owner should possess. Who was this guy?

"Are you all right?" He crouched down in front of her and lifted his hand toward her neck.

She slapped it away. "Don't touch me."

"You needn't be frightened."

She thought she knew him, but Malcolm had been right. "I don't even know who the hell you are." Not at all.

Malcolm lifted his hand again.

Heather stiffened and pressed her back into the wall.

He cupped her cheek and looked into her eyes. "Heather lass, from the moment I found you, have you had any reason to be frightened of me? Have I not done everything I can to make you feel comfortable? I promise you nothing's changed."

In the distance, sirens sprang to life. The intruder began to stir.

Malcolm claimed nothing had changed, but he was so wrong. Everything Heather understood, everything she'd believed since waking up in the hospital, was brought into question. She'd been a passive participant in her own case. She'd pushed thoughts of danger out of her mind so she could entertain the emotions that surfaced with her Highland hero's every glance, touch, or kiss.

No more. She'd focus on her own safety, her own physical survival. Her heart had no place in her thoughts at the moment or until further notice. Logic must rule.

ॐ

Malcolm stood with Cam and stared at Heather through the one-way glass of an interrogation room. She sat on a wooden chair with her knees pulled up to her chest and a cup of coffee clutched in her hands.

He hadn't wanted to tell her about his occupation at all, but this was definitely not how he'd wanted her to find out.

"What are you going to do?" Cam asked.

"Nothing. This is your job, not mine." He waved toward Heather. "Look at her. She's clearly not safe in my care."

"You need to take another look." Cam pointed to her. "That lass is alive because of you. The way I see it, she's safer with you than anyone else."

"She's not." Malcolm shook his head.

"Why? Because you care for her?"

He snapped his head toward Cam and narrowed his gaze. "Aye. Too much time thinking about taking her to bed instead of how best to protect her."

"You did protect her, you daft bugger!"

Cam didn't understand. People got hurt when feelings entered into the mix. Hadn't Malcolm witnessed it firsthand? Wasn't that the exact reason he'd quit the IPN?

It was best to keep emotions well guarded, hidden inside a vault deep in the soul. Emotions made him weak, and weakness caused failure.

"I've said it a hundred times already. I'm not the man for this job."

"And yet you're still with her. Have you ever thought that if you do care about her, it makes you the best man for the job?"

"No." He'd started caring for the mother and bairn he'd been sworn to protect in his last IPN assignment, and where had it gotten them all? With the mum in hospital, the bairn traumatized, and him in a review session with his superiors.

"Right then. Will you be telling her she's on her own, or will I?"

"What do you mean?"

"The department can't afford round-the-clock protection for her. You know that."

Malcolm clenched his teeth together, glared at Cam, and glanced back out at Heather. No, he'd not be leaving her to fend for herself. As much as he hated the idea, he'd take her home with him...again. "Sometimes I hate you, Cam."

"Aye, I know." He shooed Malcolm out of the room. "Go on."

He walked out, gripped the handle to Heather's room, and pressed his forehead to the door. "Professional, professional."

She'd been off-limits to him before simply because she didn't know who she was, but now she was off-limits because he had to keep focused. He couldn't be a professional if he kept thinking of her as a woman, a companion, a lover.

When Malcolm entered the room, Heather stiffened, but didn't turn to him. "Heather." He set his hand on her shoulder. "We can go."

She slid out from under his fingers. "I'm not going anywhere with you."

"Going to solve this mystery on your own then, are you? Going back to your flat, then?"

"No, but I...." Whatever thoughts raced through her head, she refused to share them. Instead, she sipped more of her coffee and kept her gaze focused on the far wall with the window. Outside, darkness crept over the horizon, squeezing out the orange and reds of the late afternoon sky.

"What's wrong?"

"Every time I close my eyes, all I can see are your fists pounding into that man."

Malcolm crouched before her and lightly bumped his fist on her knee. "He was there to hurt you. I wasn't about to let that happen." When she said nothing, he continued. "Heather, I'm still the same man."

She shook her head. "Oh no, you're not. Where I come from, B and B owners don't have moves like that, don't know how to handle weapons like experts, and don't talk in code like spies."

"I'm not a spy."

"But you're not just a B and B owner either."

"No, I'm not." He reached into his back pocket.

She tensed.

He hated that. It made him feel like a failure all the more.

From his wallet, he pulled his business card. IPN—Malcolm Fraser, Personal Protector. He'd thought he'd given it up. Apparently he couldn't even do that correctly. "This is my proper job."

She ripped the card from his fingers. "International Protective Network? I've never heard of it."

"It's a real business. You can ask Cam."

Her wide eyes turned to him. "So why didn't you tell me about this before?"

He shrugged. "I didn't think it mattered. Most people have one of two reactions: They're either obsessed with asking questions and getting details, or they're frightened. I didn't want you to be in either category." He eased the coffee mug from her hand, set it on the table, and took both her hands in his. "Heather, despite what you don't know about me, I am still one of the good guys."

"Logically I know that. Inspector Cameron wouldn't leave me with you if you were any danger to me." She sighed. "It's just everything I know has been turned upside down again, and I'm even more lost than I've been over the last couple of days."

"You trusted me before."

"Yes."

"Then put your trust back in me and let me take you home."

"I'm not staying in that flat, not now."

"No, you're not. You're coming back to Glenhalish with me."

"I thought the reason we drove down here was for you to get rid of me."

He should tell her something to soothe the hurt in her voice. But he couldn't. To explain his own fears would only open up more wounds he'd long past sealed shut.

"The man from your apartment claims he's working alone."

"You don't believe him."

"No, I don't."

She studied his business card once again, the edge of the cardboard flickering under her fingernail. "So you're my bodyguard then."

"Aye, unofficially."

"I can't pay you. I know we found expensive items in my apartment, but I don't really know yet what kind of money I have."

He gripped the arms of her chair. His jaw tightened. If she'd punched him, it would have hurt less. "I'm sure we can come up with some agreement on a fee when this is all over." He stood up and walked toward the door. "Let's go. We have a long ride ahead of us."

CR

The ride back to Glenhalish was quiet. Malcolm shared what he could with her about his call to his colleague Ian and about Cam's interrogation of Richard Sutherland, the man who'd grabbed her.

Visions of Malcolm played over like a continuous movie in her brain, from the gentle way he supported her in the hospital, to the beating in her apartment. Two things she could not ignore: he'd always, always treated her with care, and tonight he'd saved her life again.

And she'd insulted him with that crack about payment. God, she couldn't wait to get home and under the covers. Maybe, if she was lucky, she'd sleep until the police found out who Sutherland worked for, and she'd wake with all the missing pieces of her memory.

But Heather tossed and turned throughout the night. With the lights out and her eyes closed, all the boogey men from her life attacked her memory at once until she bolted upright in bed and left the room behind.

She slipped into the study, the room between hers and Malcolm's, and flipped on the lights. It would be a few more hours before the house would come to life with Mary and the girls preparing breakfast for the eager tourists who had no cares in the world. None of them had been attacked. None of them had been close to dying.

A shiver raced along her spine. Heather walked straight to the wet bar, grabbed a glass and the bottle of Glenmorangie whisky. The neck of the bottle clinked against the rim of her glass as she poured. Without putting the cap on the bottle, she took her first swig. The liquid burned as it traveled through her system, but she welcomed it. It meant she was alive.

"Can you not sleep?" Malcolm spoke softly.

"No, too many thoughts." Heather whirled around with the glass in her hand. He stood in the doorway with gray sweatpants on and no shirt.

Her mouth went dry. She'd imagined him to be fit, and after the fight with Sutherland, she expected as such, but the contours of his abs stirred to life every sexual need within her. *Good God,* he was beautiful. Her fingers itched to trace the muscles of his chest, to see if they were as hard as she imagined. An ache sprang to attention behind her breasts, between her thighs.

He wandered casually toward her. "Sutherland?"

"Among other things." Like how to keep her hands to herself. Another sip.

"Are you sure this will help?" He tapped his finger on her glass.

"It can't hurt." Another sip. Her eyes remained fixed on him, on the chest inches from her, on the overnight stubble covering his chin.

She closed her eyes and gulped down the last of the harsh liquid.

Glass clinked against glass.

When she opened her eyes again, Malcolm held the bottle. The liquid swished as he poured himself a drink and then refilled her glass. Once he returned the bottle to its place on the bar, he clinked their glasses, said, "*Sláinte*," and took a sip.

"I'm sorry, Malcolm."

"For what?"

"For doubting you in Edinburgh, for that comment about payment. It was like the first test of my faith in you, and I failed. For that, I'm sorry."

"I've already forgotten it." He cupped her cheek and brushed the pad of his thumb along her skin for a few seconds.

Not nearly enough.

"I'm confused, Malcolm. For a man who claims to want nothing to do with me, you've made it a point to spend a lot of time with me."

"It's not that I want nothing to do with you. It's that I have nothing to offer you."

She grabbed both their glasses and set them on the bar. She caressed his cheek. His stubble prickled her skin and stirred her hot desire. She might not know everything, but at this moment, in this room, she knew she wanted this man. "Why don't you let me be the judge of that?"

"Heather lass, it's as I told you—"

She pressed her finger to his lips, her palm to his chest. The heat of him seeped inside her skin and shot a zing straight between her legs. "Malcolm, I'm not a child."

"Aye," he said, his words rough with desire of his own, his accent thicker. "I know."

"I almost died yesterday, and this time I remember it." She stepped into the space between them, pressing her body with all its softness against his hard planes.

Malcolm sucked in a breath.

The feel of his erection against her belly, of his magnificence hardening with each movement she made, gave her a rush. She stroked both her hands down toward the elastic band of his sweatpants, and then back up. "I don't want to remember it." She wrapped her lips around one flat male nipple and used the tip of her tongue to move to his other nipple. "I want to remember something better." She rolled her hips against him.

He lifted her chin and forced her to meet his gaze. "I want you more than you can even begin to imagine, but if I take you to bed, I want you to be sure."

She slid her hand over his shoulder and tickled the back of his neck. "Malcolm Fraser, you are the only part of my life I am sure about right now."

His hazel eyes flared with hunger. He lowered his head and kissed her. She pressed her tongue to his, teased him, tasted him, shuddered with what was to come. He moved his mouth along her chin and down her neck while his hands roamed over her curves. Together they moved away from the bar and stopped by the desk.

Oh, no, he could not stop now. "Malcolm, please."

With a wicked grin, he pressed his finger against her mouth. "Hush, lass." He grabbed his wallet off the desk, pulled something out of it, and held up a condom. "Now, where were we?"

He tugged her with him across the floor, settled on the couch, and guided her down with him. She straddled his thighs, the hem of her nightshirt bunching at her waist. He slid his warm, rough hands under her top. As he moved them up over her belly, the material bunched more. He cupped her breasts and rubbed his thumbs against her nipples.

Heather pulled the shirt over her head.

Malcolm's teeth grazed her nipple just enough to elicit a moan from her. He slipped a pair of fingers under her panties and pressed against her clit. Moisture coated his fingers instantly. "Bloody hell, you're wet."

"For you." She kissed his mouth as they both worked to free her last bit of clothing. When she settled back in his lap, Heather arched into him. She wrapped her arms around his neck and whispered into his ear, "All for you."

There might be huge holes in her memory and even bigger questions about her future, but the present was something she could control. Heather wanted him, all of him, in her, on her, around her. She needed him to release the ache growing inside her—the hunger that had been building since he'd first started treating her like precious gold.

Malcolm groaned even as Heather's hips tilted again against his already hard cock. This was madness.

And so perfect.

Heather slipped her fingers inside his sweatpants.

Bloody hell, he wasn't going anywhere except deep inside her.

She shifted back a bit and pulled his cock free. Her gentle fingers danced over the length of him, covered him with the condom, and guided him to her opening. She sank onto him, one maddening inch at a time. "Heather lass." Her hands flattened against his chest, stroked down the front of him, and back again as she rose and descended again.

"Hush, Malcolm." She pressed one finger to his mouth. She replaced her finger with her lips, covering his mouth, enticing his tongue with her own. His hands drifted to her back and skimmed along her spine. Her skin was so soft, smelling of sweet lavender.

She moved over him, faster and faster, up and down his shaft. He slipped one hand between them and fingered her clit—plucked it, pinched it, rolled it between his fingers until she whimpered against his shoulder. Her body shook as her release built. Her cries of pleasure sank into his skin along with her teeth as she came.

His own release spilled seconds behind hers.

She collapsed against him, her breasts pressed firmly against him, her head tucked under his chin. He stroked her hair with one hand and her back with the other. "Heather lass, are you all right?"

Her lips brushed against his skin as she answered, "I'm perfect."

Aye, lass, perfect for me.

But she wasn't his. Couldn't be his. As much as he loved spending time with her, and as much as he'd enjoyed being with her, he'd not risk her life or his heart. This had been a physical act only, one to bring her pleasure and remind her how grand it is to be alive, nothing more.

Yet, the tight bonds he'd created around his own heart loosened. *Bugger,* he'd forgotten he had one.

Chapter Seven

*H*eather awoke alone a few hours later to the sounds of rain splattering against the window in her bedroom. She curled up under the covers, relishing the aches of her body after having sex with Malcolm. It had been magical, better than she could have dreamed on her own. She stared at the mist-covered hills and sighed. For the moment, her world felt perfect.

She showered, dressed, and descended to the kitchen. The Kierlain House was all but deserted. A few tourists had chosen to stay in by the fire instead of traipsing through rain and wind to get to an historical site. She chatted with the young couple sitting so cozily by the bay window until Malcolm came in from his morning run.

She jumped up and rushed to the doorway like a giddy teenager, but she couldn't help it. "Good morning." She smiled.

"Good morning." Malcolm spoke loud enough to include the tourists in his greeting. He stared at her for a second. "Did you sleep well?" he asked as he pulled his windbreaker and his hat off.

"Very well, thank you." Heather blushed. "How was your run?"

"Great, thanks." He turned away from her.

Her chest tightened. "Malcolm," she called when he started up the stairs.

He stopped.

Heather reached out and covered his hand on top of the railing. "Is everything okay?"

He tensed. "Aye." He pulled his hand free. "But I've errands to run with Jamie and Duncan MacInnes."

With that, he jogged up the stairs and left her alone. She hugged herself as a thousand thoughts raced through her head. Had she been wrong to sleep with him? She'd needed him and quite honestly, how could something so beautiful be wrong?

No, she'd not look back and regret what they'd done. She had too much to do to let his behavior bother her.

By the time she finished her breakfast, Mary had arrived to start her work. Heather jumped right in to assist, aiding guests, answering phones, helping in the kitchen. She had to do something to earn her keep, she told Mary. The day passed quickly and for the first time since waking up in the hospital, Heather felt useful.

Malcolm came and went several times during the day, but not once did he stop to talk with her.

And every time she approached him the following day, he made some excuse and ran out of the house.

By the third day, she was ready to tear her hair out. What had she done? What was he doing? If he had no intention of being around her, she might as well take her chances in Edinburgh with the police.

After Heather had tea by herself, Malcolm entered the house and went straight to the study. She followed him into the room and closed the door behind her.

He looked up from the book he held. Both eyebrows rose.

"What is going on?" She placed her fists on her hips.

"What do you mean?" He started back toward the door.

She planted her legs apart and stayed in his way. "I want some answers."

He crossed his arms and huffed. "Aye? And what answers would they be?"

"You can't keep ignoring me."

"I'm not."

"You are. Look, we're both adults, and I have no illusions that because we had sex we'll start a relationship, but at least be man enough to admit you've been behaving like a jerk."

What the devil had he been thinking? Ignoring her these last couple of days hadn't been wise. Malcolm had meant to cool the edges of his desire, but he only fueled her anger and his own longing for her. How could he need her so much so soon?

He closed the book he held and set it on the desk. "I'm sorry, but I cannit concentrate on keeping you safe if I'm thinking about you naked and in my arms."

Her eyes flew wide. Her mouth dropped open. "That wasn't what I expected."

"I have to think of your safety first."

"But I am safe with you."

"No, you're not. When we arrived at your flat, I was focused on you, not on keeping you safe. Because I let down my guard, Sutherland came close to taking you."

"But he didn't because you stopped him."

"It's not enough."

"I don't understand. The man's been arrested; I'm still in one piece. What's not enough?"

"He was not the main threat to you. There's someone else. I feel it. I can't do anything to take me focus away from finding that man."

"So, you refuse to allow yourself any fun while you're 'working'?" She air quoted the last word. "Even when you know we're both safe?"

He folded his fingers into a fist and turned away from her. He stared toward the window and prayed for the right words. "You don't understand."

"You're right. I don't get it at all." Slowly, her feet scuffed across the floor. He sensed her at his back seconds before she pressed her hand on his shoulder blade. "But I want to."

He closed his eyes and inhaled her scent. Oh, how he'd missed her—missed her gentle touch, her unyielding faith in him, her straightforward talk.

"In my job, distance is key. I cannit feel anything for my clients or my role is compromised. When that happens, people get hurt." He'd laughed with the bairn and the mum in Los Angeles for only a few moments and had missed the signs of the approaching assassin. "I must remain objective at all times. To have feelings for you puts you in danger."

"You're not a robot. You're human. You're allowed to have feelings."

"No, I'm not. You're not safe then."

She cradled his cheek in her palm, her soft fingers cool against his stubbled chin. Instantly memories of her hands on his chest, his back, his cock...*Christ,* he was getting hard just thinking about her.

"Malcolm, when my safety was on the line, you shifted into professional mode. You were able to handle both."

He shook his head.

She turned his head to her. "I trust you."

That alone put her in more danger, but the confidence in her eyes soothed him. Made him believe perhaps he did deserve her faith in him.

Oh, how he wanted to. Another layer of his hardened heart fell away.

He leaned forward and pressed a gentle kiss to her cheek. He didn't trust himself with her mouth. To kiss her thoroughly would stir his desires to get them both naked again, to explore her curves, her soft skin, to find new and exciting ways to make her moan. "Thank you for your confidence."

He only hoped he could be worthy of it.

She smacked her palms against his chest. "Now, you get back to work, and I'll leave you alone. I promised Mary I'd help with some of the accounting records."

"You don't have to do that."

"I know, but I like to help." She started back to the door and pulled it open before she turned back to him. "Just so you know, I expect you to have dinner with me later. A girl shouldn't have to eat alone."

"I'll be there."

Every moment he spent with Heather over the next day and a half was better than the one before. They spoke of memories that stirred her own. They shared duties around the house and helped Jamie set up the pub for the MacDougall clan gathering.

Heather continued to firmly plant herself deep inside Malcolm's life.

And he liked it.

⁓

Malcolm entered the study quietly. Heather lay asleep on the couch, a book spread across her chest. She slept soundly and from the softness of her features, he gathered, peacefully. Her body curled to fit against the too small couch, but her feet still hung over the side. Her fingers peeked out from the cuffs of her sweater.

She was beautiful in his eyes, and he was powerless to stop the effects she had on his heart. When others would have long since given up on him, Heather persisted, encouraging him to share himself with her. Each day he felt closer to her than the day before, and each day he tried to give back some of the happiness she'd shared with him.

He'd had plenty of women to warm his bed, but he'd given none of them his heart. None had earned his trust.

Until Heather. She accepted him as he was. She wasn't stupid. She knew he had many dark secrets but she hadn't changed toward him. He grinned. If anything, she was much more brazen with him than any woman had ever been, standing up to him to share her opinions.

Learning to put faith in her had not been easy, and sometimes he wasn't sure he was up for the challenge. He'd lived a cynical life far too long, been alone for far too long. But as he crouched beside her and pushed the hair from her face, he answered his own questions. The challenge would be worth it if only she stayed with him forever.

He watched her for a few more minutes. She began stirring, moaning with a creased brow.

Malcolm reached out to soothe her. She shrank away. "It's all right, lass. It's just a bad dream."

Her gaze flew around the room before locking with his. Slowly, the tension eased from her body, and she sagged against the back of the couch.

"You don't have to come to the gathering if you don't want to."

"I'm going." She yawned and lazily turned to the clock. "Give me ten minutes to pull myself together, and then I'll be ready to go."

"I'll be in the kitchen."

Malcolm was just giving last minute instructions to the evening maid when Heather appeared with three minutes to spare. *Pull herself together*, she'd said. She had changed from the jeans and sweater into a black hip-hugging skirt and a golden brown sweater. She'd pulled her hair out of the ponytail to let it float around her shoulders and down her back. The sight of her took his breath away.

"We'd better go." He rushed forward and helped her into her coat. If they stayed here much longer, he'd surely carry her to bed and forget all about the party.

ఇ

When they arrived at the pub, music poured out of the walls along with whoops, hollers, and clapping. Heather stopped outside the door. Malcolm held the handle but didn't open the door yet. "What's wrong?"

"I've been in Glenhalish for a week, and I feel more at home than I ever remember feeling anywhere else."

"I'm sure you were happy in your other life." He let go of the handle and stuffed his hands in his pockets. "You, Ms. Optimism, Ms. I'm Going After What I Want to Hell With the Rest of the World."

Heather shook her head. "I have enough of my memories back to know I wasn't. And you know what really scares me?"

"What?"

"That once I get my all of my memories back, I'll be miserable."

"Then you change your life and do what makes you happy. You put that first. As for now, just relax, enjoy what you have here, and deal with your other life when you get it back."

"Oh, I do enjoy my life now. That's the thing. You make me feel safe and comfortable and desirable and like I belong here. I couldn't ask for anything more, and I can't imagine anything better."

He ran his thumb down her cheek and pinched her chin. "You do belong here for as long as you like. Always remember that." He pulled her flush against him and lowered his head to kiss her. She felt the hard line of his cock against her belly and grew wet with desire.

The door swung open behind them, and several people yelled out to them.

66

Malcolm touched his forehead to hers. "We'd better go in."

Because the sooner they entered the pub, the sooner they could go home, and she could have what she most wanted. Him, inside her, taunting and teasing her body into wave after wave of unending pleasure.

The MacDougall family, along with most of Glenhalish, sang, drank, and danced to celebrate the matriarch's eightieth birthday. Heather reveled in the man beside her. It was as if whatever demons had possessed him had taken the night off. Malcolm introduced her to more of his friends, spun her around the dance floor, and shared more happy memories of his younger years.

After another round on the dance floor, Heather sent Malcolm to the bar for drinks. She sat next to the matriarch in the only free seat. The older woman leaned closer to Heather and talked over the music. In Gaelic, she commented, "True love is so rare these days. You and your husband give me hope in the future."

"He's not my husband," Heather corrected.

"Perhaps he should be, aye?" The old woman's eyes twinkled.

"Another round on the floor, Auntie?" A young MacDougall, a year or two younger than Heather, approached the older woman with an arm held out for her.

The woman took the man's arm and stood. Turning back to Heather, she said, "Hold close what you have, for it is a beautiful gift." She winked and moved out to the dance floor.

Heather scanned the crowd and found Malcolm standing with Jamie and a few other Scotsmen across the pub. Her heart fluttered. Was this old woman speaking the truth? Did she and Malcolm have something special? Something worth pursuing? She knew eventually they'd find whoever tried to kill her, and then she'd be free to go home. But was that life something she'd want back?

Butterflies roamed free throughout her stomach as Malcolm excused himself from the other men and made his way back to her. The elderly MacDougall danced her great-nephew over to him, and she touched his arm. Malcolm leaned over to hear her above the music. His eyes flashed over to Heather and a wide smile broke out on his face. He turned to say something to the woman and closed a fist over his heart.

She would have given anything to hear what had passed between them. When both Malcolm and the woman turned smiling faces to her, heat rush to her cheeks.

Heather accepted the cool drink from him when he took the seat next to her a minute later. She leaned closer to him and brushed the back of her hand between his legs. "Thank you."

He stilled for a moment and then turned to her. "You're a naughty little lass, aren't you?"

"Oh, I don't know." Behind her fingers, he grew tighter, harder. "Then again, perhaps I am." She slid her fingers to the zipper. "Maybe you need to put me in my place." She leaned more against him and took his earlobe between her teeth.

He gripped her hand and pulled her out of the seat.

"Are we going home?" she asked.

"We'll not have time." With his fingers entwined with hers, he led her through the hallway toward the bathrooms and through one of the closed doors.

The room was filled with boxes and bottles and metal shelving units. It smelled of dust and liquor. Malcolm closed the door and locked it. He slid behind her, his arms wrapping around her, pulling her flush against him. He slipped one hand under her sweater and cupped one of her breasts. The other hand slid under her skirt and slid against her clit. "You're a wicked lass."

She shivered in his arms as he inserted three fingers into her. He caressed her breast, teasing the nipple into a hardened, straining tip. Against her backside, his cock grew harder, tighter. The feel of him surrounding her, owning her, claiming her body, set off sparks inside her and sent waves of warmth between her legs. He stroked his fingers inside her, touching that most sensitive spot until her whole body shuddered in his arms. Heather bit her lip to keep from moaning loud enough to attract attention, but still a weakened moan escaped.

Malcolm did not relent. He wrapped his front arm completely around her chest, resting comfortably under her breasts, and he pulled his fingers free from her body.

Instantly she moaned again at the loss.

The zip-zip noise behind her overshadowed her own heavy breaths.

The sound of Malcolm ripping open a condom wrapper made her body hum in anticipation.

Her skirt remained bunched at her waist, but her panties slid down her legs. "Malcolm, I need a minute." Indeed, her legs still moved like jelly, and her heart rate hadn't calmed from her first release.

"You'll not get it." Malcolm leaned her over the boxes and slid his thick, hardened cock inside her from behind. Fast.

Heather gasped at the sensations of him traveling into her moistened walls, stretching her body. She did moan then, louder, longer. He surrounded her, owned her at the moment, and she didn't mind. Not one bit. She braced her hands on the boxes and surrendered control.

He pushed inside her again and again, faster, harder, completely. His chest pressed against her back, his mouth gently sucking and nibbling the skin of her shoulder.

She closed her eyes and surrendered to the sensations he gave her. She felt like she was floating toward the sun with too much love inside her heart, her soul. Higher and higher she rose, louder and louder she moaned, as he continued to slam into her until she touched the sun, and her body exploded. Wave after wave of her release rocked through her body. Seconds later, Malcolm joined her on the journey.

She collapsed against the top box with Malcolm still inside her.

"That should teach you to tease me in public."

"Are you kidding?" She grinned and turned her head back to him. "If this is my punishment, you can definitely expect much more teasing. That was amazing."

"Aye." He chuckled into her ear. "We are good together, aren't we?" He leaned in to kiss her and slid out of her body.

Yes, they were great together, in every sense of the word. For the first time in days, Heather felt like a whole person. At the moment, she couldn't imagine a more perfect life.

The challenge now became convincing Malcolm they were meant to be together. Heather hoped she was ready for the battle.

⁂

Heather carried her books and notebook down the stairs. Despite the wonderful time she'd been having with Malcolm, she needed to start working on her schoolwork again. Her Ph.D. had become very important to her, and she refused to fall behind because of someone coming after her.

She wandered down the hallway and listened to an elderly tourist ask the same questions of Malcolm as she had asked earlier that morning. Heather turned the corner and stopped behind the stranger studying the large painting on the far wall of the common room. "Hello."

"I hope you don't mind, I was just admiring the—" The man stopped speaking once he turned around. "I can't believe it."

He was handsome, well dressed, and an American.

"That particular painting depicts Bonnie Prince Charlie's arrival in Glenfinnan back in 1745," she explained. "Are you familiar with Jacobite history?"

"Yeah, somewhat." He flashed a brilliant smile revealing a precious dimple in his chin.

"Then I won't bore you with my rendition." She chuckled. "I'm Heather. Welcome to Glenhalish."

"Thank you."

"Did you come in with the tour?"

He didn't answer at first. He only watched her, glanced down the entire length of her body. He moved toward her with open arms. "No, Heather. I came for you."

Every nerve went on high alert. Heather backed up. "Uh, wait a minute."

The stranger continued toward her. "It's me, honey. Don't be afraid."

She took another step back and bumped into Malcolm. His hands cupped her elbows and then moved her behind him. "Can I help you with something?"

"I'm sorry. I'm just so happy to see her alive and well. The police warned me she might not remember me," the man babbled. "Heather, I've been so worried about you."

"Who are you?" She peered around Malcolm.

"I'm sorry. I should've told you that first. I'm Lucas Denton." He said his name like it was supposed to make everything clear.

Malcolm glanced at her for a confirmation she couldn't give. "And who are you to Heather?"

"I'm her fiancé."

Chapter Eight

The room began to spin. Heather's body was already weaving. This couldn't be true.

"Her fiancé?" Malcolm almost spat out the words.

"I need to sit down," she said.

Lucas awkwardly raised his hands to help, but Malcolm took the lead and walked her to the couch. Sadly, he took his hands off her too quickly and remained standing.

"I've been out of the country on business for a few weeks," Lucas explained as he sat beside her. "I didn't realize you'd been hurt until one of your friends called me."

"But my apartment in Edinburgh. There were no signs of you there."

"That's your home away from home. We live in New York. When you decided to do your research on the Shetlands and Orkney Islands, we though it best to set you up in the apartment. We agreed I would visit you in between business trips."

"When did you last speak with her?" Malcolm crossed his arms.

"We spoke the second week of August. She was planning to make another trip to Orkney to finish up the details of her research." Lucas turned back to Heather. "You'd told me you'd be there two to three weeks wrapping up, depending on the weather. You were supposed to call me when you got settled back in Edinburgh."

Malcolm reverted back to his thick Scottish brogue. "Did you not think it odd when you hadn't heard from her?"

Lucas looked to be biting his tongue. He steepled his fingers together and breathed deeply before answering. "I was in Cairo for two weeks and knew she'd call me when she could. You have to understand my fiancée and I lead very busy lives. Sometimes we don't see or speak to each other for weeks with her out on a dig or me on a business trip."

"My *fiancé*." Heather spoke as if repeating the word would help her absorb it that much quicker.

"Right."

She was almost afraid to ask the next obvious question, but she had to know. "Any children?"

"Not yet. We talked about it but decided to wait until you finished school." He set his hand on her knee and ran the other over her shoulder.

Heather stiffened.

Malcolm dropped both hands and curled his fingers. "You'll take your hands off her."

She resisted the urge to jump up and throw herself in Malcolm's arms.

Lucas glanced at Malcolm and then at her. "Of course." He pulled his hands back. "I didn't think about you not remembering me. It's understandable you're a little uncomfortable." He studied her with his eyes, but the feeling remained as filthy as if his hands drifted over every intimate spot of her. "It looks like you've been well taken care of. Other than the memory loss, I mean. You don't remember anything about our life together?"

"Malcolm, Jamie's just rang." Mary stepped in the doorway. "Oh, sorry. Should I come back?"

"It's all right." Malcolm motioned her inside. "Have you met Mr. Denton?"

"Aye, when he came in earlier. Jamie's wondering where ye are. The game's about to start. Do you want me to ring him back and tell him you'll not be there?"

"I'll take care of it," he answered.

"Right." Mary walked away.

"Mr. Fraser, if you have plans, don't let us stop you," Lucas piped in. "Heather and I have a lot to catch up on."

Her eyes widened and panic filled her chest again. Surely Malcolm wouldn't leave her alone with this man, would he? *She* wouldn't leave herself alone with him, never mind anyone else. "Why don't you come with us? You can fill me in on who I am while the guys watch the game."

"All right. Whatever you want," Lucas agreed.

She didn't want him here at all, but for now she'd put up with him. At least in the pub she'd have Malcolm by her side, Jamie behind the counter, and half of Glenhalish to keep her safe from her fiancé.

Damn.

CS

Mary must have called Jamie as soon as she, Malcolm, and Lucas left the Kierlain House because as soon as they entered the pub, Jamie held out a dram of whisky. "Good to see you, lassie. I thought you might be needing this." He winked as Heather reached for the glass.

Lucas set his hand on her forearm. "My fiancée doesn't drink."

"Aye, but our Heather does." Malcolm pulled the other man's hand off her.

"A lot's changed." She accepted the drink and swallowed it in one gulp.

Her fiancé's jaws clenched as he exhaled sharply. "Why don't we find a table, and your friend can grab our drinks? Is that all right, Mr. Fraser?"

"Aye, I suppose." He leaned onto the bar.

Once Heather and Lucas gave their orders, they walked to a table toward the back of the room. Around them, men cheered and yelled as one of the teams scored.

While Lucas droned on about his import/export company, Heather focused on Malcolm. He was her rock, holding her heart. He would help her through this disaster.

"Heather." Lucas reached across the table and took hold of her hand.

She fought the urge to yank her arm back. His skin was soft, cool to the touch. Not like Malcolm's warm and strong and utterly masculine hands.

"You have a life with me in New York."

"I have a life here in Scotland, too."

He waved his hand as to dismiss her thoughts. "That's only until you finish your degree. Then we have our wedding and can begin our family."

His cell phone rang.

Saved by the bell?

"Excuse me. I need to take this."

 C3

Malcolm turned away from Lucas and Heather and back to Jamie. "I dinna trust him."

"Now wait a bit," Jamie cautioned. "Dinna pick a fight straight away. See what he has to say for himself first."

"No, Jamie," Malcolm added while turning a watchful eye on his woman and her supposed fiancé. They'd claimed one of the last two open tables, in a far corner away from the noise and crowd. "There's something about him I don't like. If I had a fiancée like her, I wouldn't be out of contact for weeks at a time."

Jamie slowly, deliberately cocked one eyebrow at him and smiled.

"What?" Malcolm snickered. "What's the point in being engaged to her then?"

Jamie set their drinks on the bar. "You don't think he's responsible for her near drowning, do you?"

"I don't know what to think." Malcolm scrubbed his hand over his face. "I'll have Cam check his alibi for the night of the attack. He says he was in Cairo, but something's not right."

"Is that the personal or professional Malcolm talking?"

"Both." Which only made things more difficult. He'd allowed himself to care for her, he'd opened his hardened heart, and here again his pain made him question his own instincts. "Bugger."

"Take it one hour at a time. Your lass cares a great deal for you."

"Aye, but is it enough?"

"Who knows, laddie? For now, though, go over there and protect your woman."

Malcolm grabbed the three drinks and headed across the bar.

While Lucas talked business, Malcolm set the drinks on the table and sat beside her. Her usually bright eyes stared wide, as if she were caught in headlights. "Everything all right?"

"How can I be engaged to him? I feel nothing with him, nothing good anyway."

His jaw clenched. "Has he given you reason to be frightened of him?"

"No, but think about it. There were no signs of him at all in my apartment, no pictures of us, no bridal magazines or information a regular bride-to-be would be hoarding."

His whole body tensed. He stared across the table at the man claiming to be Heather's fiancé. She had excellent points, ones he hadn't thought of.

Lucas' phone conversation began to wrap up. Malcolm rested his palm against Heather's back and leaned closer to her ear. "Don't worry, lass."

And just like that, a bit of tension seeped out of her body. Whether his words or his touch, Heather believed him, believed in him, trusted him.

He hadn't lost her.

"Sorry about that." Lucas stored his phone in his pocket. "So, Heather, how about after we eat, we get your things and move them into my hotel room?"

Hell no.

Her head snapped up from her pint, and her jaw dropped open. She glanced first at Lucas and then Malcolm and then back to Lucas. "I...."

"That's not going to happen," Malcolm said calmly.

Lucas narrowed his gaze. "Forgive me, Mr. Fraser, but it's not your choice."

"You're wrong. It is my business, you see. The Edinburgh Police have put her in my care and until they tell me to let her go, she'll stay where she is."

"What qualifies you to keep her safe?"

"I'm the one who saved her life."

"More than once," Heather added.

Lucas sat back in his chair. "Fair enough." He nodded. "I can see where you're both coming from. You've been together for several days, and here I am, a complete stranger, eager to take her away. So how about this? Heather, at least spend some time with me, get to know me all over again and maybe more of your memories will resurface."

"I think that's fair. Malcolm?"

"Aye."

For the next day and a half, Heather spent most of her time with Lucas, trying to reminisce about a supposed love she no longer felt for him. She remembered their life together, the friends they had, but deep inside her soul, she couldn't shake the feeling something was wrong with this picture. If she was going to marry anyone, she'd be standing next to Malcolm, holding his hands, and repeating vows to love, honor, and cherish him. Not Lucas.

Malcolm always remained close by, always with a legitimate sounding excuse. But he hadn't welcomed her to his bed since Lucas arrived. She missed Malcolm, missed the feel of his body, the scent of their lovemaking, the adventure of exploring new and exciting ways to bring each other to completion.

Something inside her soul whispered this wasn't right. Heather would have to take matters into her own hands. Her decisions would affect all of them, but for once, she decided she would listen to her heart and do what she wanted instead of worrying about everyone else.

She pushed the covers off her body and climbed out of bed. Already her heart rate picked up speed. Her limbs shook, but she'd not back down. She deserved to be happy. She deserved to know if Malcolm would be part of that happiness.

Light slipped out from under his bedroom door. She raised her fist and knocked.

"Hold on." Shadows flickered under the door and seconds later it opened. "Is something wrong?" As usual, he had no shirt on and a pair of sweatpants.

Yes. He held her heart hostage. "We need to talk."

He stepped back and motioned her into the room. His gaze drifted the entire length of her. Once she stood in the center of the room, he closed the door. "What is it?"

"Ever since we met, you've been advising me to put my own needs first. Well, here I am doing that." Her pulse rumbled now, like a freight train along tracks. She wrung her hands. Could she go through with this?

Yes. She had no choice. She straightened her spine and looked him in the eye.

"I don't understand," he said.

"I've had enough time to think about it." She licked her lips. Good grief, this was harder than she'd anticipated. "I want you, all of you—the good, the bad, the ugly. You make me happy, when you're not being a jerk, and I want us to see where this attraction takes us. I can't imagine my life without you anymore, and frankly, I don't want to. So, I need you to make a choice. If you want me, claim me and let me in. If you don't, let me go." There. She'd said it. The hard part was over.

But he stood silent for too many minutes.

Her confidence dwindled. Her heart squeezed. She fought the urge to run from the room.

"Heather lass," he began, his voice thick with emotion. "You're already in here." He closed his fist over his heart.

Every bone melted in her body. Her chest exploded with...love? Yes, she loved him. She rushed into his arms. They kissed like they were starving; hands roamed everywhere as clothing disappeared. Malcolm swept her into his arms and carried her back to his bed. He wasted no time sliding over her body, the length of him pressing down on her. He palmed her breasts, kneaded the sensitive skin, and tweaked the hardening nipples. He pulled his mouth from hers and began a trail of fiery kisses along her neck, down her chest, and into the juncture of her thighs.

She gripped the sheets on either side of her and lost her mind. "Oh, Malcolm." Already her body wept for him as his mouth moved over her clit, sucked it, and nibbled it. Tears began streaming out of her eyes.

But his exquisite torture continued as he slid his fingers deep inside her until she bucked against the mattress, and her release rushed through her body.

When he covered her body with his again, he whispered, "I love watching you react to my touch, lass."

"Well, then, don't stop now." She wrapped her arms around his neck, her legs around his waist. "We've got a long night ahead of us."

Malcolm reached into the top drawer of his nightstand and pulled out a handful of condoms. "As you wish." They worked together to cover him, and then he slid inside her, slowly, and claimed her, body and soul.

C3

"Are you at home?" Ian MacKenzie, Malcolm's other best friend and IPN colleague, asked the next day over the phone. His voice held a hard edge.

Malcolm knew that tone. He gripped his cell phone tighter as he stared out of the kitchen window with a cup of coffee in his hand. "Aye."

"Are you sitting down?"

Adrenaline started to simmer within his blood. "What is it?"

"A package arrived this morning at your lass's flat, from Skara Brae."

"And?"

"I'm faxing you some documents from the package. You'll want to see them straight away."

Malcolm set the coffee down and started up the stairs. "Why is that?"

"All evidence points to Denton as the one who wanted her dead."

"What?" Malcolm gripped the banister, trying to blink away the red rage in his vision.

"There's a letter from a friend talking about how Heather had broken the engagement months ago."

Bloody hell. He released the banister and jogged the rest of the way up the stairs.

"And mixed in with her research are papers looking suspiciously like proof his company has been doing some illegal activity. I've already called Cam, and I've got our favorite technical analyst working on getting more information for us."

"Thanks, Ian." As Malcolm walked into the study, the fax machine beeped. He grabbed the papers. "I'll call you back in a bit."

"Right."

Malcolm studied the pages of names, dates, cities, and codes. Then he read the letter. Heather had apparently called off the wedding months ago. Lucas had been bullying her to reconsider, but she'd refused, choosing instead to take care of herself.

His chest constricted. Her instincts about Lucas had been right.

Malcolm stared across the room. He wanted her in every sense of the word, in every bit of his life, in every room of the house. All her courage urged him to take a chance. Every moment with her melted more of the ice around his heart. And he'd rather have her in his life, to experience the love he'd only ever dreamed of than to never explore it at all.

But first, they had to put a stop to Lucas' plan.

He stood, held the pages in his hand, and started down the stairs. Mary hummed while dishes clanked in the dining room.

Malcolm stopped in the doorway. "Have you seen Heather?"

"No, lad, not for a while."

He rushed through the house, room by room. With each empty space, his confidence dwindled. Where could she be? If he'd allowed her to be harmed because he thought too much of making love to her, he'd never forgive himself. In the kitchen, Malcolm picked up the phone and called Denton's hotel. "Please don't be there," he whispered as he waited for someone to pick up.

The front desk clerk hadn't seen her today, and neither had Jamie in the pub. Malcolm slammed the phone down and stared out the bay window. "Where the hell are you?"

His heart leapt. A lone figure stood at the water's edge by the breach way. Dark hair, the plaid Heather liked to wear. Fraser colors.

He smiled and started for the door, the fax gripped tightly in his hand.

As he pulled the door open, his world grew dark, his vision tunneled. Lucas Denton approached her from the footpath by the Glenhalish Monument.

Chapter Nine

The wind howled despite the warm sunshine. Heather pulled her pashmina tighter around her. If this was any indication of the winter to come, she knew it would be cold. But Malcolm would be there to warm her body and her heart for the rest of her days.

The water lapped lazily against the rocks. A lone boat bobbed about half a mile out, no doubt one of the neighbors fishing. Maybe she had decided to study here once she fell in love with the land. Surely her home in the States couldn't have scenery this beautiful.

The States. Her other life, parts of which, she no longer wanted. Soon she'd have to share her decision with Lucas. He deserved to hear the truth.

She breathed in the loch air and sighed. This was the life she wanted, one with Malcolm and the Kierlain House with the occasional trips to Edinburgh and Glasgow. At this moment, she couldn't imagine wanting a life somewhere else.

"Heather, I'm glad I got you alone." Lucas stalked toward her from the northern end of the loch.

"Hi, Lucas." Well, no time like the present to break off their engagement. "I'm glad you're here too. We need to talk."

"There's no time, sweetheart. We need to get out of here." He grabbed for her hand. "You're not safe here."

She yanked her hand away. "What're you talking about?"

"Your life is in danger. Please come with me now, and I'll explain on the way back to Edinburgh." Like dealing with a petulant child, he gripped her elbow hard and pulled her toward the tree-lined path.

"Wait a minute, Lucas."

"Fraser is behind your attempted drowning. He was hired by one of my former employees to kidnap you for ransom."

"That's crazy." Malcolm, who treated her well every single day, who made love to her like she owned his heart, could not be responsible for this.

"Heather!" Malcolm thundered toward them, a storm raging in his eyes, his beautiful body tense.

"Stay away from her, Fraser!" Lucas jumped in between her and Malcolm, his arms out to both sides. "I won't let you hurt her anymore."

Malcolm stood still, calm. His voice held the thick Scottish burr, but no hint of panic. "I'll not hurt her. She knows that."

Heather stayed where she was but asked, "Lucas, what makes you think Malcolm's responsible?"

"Sweetheart, I know it's hard to accept, especially when you've been so vulnerable, but this guy was only using you to get to me."

"Listen to the desperation in his voice, lass. Ask him for proof."

"Lucas?"

"I have proof in the car. I'll show you on the way to Edinburgh. Please, sweetheart. Let me get you safe."

"He can't give you proof because it would point to him. Heather, Lucas is the one who tried to have you killed," Malcolm explained.

Her stomach dropped. "What?"

"Don't listen to him," Lucas said. "He's just trying to take suspicion off himself."

"My friend Ian faxed papers left for you at your flat this morning from Skara Brae. One was a letter from your friend talking about how you had called off your wedding. The others were papers you picked up at Lucas' office when you were doing research. He wanted you killed because he worried you knew too much."

She glared at Lucas. "Too much about what?"

"His illegal business," Malcolm said.

"Heather, you can't believe that. You know I love you."

"I don't know what to believe," she mumbled out loud and stepped away from both men.

"I'll only tell you what's true," Malcolm said. By his sides, his fingers curled and uncurled. Papers crackled under his fingers.

"He'll say anything to get you away from me. Please, baby. Don't listen to him." Lucas leaned toward her.

Malcolm held out his hand, as if to reach for her. Or to stop Lucas. "That's right, lass. Dinna listen to me or him. Listen to your heart."

All the doubts and anxieties she'd had about Lucas from the moment he stepped into the Kierlain House came flooding back. She faced him and saw the desperation in his eyes as he awaited her answer. She then looked back to Malcolm and saw only truth and honesty. She knew he believed in her enough for her to make the right decision.

"How could you, Lucas?" Without another glance, she started toward Malcolm.

"You ungrateful bitch. I gave you everything, and this is how you treat me?"

"No!" she screamed as she whirled around. "You gave me nothing but social expectations for my role as your wife. I deserve to be happy. You're nothing but a money-hungry, power-hungry man, and I will do everything I can to make sure you rot in jail."

Lucas pulled a small handgun from his coat pocket and pointed it at her. "I'm sorry. That's not going to happen. I've worked too long and hard to let either of you ruin my business."

"No!" Malcolm started forward.

Lucas turned the gun on him.

Her whole body shook. Damn. She swallowed the lump in her throat. "It's over, Lucas. You shoot me, Malcolm will kill you. You shoot him, I'll fight you as much as I can."

"I'm not worried. You, I can handle." He kept his weapon trained on Malcolm.

Rage, hot and swift, consumed her. "Not anymore." She rushed forward.

"Heather, no!" Malcolm hollered.

She slammed into Lucas' side.

His arm shifted, and the gun went off.

Out the corner of her eye, she watched Malcolm duck.

Lucas tossed her to the ground. Her head slammed against the hard-packed earth. Pain splintered across her skull. Her vision blurred. Pebbles dug into her palms.

Malcolm knocked the gun from Lucas' hand. It dropped in between rocks. He growled like a pit bull and threw punches at Malcolm's midsection, at his jaw.

Fear seized her insides. Both men crashed to the ground. Malcolm struggled to gain control, but only for a moment. Her man had to win.

Malcolm gained the upper hand and tossed out punch after punch to Lucas' body until he no longer moved.

Then he stood and glanced her way. "Heather, are you all right?"

Her voice was lost. All she could do was nod. She scrambled to her feet and pushed herself into his arms.

He gathered her close. "You know that was daft, aye?"

"No, we're a team. I had to do my part to save the man I love."

She pressed her hand to his shoulder and brushed her mouth over his.

He returned her kiss, but not before he sucked in a breath through gritted teeth.

Moisture coated her fingers. Lead lined her insides. She pulled her hand away from him and gasped. Blood! "Malcolm, you're hurt!"

He winced as she fingered his wound. "It's only a scratch. I'll be all right."

"You need to see a doctor."

"I have all I need right here."

Chapter Ten

*H*eather wandered into the study with her hands behind her back. "How's your shoulder?"

Malcolm smiled, as he did often nowadays. He'd never tire of looking at this bonnie, amazing woman who had believed in him, trusted him, showed him what unconditional love was. "Heather lass, it was only a scratch. Even the nurse in the Accident and Emergency Department thought me a fool for getting it treated."

"Well, I don't care. I needed to know you were okay." She remained on the far side of the desk and tilted her head to see his day planner. "What are you doing?"

"I've called the IPN. I'm returning to work on Monday."

She nodded. "That's good."

"You're all right with that?"

"Yeah. You'd be a fool to give it up when you clearly are the best man for the job. Besides, with you at work, I'll be able to finish up my thesis." She swayed her hips as she rounded the desk, her hands still couched behind her. "And Monday's good. It means I have you for the weekend." With a devilish gleam in her eye and a wicked grin, she pulled a sheer blue scarf from behind her.

Malcolm's cock instantly twitched as the possibilities for sexual adventure streamed through his brain. He clasped his hands together, raised his eyebrows, and offered her his wrists.

"You're a naughty lad, Malcolm Fraser, with some very naughty thoughts." She smiled, maneuvered around his chair, and slid the cool fabric over his eyes. The scent of her lavender soap teased his nose. He could still see out of the scarf even after she'd wrapped it around him twice, but he wouldn't tell her. He'd let her lead him anywhere she wanted.

Indeed, she truly did have him, body and soul. "Aye, and will you help make those naughty thoughts come true?"

Her breath stirred over his ear. "Perhaps." She grabbed his hands and tugged him to his feet. "Now, follow my directions and trust me to lead you."

"All right."

She led him out of the room and down the hallway toward the room she'd occupied when she first arrived. But they turned left instead of right.

A sharp squeak preceded a rush of crisp, early evening air. The roof.

"Now, this could get tricky, but you have stairs to climb."

He'd traveled up and down these stairs thousands of times as a lad. He climbed them now with ease. Wind whistled and rustled his hair as he emerged. Heather came up behind him and closed the door. Again she took his hands. "A few more steps…almost…there." She pressed her palms against his chest. "You can take the blindfold off."

He pulled the fabric from his eyes. A beautiful sunset painted the sky to the west and a few stars twinkled overhead. Before him lay several blankets, a bottle of wine, and two glasses. A few candles flickered in the breeze. "What's all this for?"

"I wanted to see a sunset with the man I love, and I wanted to make love outside."

"I think I can handle that." He nodded and wrapped his arm around her. "I am a professional, you know."

"Oh yes." She pressed her sweet curves against his body. "You're definitely an expert." With a wicked gleam in her eyes, she drifted her hands toward his crotch. "And I think it's time for another lesson."

He held up the scarf. "Tonight's lesson will be to find as many uses for this as we can." He claimed her lips, captured her heart, and caressed her soul.

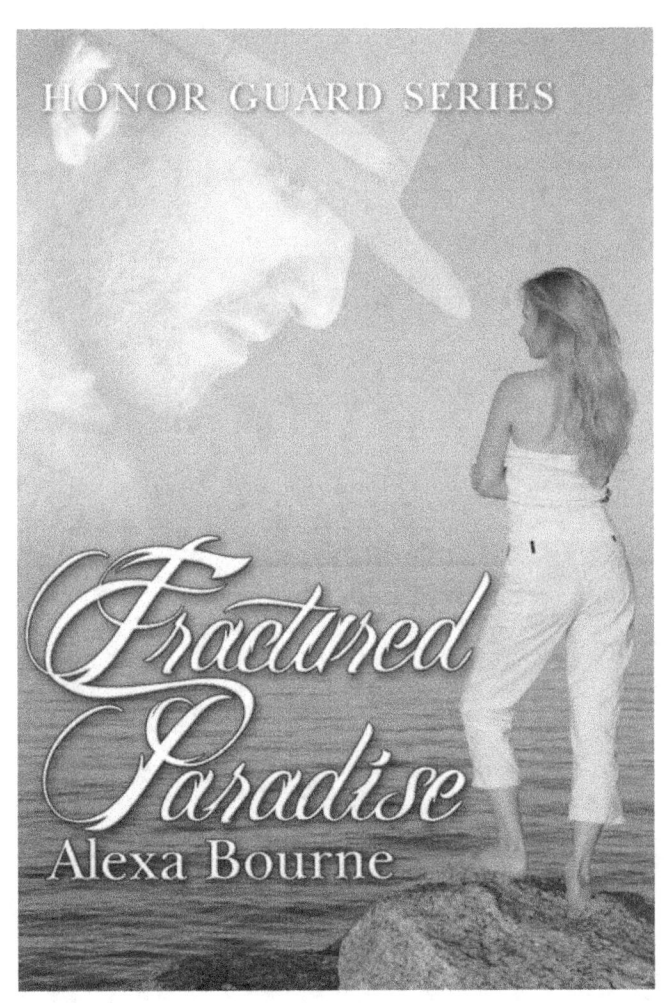

Fractured Paradise

Chapter One

*I*n a perfect world, Rachel Grant would be sitting on the back porch of her grandmother's English cottage sipping a pint of lager while watching the boats ferry tourists across the North Sea.

But this wasn't a perfect world.

The small cottage she'd been sent to "tidy-up" stared at her with broken windows, exterior walls missing wooden slats and stone, and a thousand years of neglect. Uncontrolled grasses choked the once vibrant and sweet-smelling gardens. Her sanctuary, Nan had called it? Maybe sometime in the last century.

She dropped her suitcases and flexed her fingers. She'd come to do a little dusting, a little washing, and *poof,* she would have the cottage ready for her grandmother's return. But this eyesore required extensive renovations. As a technical analyst for the International Protective Network, Rachel worked with computers and digital research. Manual labor was way out of her comfort zone.

Thunder crackled above, and she squinted up to the sky. An impending storm prepared to drench her at any moment—not that it would make much difference. When she'd rowed out to this isolated, pathetic piece of dirt, she'd soaked herself through. She shivered against the cursed wind, ran her fingers through her hair, and blew out a slow breath. *Now what?*

She'd given up her seat in front of a flat screen and a keyboard back in Edinburgh to execute her nana's fanciful ideas of returning to Sunderland. Rachel had agreed only because it was for Nan, but….

"This, I did *not* sign up for." Tears pricked at the corners of her wind-burned eyes, threatening to rip her resolve to shreds. Getting here had been hard enough. It wasn't fair that her island of paradise looked like the summer cottage from a teenage horror movie.

She took a cleansing breath. No panicking allowed. Solving problems was her specialty, after all. "Well, computer problems, anyway," she mumbled.

"A bit of a disappointment, I expect." A rich, deep voice with a twinge of an English accent drifted from behind her.

She whirled around. Her hair whipped against her cheeks and made her wish for the hundredth time she hadn't packed all her hair clips.

"Sorry. I didn't mean to frighten you."

The stranger paused beside the edge of the clearing, and her heart stuttered. Although no one would mistake him for a Hollywood leading man, the guy could command attention by stepping into a room. Or onto an island.

"That's okay. You didn't." She permitted her gaze to wander over him.

He kept his hands stuffed into the front pockets of faded jeans. The wind tore at his gray long-sleeved shirt, outlining the contours of a well-defined chest. Unruly light brown hair touched his collar. High cheekbones accented his deep-set eyes. Not friendly eyes, but no threat lay behind them either, at least none she could uncover.

He pulled a hand from his pocket and held it out. "Aidan Camden of Dawson Tours, your neighbor from across the water." He tipped his head toward the way he'd come.

Camden. His name sounded familiar, but why? She shook his hand with a hint of hesitation. "Rachel Grant."

His fingers warmed her skin, his grip strong and confident. Awareness trailed along her arm. Then again, it could be the accent that made her skin tingle. British accents never failed to stir her emotions.

A trace of a smile danced on his lips. "Aye, the American."

Huh. "You know of me?"

A low rumble of laughter slipped from his mouth, the sound relaxing her from deep within. "Word travels fast here. I saw you paddling your way out."

Paddling? No, he'd seen her fighting with the oars. Until today, she'd never set foot on a boat, much less held an oar. But she would consider swimming across the Atlantic Ocean if it would make Nan happy.

"Tell me, Mr. Camden, are you in the habit of following foreigners?"

"No, lass, but you're all the talk of the Roker area. The mighty Grant descendant come to see about selling the family cottage."

Selling? She lifted one eyebrow, pulled on her lower lip, and turned to stare at the building. Nobody in his right mind would plunk down hard-earned British pounds for this place.

"I was beginning to wonder if your family would ever agree to sell it," he continued as he moved past her toward the wreck. He set his hands on his hips and gazed at the rundown building.

Rachel aimed her eyes lower, to study the back of him, until an uncomfortable knot formed in her stomach.

Camden. Aidan Camden.

Alarms sounded in her head. She folded her arms across her chest. "So you're the one."

"Eh?" He turned back.

"My grandmother said someone's been harassing her to sell." Okay, harassing was her word based on Nan's ranting and raving, but still. "It's been you, hasn't it?"

He recoiled as though she'd slapped him. "I've done nothing of the sort. I've only inquired about purchasing the property since no one's been here in years."

The need to defend what belonged to her grandmother surged within her. She curled her fingers into fists. "Mr. Camden, I'm sorry you've been misinformed. I'm not here to sell my grandmother's cottage. I'm here to get it ready for her. I'm bringing her back."

His kind expression slipped away, replaced by a face cut in stone. He straightened to his full height. "For what?"

"To live, of course."

"Is she mad?" His lip curled as he pointed toward the cottage. "Just look at it. *You* can't stay in there, never mind your gran."

Planting her hands on her hips, she perused the dump before them. He had a point. The cottage definitely needed life support. "I admit it's not what I expected." No, her relaxing two-week vacation plan had gotten a huge wrench thrown into it. "But I'll make it work. Somehow." Because that's what people counted on.

Nan had asked her to embrace the possibilities, and that was exactly what she'd do. So what if the temperature was a bit on the cool side and the clouds threatened to burst open at any minute? Just because the weather and the cottage weren't perfect didn't necessarily mean this vacation would be bad. She worked with people who could do absolutely anything they put their minds to. "I can handle this." She would assess the damage and map out a plan to accomplish her goal. *Problem solved.*

Slowly, she walked toward the front entrance. When she turned the handle and pushed, the door fell off the hinges. Its bottom edge thumped against the ground while the top half teetered forward, threatening to crush her.

Rachel shot her hands above her head.

Camden came to her side and braced the door. "Mind yourself."

"Thanks." She glanced up at him.

Hazel. His eyes were hazel with a strand of gold threaded in them rivaling the rays of a midday sun. And if she wasn't mistaken, a bit of tension cast shadows along his features that had nothing to do with the weight of the door.

In the front yard, he'd looked tall, but standing so close to him, she could see he stood a good few inches above her, which placed him at about six-two. He'd appeared thin, but the width of his shoulders set that notion aside, as did the bulk of muscle straining against the sleeves of his shirt. And those eyes—invasive, as though he tried to search out weakness within her.

A shiver curled down her back.

She cleared her throat and broke eye contact. She had enough to think about. Good-looking men came, wreaked havoc on trusting hearts, and went. This geeky computer girl needed to focus on family.

Camden leaned the broken door against the wall and took a step away from her.

Good. She needed to concentrate on the house, not on Camden. He was the enemy, after all. He'd had his estate agent call Nan, send her letters with legal mumbo-jumbo she didn't understand, and panic her into contacting Rachel for help. Sure Camden was polite now, but she had no doubt he would put up a firm fight.

She wandered into the kitchen and swiped her fingers in the dust on the counter.

"Your family hasn't been here in ages. Why would your gran want to come back at all?" He opened cupboards and drawers, glancing inside each one.

What does he expect to find?

"My grandmother loves Sunderland and all her memories tied up in the cottage." Although, Rachel's own recollections held a beauty long lost to the building she currently stood in. "I can assure you, Mr. Camden, she's not interested in selling."

He picked up a forgotten plate and blew a breath over it. A dust cloud swirled around him before he returned the plate to the counter. "Aye, perhaps, but your parents are willing to consider it."

She bristled, with knots forming in odd places in her chest. "My parents?" But the cottage wasn't theirs to sell.

Camden stuffed his hands back into his pockets and glanced at the ceiling, as though studying the damage left there by too many thunderstorms. "I offered to take it as it is. I thought your arrival meant they intended to proceed."

She wanted to be angry with him for trying to charm—Nan's word—the property out from under her grandmother's nose, but she couldn't. Her sense of righteousness, ingrained in her since birth, won out. He had his own reasons for wanting the land, and as much as she was dying to know, he owed her no explanation. She had to respect his reasons even if they didn't agree with her own agenda.

But he's not getting this cottage.

"No, sorry. Legally my grandmother is still the owner," —as far as she knew— "and she has every intention of returning." And Rachel would do whatever she could to make sure her parents didn't yank the cottage out from under Nan's feet. Just because she was old didn't automatically make the woman senile. "Why is the cottage so important to you?"

Those hazel eyes couched a mixture of reverence and sorrow. "I'm afraid that's private."

She regarded him for a few seconds, trying to see past the guarded wall he'd erected. What secrets did this Englishman hide? More importantly, why should she care?

She couldn't.

She passed into the bedroom just off the kitchen and ran right into a mass of cobwebs. The silky threads clung to her skin, catching on her lips and lashes. Shaking her head, she spat them away and brushed her hands over her face. The skin on her arms tingled, as if hundreds of spiders crawled over her.

Camden closed the few feet between them and picked another strand of the web from the side of her face. His barely-there touch left her with an odd sensation.

"Thank you."

She stepped away and continued room to room, calculating all the work she'd have to do to make the place livable again. Broken furniture, dust everywhere, boxes of junk strewn across the floors. Patches of the ceiling sagged here and there. The window on the far side of the living room would be beautiful if not for the crack down one panel and the caked-on mud obscuring the view of the sea.

She sighed.

Camden traipsed to her side. "You know you'll not be able to stay here, aye?"

She shrugged. "Not at first, anyway. I'll spend a few nights at a hotel while I clean and start repairs. Then I can spend the last few days here before I go get Nan. I can always continue repairs when we get back."

"So you're to stay with her, then?"

"Yes, to make sure she's taken care of and to handle any problems that arise."

"Such as me?"

She glanced up to him and found a contagious smile. "I hope not, Mr. Camden."

"Call me Aidan."

She wouldn't. First names were a bad idea with a man like him. He wasn't interested in making friends. He only wanted the cottage. She'd been down this road before. At least Camden didn't cover up what he was after. Not like Trevor Layton, who'd wined, dined, and bedded her just to insinuate his way into her father's powerful circle of surgeon friends. Even now, a year and a half later, the memories of her engagement still left a bad taste in her mouth.

Forget both of them.

"I'm sorry you've been misinformed, Mr. Camden, but we're staying, and there's really nothing you can do to change our minds."

"You can't understand Sunderland life after a short holiday here."

Her insides knotted, but she stood her ground and kept her gaze locked with his. Too often in the past she'd surrendered to Trevor's stare. But she was guilty of nothing—then or now. Today she would not be the first to look away.

"Thanks for the vote of confidence." Rachel always found a way to accomplish whatever she set out to do. Of course, that usually involved technology. "If you don't mind, Mr. Camden, I have a lot of work to do, and I really need to get started."

But he didn't move. Instead, his gaze swung out over the window. Some emotion weighed down his shoulders. Regret maybe, or longing. "I'd forgotten how beautiful this view of the lighthouse is."

She bent forward and tried to see what he saw. "It's gray and cloudy."

A soft chuckle left his lips. "Aye."

The sound tugged at what heartstrings she had left. "So you haven't been out here in a while." Even as the words left her mouth, she knew they were a mistake. Fishing for information would not help get him out of the cottage.

"No, not in a few years." It seemed as though some memory held him rigid.

The pain overtaking this strong Englishman rattled her nerves. *Do not ask anything else, Rach. You want him to leave.* "Then why do you want the cottage?"

"My wife always loved this place."

She let out a short, silent breath. "I'm sorry, but she can't have it."

"Aye, I know." Camden turned his gaze to her, a low fire crackling in his eyes. "She's dead."

Rachel stilled. A leaden weight dropped from her stomach to her toes. He had her attention now. All of it. What was she supposed to say to that?

Prickly silence hung on the stuffy cottage air between them.

"I'm sorry for your loss." She held out her hands in a gesture of surrender. "Look, let's work together to find a solution, something that benefits us both."

Aidan wanted to kick his own arse for telling this blasted American about Brooke. It was none of the lass's business. "A compromise is out of the question."

Too late in his marriage he'd promised to look into buying the cottage for Brooke. Cancer stole her away before he'd ever gotten a response from the Grant family. He'd vowed to her while she lay on her deathbed he would continue with their plans for the cottage. He needed this property signed over to him if he ever hoped to find peace again.

Emotion had no place in this discussion. For him to get what he wanted, he had to think clearly, be smart. "Fixing this cottage isn't pulling out a few weeds, washing some windows, and sweeping the cobwebs away. There's hard labor here, and you're only one woman."

"Yeah, but I can do it."

Such confidence, she had, in the face of impossible odds. Like his Brooke.

Yet, so very different. He studied Rachel, with her dark blue sweater and those classic American jeans. His gaze soon drifted to her long, blonde hair, falling round her shoulders, to her storm-tossed green eyes. Aye, that phrase sounded daft, especially from him, but there was no other way to describe them.

Nonsense! He needn't worry about the woman's eyes. What happened to him being smart?

She propped her fists on her slim hips and her bottom lip jutted out like that of a cheeky bairn. Her breasts rose on the heels of a deep breath.

He closed his eyes for a moment and rubbed those images from his head.

"I may only be one woman, but I'm a very determined one."

He nodded. "Aye, you are that." *And stubborn.* Against his will, a hint of a smile forced its way to his mouth.

He needed to pick his battles. This wasn't one to fight. The right time would come. Indeed, perhaps the best way to get rid of Ms. Rachel Grant would be to leave her alone. After watching that display of her rowing out to the island, he knew one of these times she would upset the boat and land in the cold, harsh North Sea. Surely after that, she'd not want to stay. She wasn't prepared for the work before her.

Aidan walked to the door, opened it, and peeked out at the sky. The mists rolled in over the Roker Pier Lighthouse again along with the darkening clouds. A perfect match to his mood. He peered at his watch and turned around to face his intruder. "I'll be on my way. I've an afternoon tour to look after. Take care crossing back to the shore."

"I'll be fine, thanks." She rubbed her arms. "I am sorry you've been misled."

After crossing the threshold, he stood outside the cottage once again, and shrugged. "No matter."

Her lips curved into a bonnie smile. "Have a good day, Mr. Camden."

Something stirred within him. "You as well, lass."

Aye, walking away was the right decision. On his own he would be able to reevaluate his options logically and put to rest these daft emotions she'd ignited.

Chapter Two

*R*achel had come to the United Kingdom years ago to accept the job of a lifetime. She'd come to this *city*, if you could call it that, today at Nan's request. Tonight, she came to the Thrush and Hound Pub because she seriously needed a drink.

Hopefully, the pint of lager sitting in front of her would help ease the panic that had settled into her bones after an afternoon in the cottage. She was beginning to think she'd bitten off more than she could chew here. How the hell had she let Nana talk her into this?

She should be in her element, searching through digitized documents for the bodyguards of the IPN, instead of carrying out this ill-fated secret mission for her grandmother.

She sipped her lager, took a deep breath, and scanned the pub. The building was twice the size of that dilapidated cottage, and with a much cozier atmosphere. It sported wooden tables and pictures of when Sunderland shipyards were in full swing. An area with darts and a big screen TV lay on one side separated by an ornately carved wooden railing. A sense of warmth welcomed her from the moment she'd stepped inside.

Then again, maybe that was just what she'd hoped to find after the strange encounter with Aidan Camden. She set her pint back on the bar and traced lines along the glass with her finger. Clearly, he didn't want her around now that he knew she didn't intend to sell the cottage, and yet she couldn't stop her hormones from reacting to him.

The bell on the front door of the pub chimed. The bartender looked up from loading glasses in a dishwasher and waved. "Hello, Aidan. What can I get you?"

Rachel's stomach flip-flopped, and she sat up straight. So much for relaxing tonight.

His voice, so deep and rich, drew closer. "As if it's different from any other day, lad."

"A pint it will be, then." The bartender shifted to the cupboard, retrieved a glass, and pulled on one of the beer taps. Camden took possession of the stool next to her despite all the empty ones along the bar.

She turned her head toward him.

Big mistake.

He fixed those hazel eyes on her and flashed a heart-stopping grin. "Hello again, Rachel." Her name rolled off his lips like a sweet caress.

Her insides melted even as her brain ordered her to ignore the reaction. Good grief, what was wrong with her? Camden equaled the enemy. Trevor had wanted her dad's social circles. Camden wanted the cottage. They weren't that different.

It had to be the accent. Although, why did everyone she'd met in Sunderland sound a lot like her colleagues in Edinburgh?

"Hello," she said.

His gaze fell on the overnight bag that lay between them. "Decided to put the cottage behind you, then?" A lilt in his voice revealed his hope.

"Just for tonight." She glanced down at her bag. Remembering the state of the cottage, she added, "And maybe tomorrow."

"Thanks, Bradley." Camden grabbed his pint and took a sip. "Daft lass," he chided under his breath, but the smile took the sting out of his words. "Do you really want to risk your Nan's health by bringing her back to that?"

"Mr. Camden, I'm not stupid. I won't bring her down here if it's not ready."

"Will you not call me Aidan?"

"Why should I? We're not friends."

His hazel eyes gleamed with mischief. "Aye, but we're not enemies, either."

"True enough, *Aidan.*"

"Of course, with the cottage, you do have another option."

Leaning her elbow on the bar, she cradled her cheek in her palm. He was nothing if not persistent. The grin refused to wait and tugged at the corner of her lips. "Even if I wanted to, it's not mine to sell."

He crossed his arms. "I'll make your gran a fair offer. Think on it, lass. The two of you can enjoy your holiday, get out and see the sites of northern England. Then you can tell her how charming I am and how she'd be absolutely daft not to sell to me."

After the hours she'd spent this afternoon knee deep in dirt, dust, and debris, he offered a serious temptation. But Nan had a plan, and she was counting on Rachel to see it through.

"I can see the wheels spinning in your mind." He raised his glass. "To a new partnership."

She held on to her glass and pulled it to her chest. His gaze followed for an instant before settling back on her face.

Typical man. "I haven't agreed to anything."

"Aye, but you will. You'll see. When you wake up tomorrow faced with the reality of the cottage repairs, you'll make the smart decision." He held out his glass, raised it again, and took a deep drink.

"Don't bet on it. I have no intention of abandoning the cottage."

The bell to the pub chimed again. He slipped a lazy glance toward the door. "I see you've inherited one trait from your Grant ancestors."

"What's that?"

"Stubborn pride." Sliding off the stool, he pulled the pint glass with him.

"Did I hear you say something about a Grant?"

A stocky young man in his early twenties and an even younger man stopped next to them at the bar. Both towered over her. The two newcomers shared the same unruly chestnut-colored hair, chiseled features, and eyes infused with trouble.

All four men exchanged greetings, then all eyes returned to her.

"David and Adam McAndrew, meet Rachel Grant." He gestured

toward her. "From America."

"I work in Edinburgh, actually."

David's bushy eyebrows lifted, and his gaze slid back to Aidan. "The plans are coming along, then?"

Bradley poured two more pints.

"Not quite." Aidan held a forced smile. "She's here to *restore* the cottage so her grandmother can come back to live in it."

"Is that so?" A dark expression slipped over Adam's face. "And your family's left a wee thing like you to see to the repairs, have they?" He fished in his pocket and handed Bradley some money.

Wee thing? At five-nine with about fifteen extra pounds on her, she had never been called a wee anything. She straightened her back and lifted her chin. "They know I can do anything I put my mind to."

"But you fixing the cottage on your own, that I'd like to see." David smacked his brother in the chest as both men snickered. Aidan had said as much to her on the island, but here he remained silent, holding allegiance to neither side.

Tension crept up Rachel's spine, the kind that surrounded her when one of her IPN operatives dared to question her research abilities. She had no tolerance for people with no faith.

"Not only that, but I'll be able to get the job finished in record time. Wait and see. I'll be sure to invite you out to the island when it's done," she snapped.

"Lads, let's away." Aidan thumped David on the shoulder.

The brothers grabbed their beers off the counter.

"Aye, and leave Miss Grant to her grand fantasy." David allowed Aidan to steer him to the back of the pub.

"Luck to you then, miss," Adam said on the heels of another chuckle. He followed the others to a corner table.

Turning back to the bar, she took a swig from her pint glass. She'd get the work done, go get Nan at Heather Oaks, the sheltered accommodation facility in Edinburgh, and then relax. Cleaning the cottage would be her first step. If she could just do that, then everything else would surely fall into place.

That settled it. She would finish her drink, go check in at the Hastings Hotel, and retrieve her laptop. She would research Camden, the McAndrew brothers, and businesses to assist her efforts in this…city. The sooner she could get the work done, the sooner she could leave and return to civilization.

Aidan sat with his back against the wall. As he watched Rachel bend down and grab the overnight bag by her feet, he itched to say something more to her. Perhaps goodnight or good luck. Or maybe just goodbye. Instead, he curled his fingers around his glass and sipped his pint.

David glanced over his shoulder and then slid him a punishing glare. "Why do you look at her that way?"

"What way?" He snapped his gaze back to the boys.

"As if you want to set things right for her." The lad scowled.

"Don't be daft." He rolled his eyes, picked up the cocktail napkin, and tore it into jagged strips.

"Do you not want the cottage anymore?" Adam asked.

No, he'd never wanted it. "Aye, I do. Your sister's dream for it," — haunted him still— "stays fixed in my mind. I'll not dishonor her." His conscience wouldn't allow it.

David bent farther over the table and lowered his voice. "Then why do you want to aid the enemy?"

"That woman's not the enemy. She has more right to be in the cottage than Brooke and I ever had."

"But you and Brooke had grand plans for it," David said.

No, their sister had had those plans. Aidan had never wanted to leave London to return to Sunderland. Another difference between husband and wife. Another sword point to hold his soul captive.

Rachel wandered toward the door, set her palm against it, and glanced back at him. Was that some sort of plea across her face?

Horrid sensations twisted his innards, yet he couldn't pull his gaze away. Why did her eyes have to seek him out?

"Those Grants haven't been here in years. Can you not fight for it?" Adam shifted in his seat.

"Aye, I can." He watched the lass slip out the door. "But I'll not need to."

"Eh?" the brothers said in unison.

"She thinks she'll be able to restore the cottage, but she'll not have the strength to do it." The lass didn't belong here. With luck she'd realize that soon, and he'd own the cottage outright.

"You'll not help her, will you?" Adam's voice held on to the anguish of a brother's broken heart, as if letting the cottage go would betray Brooke's memory.

Perhaps it would.

"No, but I can help her see what a daft idea she's got in that head of hers." That stubborn head with its waves of golden hair falling around that firm chin, and those piercing green eyes. Lovely eyes that just might cause him a twinge of guilt when he claimed the cottage.

No. He carried enough guilt for failing his childhood sweetheart. The American was the weak one here. He was not.

Gulping the rest of his beer, he stood. "Another round, lads? This one's on me."

È

The next morning, Rachel glanced out the window of her Hastings Hotel room and sighed. The sunny scene was very different from the torment of last night's downpour. "Sunderland, let's work together today, all right?"

Ten minutes later, she bounded down the front steps of the hotel. Scattered clouds set high in the sky. Banners swayed in the breeze. Any remnants of last night's thunderstorm had disappeared, leaving behind a perfect picture before her.

She roamed along Fawcett Street in the direction of the Sunderland Bridge. Sunlight spilled on the streets, reflected over the Stadium of Light soccer arena. *Football*, the English would correct her.

She smiled, remembering how huge this street was when she was little. Now, it would only take a few steps to cross. The memory of skipping across while holding her grandmother's hand brought her heart peace. How could she have forgotten what she loved about this place?

Bits of Nan's stories resurfaced from far off places in her brain, of days her grandmother wandered along that bridge with a pastry on her way to see her own grandmother. Today, Rachel chose a sausage roll from a nearby Gregg's Bakery for her stroll across the bridge. The cottage was only about two miles away, and the exercise would do her good.

She took the stairs just off the bridge, intending to stay along the edge of the River Wear. Had she really only been seven the last time she'd followed that path? She had come here to spend the summer with her grandparents while her father performed surgery and her ten-year-old sister, Vicki, toured the States with their mother and participated in various beauty pageants. At first, Rachel had been upset her mother had sent her away, but after hearing how miserable her sister was, and after the magical Grant outings to the Hylton Castle ruins and Marsden Grotto, she had decided to be relieved. Nan always made her feel special.

As Rachel passed the Roker Pier Lighthouse, she spotted her rival exiting the grocery store a few blocks away. He carried a brown paper bag.

Her stomach curled. Tingles sparked behind her breasts and shot right into her abdomen. Damn it, why did her body react every time she ran into the man? E-n-e-m-y. No matter how attracted she was, Aidan Camden was no man for her to deal with. Not now, not ever.

And yet, she still hurried her pace to catch up to him. "Good morning."

"Hello." Aidan stepped into line with Rachel and allowed his gaze to float over her. She looked much more casual today, with a well-worn pair of jeans and a sweatshirt to match her eyes. Her hair fit into a ponytail. "Back for more punishment on your island?"

They passed various guesthouses, walking side-by-side as if old friends instead of two strangers who vied for the same thing.

"It's a new day. I have plenty of hours to get quite a bit done in the cottage before the sun goes down."

"What's brought on this attitude? When you left the Thrush and Hound yesterday, you looked quite defeated."

She leaned toward him. "You'd like that, wouldn't you?" A brilliant smile curled her full lips.

"I want the cottage. I don't want you harmed in the process."

She halted in the center of the Dawson Tours parking lot. For a second their eyes locked in some kind of strange connection. Something stirred within him, hot and hungry.

"I almost believe you," she said.

What was it about this woman that prompted him into action, into banter he'd never been comfortable sharing with Brooke? With his free hand, he reached up and caught the loose strands of her hair in his fingers and tucked them behind her ear, his fingertips lingering against the shell.

"Thank you." She allowed that tongue to swish over her lips, moistening them, taunting him, all but begging him to taste them for himself.

He snatched his hand away and stepped back. Where had those thoughts come from? He could not have anything physical with her. Nor did he want anything to do with her. He'd loved one woman filled with daft ideas for that cottage. He'd not be swayed by another. Aidan closed his eyes and pressed the heel of his palm against his forehead.

"Hey, are you all right?" she asked.

The gentle caress of her voice was almost as deadly as the touch of her fingertips to his wrist. His blood steamed under his skin, tinder threatening to burn with an ache so deep he'd forgotten what it felt like. So long he'd gone without a woman in his life, in his bed. Perhaps this was his body's way of saying *get on with it*.

He opened his eyes and jerked backward. The grocery bag tipped to one side. "Aye," he snapped amid the crackling of the bag as he steadied it.

Her fingers recoiled, and instantly, guilt crept into his body. He wouldn't say into his heart. Brooke had ripped that out and taken it with her a year and a half ago after her fierce battle with leukemia.

Brooke. Aye. Thoughts of his wife were good at this point. Definitely would stop him from thinking about this foreigner and her effect on him. Brooke's silly notions of an island escape had all but drained the life out of their crumbling marriage. Then her illness grabbed the rest. He had promised to honor her and what they'd never had a chance to achieve from that day forward. He'd do well to remember that anytime thoughts of Ms. Grant crowded his brain.

And yet, he was sure he'd not ached like this with Brooke. Ever.

He stole a glance at her. While not conventionally beautiful, Rachel was a truly bonnie lass still. He peeled his gaze from her and focused on the Dawson Tours front door. Salvation from all she stirred within him waited, as soon as he could get to the privacy of his office.

From the corner of his eye, he noticed her staring out toward the cottage. Surely she'd give up and go home soon. Wouldn't she?

Something lent that sparkle to her emerald eyes. Defiance, stubbornness, pride. Whatever it was, she stood a bit straighter, stronger, prepared for a battle. "Nan always said if something's not worth fighting for, then it's probably not worth having."

Aidan shrugged. "Sometimes no matter how hard you fight, you still lose." She turned to him. He sensed it, but he absolutely did not return her gaze. "And then you've wasted all that time, all that effort on something instead of focusing on what you can do."

His attempts to buy the cottage, to make it Brooke's dream home, had robbed them of precious time together before she succumbed to the disease that ate away at her.

She remained silent for a long moment, and he wondered if he hadn't offended her. "Maybe you believe what you're doing is best," she finally said. "In the end, nobody can find fault with that, right?"

He knew some deeper emotion lurked behind her words, but to be truthful, he wanted nothing to do with it. Trying to console the wounded heart of a woman had nearly driven him mad once before. He'd not get involved in this woman's life anymore than he already had.

To his relief, she appeared to have less interest in pursuing those emotions than he. She folded her arms. The wind whipped her bangs from her forehead. Those potent green eyes filled with moisture. "Listen to me ramble. Sorry. We've both got work to do. Have a good day, Aidan."

Without giving him a chance to respond, she crossed the empty road and set out on a jog toward the shore. For a moment, he wished for her to come back. As if some piece of him trailed after her and left him un-whole.

But just for a moment.

This was better. She returned to the life she insisted on making and he to his. Simple. Perfect.

Then why did he stand in the Dawson Tours parking lot watching her settle into the boat and wrestle with the oars?

Chapter Three

After two straight days of working in the cottage, Rachel thought she was ready to spend her first night there. She'd scrubbed, swept, and rearranged furniture.

But now that she stood in the center of the living room with her pajamas in her hands, her suitcases against the rocker, and noises coming from the walls, reality did not live up to her dreams.

Wind whistled an eerie tune through the cracked windows despite the plywood she had managed to hammer in place yesterday afternoon. The wood burned in the fireplace, yet a chill overtook her body.

Thump, thump.

She stilled. Gripped the pajamas tighter. What the hell was that noise? It was too erratic to be branches banging against the building.

Thump.

Her heart sped up. She scanned the room. Someone knocking, maybe? But who would visit this late? And who would knock like—

Thuuummmp!

She swallowed the lump in her throat and dropped the pajamas. Spinning closer to the fire, she grabbed a poker.

The triple window overlooking the Roker Pier Lighthouse rattled. Constantly.

Stepping out of the firelight, she shifted her back against the wall and flexed her fingers around the poker.

The window over the kitchen sink started to rattle, too. At the same time as the triple one.

What the hell was going on?

The jostling stopped. Only the crackling flames spoke in the silence.

She stared at one window for several seconds and then at the other. Nothing changed. No one tried to break into her cottage. No one said anything.

But there was no way she would stay.

Rachel put the fire out, yanked on her sweatshirt over her T-shirt, and ran to the shore. Hopefully the Hastings had rooms available.

The sky held light still. As she began rowing, the wind whipped so fiercely her hair felt like Medusa's serpents dancing around her head. Water sloshed against the side of the boat, but that was probably from her ineptitude as an evening rower. The last vestiges of daylight sank behind the buildings, leaving her with unsettling shadows creeping upon her quicker than she'd thought possible. The rickety old boat creaked under her weight.

What had she been thinking?

Suddenly, a different kind of chill drifted through her. Wetness seeped through her hiking boots, making her toes curl.

She stilled her hands and straightened her back. Liquid climbed into the boat to join her.

A bubble of panic formed in the center of her chest. Whipping her head around toward shore, she spotted both her cottage and the beacon of light coming from the parking lot of Dawson Tours. Which was closer?

On the island, she would be alone until someone decided to check on her, which could take days. Quick decision—go for the shore.

Rachel rowed faster away from the cottage and mouthed the words to the only prayer she remembered from her youth. Water gushed into the bottom of the boat now, swishing around whenever she moved her feet. The shore remained too far out of reach.

She cupped her hands and bailed frantically, but she would never be fast enough to keep from sinking. Her heart thumped against her chest, in her ears, and picked up speed. "Help!" she cried. "Somebody help me!"

But no one would hear her. Her throat tightened. Just how deep was this section of the sea?

One of her oars scraped along the edge of the boat and disappeared. "No, no, no!" She stretched out to grab it, but the boat rocked beneath her, flipped up on its side, and dumped her.

An icy chill seeped into each layer of her skin as cold, cold moisture covered every inch of clothing and exposed flesh.

"Oh!" she yelped, and frigid liquid invaded her mouth, her nose, her ears. She lowered her foot to try to ground herself, but it never touched the seabed.

A whoosh sounded above her, followed by a *thwump*.

Rachel fought to reach the surface. Raising her hands, she touched wood. When her head broke the surface, she gulped in as much air as she could.

Relax. She would get out of trouble if she remembered to be smart. Opening her eyes, she blinked rapidly. Water below her. Wood above and around her. She'd emerged beneath the overturned boat.

After a good gasp of air, she ducked under and swam around the boat. Her lungs squeezed tight as the sea tried to swallow her.

Something else strong and crushing grabbed a hold of her.

Her head broke the surface again, and she gulped mouthfuls of oxygen. She kicked and kicked, shoving with her arms and fighting to keep her head up, but the liquid still flowed down her throat, up her nostrils. With every attempt to breathe, her chest burned.

She pushed, trying in vain to get the weeds off her, until she felt human fingers complete with fingernails and a thick wrist.

"Stop beating us about the head!"

She sneezed and inhaled more glorious air.

"Calm yourself, you daft woman!" the deep, rich voice ordered.

"Ai—" She coughed. "Aidan?"

"Aye, it's only Scotland's Loch Ness that has a monster."

All the fight went out of her. Allowing him to support her, she welcomed his firm hold. She coughed again while shivers wracked her body. As he swam toward the shore, his grip around her waist never wavered.

"You're all right," he soothed as another coughing fit assailed her chest.

Water rippled around her, more calmly now. She was safe. Aidan had come to her rescue. Rachel allowed her head to rest against his chest, and she closed her eyes to the night sky.

He stumbled to his feet a few minutes later. "You can stand now."

Her feet found firm ground, yet her knees still wobbled. Her hero kept hold of her until her legs solidified under her enough to make it farther onto the shore.

She collapsed onto the cool sand, coughed up the last pockets of liquid from her lungs, and inhaled the glorious smell of sand.

He rubbed his hand along her back and sat down beside her. "Easy, lass."

"How'd you know I was out here?"

"I was just leaving the office. I saw the boat sinking and you flailing about. What were you doing coming across at this time of night?"

She glanced up at the sky with its streaks of pinks and darker blues mixed behind the clouds. "It's still light out." A little, anyway, she silently added as more stars winked down at her.

"Aye, but not for long."

"I was trying to save myself some money and actually stay in the cottage, but it's too cold." Not to mention too freaky. She shivered. "I wasn't thinking."

"That's the problem. You don't think before you act."

She jerked her head back to glare at him. "That boat's been working fine for me up until tonight. I had no reason to think it would fail me now. What's it to you, anyway? Was it your boat that drifted to the bottom of the sea?"

"It's not the boat, you daft lass." He shook his head. "You could've drowned."

She frowned. One second he was scolding her and the next he worried about her? "But I didn't." Another shiver coasted down her spine. To be honest, she wasn't sure if it was the cold wind mixing with her wet clothes or the look behind Aidan's eyes.

"Come on, then." He got to his feet and held out his hand. "You're shivering."

"Not too bad," she lied easily. She slipped her hand in his and allowed him to pull her up. Her fingers pressed against his chest as she bumped into him. Wet patches of material covered warm patches of skin.

His hands sneaked around her waist to steady her while those damn eyes watched her. "Don't tell lies," he scolded on a whispered breath. "Your lips are trembling."

Slowly, he eased his hold on her, but he did not release her completely. His fingers remained at her waist. The intimate touch unleashed a wave of desire within her. This man became more of a temptation to her with every encounter.

"Maybe I'm a little scared, too," she admitted. She glanced at the island just in case she saw someone, something to prove she wasn't losing her mind.

"Don't worry. You're safe now."

Yes, she was safe from all physical danger, but this *something* between them kept sparking inside, as if just waiting for a match to ignite the flames. For a moment, she wished to forget being sensible and instead sink into the emotions he stirred within her.

No, being reckless had wounded her before. She couldn't afford to put her heart on the line again.

Yet wrapping her arms around his solid strength would feel so good, so right. She didn't give in to the craving. Despite the pull she felt toward him, they weren't anything more than rivals. He wanted what her family possessed.

He stared at her for several seconds with gentle longing swimming through his eyes.

Wait. Longing for *her*?

As swiftly as it had come, the tenderness disappeared, hidden behind some thick, heavy wall. Whatever emotions she had evoked, he'd clamped down on them before they were allowed to roam free. He took a step away from her and then another.

"Come on. Let's get you somewhere warm and dry."

"Oh, you don't have to do that. I can just…." She turned her head, scanned the shoreline. Darkness had overtaken the water.

"Stop here and freeze to death?" He shook his head. "I think not." His hand pressed lightly against the small of her back as he led her toward his vehicle in the Dawson Tours parking lot.

"Where are we going?"

He glanced at his watch then at the row of guesthouses. And then toward the center of Sunderland. "My house."

Oh no. That was not a good idea. "What about the Hastings?" She smoothed her hand over her sopping wet hair.

"They're full. Gemma…you know her, aye?"

She nodded. The woman worked at the Hastings and had sort of taken Rachel under her wing.

"Gemma told us a tour came through this afternoon. I'm afraid you're stuck with me." He opened the passenger door of his car, motioned her inside, and closed the door.

Reluctantly, she settled in and tried to focus on anything but remembering the way she felt wrapped in Aidan's arms. Well, that and her soaking clothes.

Chapter Four

*A*fter a hot shower, Rachel stood in Aidan's bathroom and stared at herself in the mirror. A T-shirt. He'd given her only a T-shirt to wear while her own clothes, underwear and all, joined his in the washer. Granted it came all the way down to her knees, but as she fingered the seam, she couldn't help feeling...naked. Already her nipples pushed against the fabric.

She opened the door, crossed her arms in front of her, and wandered slowly toward the stairs. No feminine touches lingered within his home. The scent of furniture polish lurked like background music. Dark woods, heavy curtains, and stark furnishings, and yet it still managed to look comfortable.

Just a splash of color would brighten the place up. She supposed though the décor reflected her host's personality. Serious, quiet, shadowed. The quick assessment of him squeezed her heart. Surely there had to be so much more to the man.

She walked into the living room and stopped at the edge of the couch. Her hunky Brit sat in one of the chairs next to the fireplace with his forearms resting on his thighs.

Her heart skipped a beat, and she lost her ability to breathe for a second. Yes, he wore a white shirt and a pair of striped pajama pants, but the sight of him revived every neglected ounce of femininity within her. Strong, confident and comfortable in his own skin. That was sexier than movie-star looks any day.

He pressed one palm on his thigh. His gaze traveled down the length of her body before reaching back to her eyes. "Are you ready, lass?"

She stilled. "For what?"

"To tell me why you're so frightened."

Aidan worked hard to keep his gaze on Rachel's face. Her hair draped over her shoulders, and in the firelight, the strands sparkled with a hint of golden sunrays. The clothing he'd loaned her hung loosely off her shoulders. The edge of the fabric barely reached her knees. Her legs were toned, with small feet and perfectly painted toenails. Pink toenails.

"What do you mean?" she asked.

He wanted to get up, to move next to her, but he couldn't trust himself to keep his hands to himself. "Why were you coming across the water so late at night? You're a smart woman. You know it's not safe to do."

She nipped on her bottom lip for several seconds, as though trying to decide how much to trust him with. "I heard noises in the cottage that I shouldn't have."

He frowned. "What kind of noises?" She didn't strike him as the type of woman to scare easily.

"The windows rattled."

"It is a bit windy."

Even before he finished his statement she was shaking her head. "That's not it. It was like someone was rattling them on purpose. And the rattling lasted for a couple of minutes." She rubbed her arms, wandered to stand by the fireplace. "It freaked me out, and I knew I wouldn't be able to sleep there. And if someone was out there, staying in the cottage would be stupid."

"So, you took the boat and started across."

She nodded. "Until it started filling up with water. I swear, Aidan, the boat was fine earlier in the day. I know because I check the hull for leaks before every row across. I'm a little obsessive about that." She shoved her hands through her hair. "I'm starting to think someone doesn't want me here."

"You can't think it's me."

"No, I don't. Not now, anyway. I admit at first I thought it might be you. Since you want the cottage, I thought you might stoop to that level and try to scare me away."

He gritted his teeth and rested both palms on his thighs. "I'm not that kind of man. I'd not harm a lass to get what I want."

She pushed both hands forward, as though to hold him off. "I know. I'm sorry, but then I realized you couldn't have rattled *both* windows and then rowed back to the shore and then swam out to get me. That's not possible."

"Is that the only reason you don't suspect me of trying to sabotage your efforts?"

She remained quiet, but she refused to meet his gaze.

He shot up from his chair. "Answer me, lass."

"I…. Truthfully, I don't know what to believe." She stared at his chest. "I know you want the cottage because it means a lot to you, but I don't think you'd do anything to hurt me to get it. Although I don't know whether that's my head or my heart telling me that."

"What do you mean?"

Her breasts rose with the deep breath she took. His hands itched to curve around them, to feel the silky softness of her skin. He flexed his fingers at his sides.

"This thing between us is making my head crazy." She smoothed her palm over his shirt. Could she feel his heartbeat gathering strength? "I like you, Aidan Camden, and I don't want to."

"Because I'm supposed to be the enemy?"

"Yes, and I'm afraid to give you too much power because I don't want to get hurt. I mean, to be truthful, I'm much more comfortable locked in a room by myself with my computer and keyboard."

"Rachel, you have all the power." He slid one hand around her waist and pulled her against him. "Aye, I want the cottage, but at the moment, I want you more." He lowered his head and pressed his mouth to hers.

Heated tingles ignited from Aidan's touch and zinged right between Rachel's legs.

His hand roamed down her back and under the T-shirt she wore. His palm cupped her bottom, pulled her against his erection. "You've been driving me mad since the day you arrived."

As he did her, with his British accent, his care and concern, his honesty. And of course, his magnificent body. He kissed her, touched and stroked her skin until the ache consumed her. "This isn't right, but I do want you."

"What isn't right about it?" His thumb brushed over her already swollen clit. "Tell me and I'll stop." He claimed her mouth again, and slid his tongue inside at the same moment he pushed his fingers inside her.

She rested against him since her limbs threatened to collapse. "Don't stop. Promise me you won't."

He kissed her once more and pulled away. "Come." Grabbing her hand, he led her upstairs. He rushed into the bathroom and returned to her in the hallway in record time, ripping open a foil package. "Lass, I don't know if I—"

She pressed a finger to his lips and grabbed the condom. After stripping off her shirt, she pulled his penis free. With her own hands shaking, she covered the length of him.

Aidan lifted her, pushed her back against the wall and slid inside her. Rachel squeezed her legs around his waist and rested her head on his shoulder. He thrust with long, decadent strokes, and she rode on the rhythm he set, reveling in the feel of him filling her, holding her, loving her.

His hand drifted under one breast and lifted it to his lips. He licked the hardened nipple once, twice before sucking it into his mouth. His teeth took turns with his tongue, grazing the sensitive tip until she lost all coherent thought. And then he moved to her other breast. His touch was magical, at once making her feel treasured and protected.

He pulled his lips from her breast and returned to her mouth, sliding his tongue inside, to dance with hers, to sweep along her teeth. His body moved faster, harder toward an edge she wanted, craved. Rachel slid her hand through his hair and rocked her hips in time to his movements.

A perfect match.

At her back, the wall felt cold, hard, unyielding. Against her, Aidan's body was warm, strong, and solid. Finally, finally she found her release seconds before he did. Her heartbeat knocked against her ribs, her brain had turned to mush, and the lights in the hallway appeared to have exploded into a kaleidoscope of fire.

He breathed heavily in between sweet, gentle kisses. "Are you all right?"

She smiled. "I am."

"I'm sorry I couldn't make it to the bed."

She pressed her finger on his lips. "Don't you dare apologize for anything."

"But to take you in the hallway."

She draped her arms over his shoulders and tipped her head to one side. "Do you hear me complaining?"

He kissed her forehead, her nose, her lips. "No."

"But if you really feel that guilty, you could make it up to me."

"How's that?"

"Take me to bed and show me what other talents you have."

Laughter rumbled through his chest. "Aye, I can do that." He carried her into the bedroom and set her in the center of his bed.

◌જ

Rachel may have enjoyed making love with this absolutely hot Englishman and falling asleep in his arms, but the man snored like a freight train. After blinking herself completely awake, she squinted to read the digital clock on his dresser across the room. 5:36 a.m. She rested her head back on the pillow and brushed her hand against her forehead. With him next to her, she'd never get back to sleep.

As if to prove her thought, a yawn shoved its way through her mouth. Resigned, she removed his arm from her stomach, pulled back the covers, and slid from his hold. The cool air danced on her naked skin. Goosebumps popped up along her arms. Her nipples hardened again.

Outside, gray clouds covered the sky. No rain fell yet, but she could tell it wouldn't be long. The sooner she got out of here and found another boat back to the island, the better.

She grabbed her clothes from the dryer and dressed. Selfishly, she first put on the T-shirt she'd worn the night before. It held Aidan's scent and having it close to her skin would comfort her as the reality of her cottage life returned.

She tiptoed down the stairs and searched for a pen and paper on the rolltop desk in the corner of the living room. On the top shelf was a picture of Aidan and a beautiful young woman with honey-colored hair, bright blue eyes, and a killer body. Of course, the two of them couldn't have been much more than twenty at the time, and they looked absolutely perfect together. His late wife? Happiness flooded his features in the photo so much that Rachel almost didn't recognize him.

Her throat tightened, and she brushed her fingers against the edge of the frame. How wonderful to have that much love for another human being. How terrible to lose her so soon.

Once she set the picture back down, she jotted a note to him and slipped like a coward out the front door. It wasn't that she had regrets. No, their evening had been perfect in every way. Last night had been comfort sex, to help her get over the fear rushing through her veins that compelled her to cross the water at 11:00 p.m. But that didn't change the fact he wanted Nan's cottage. And plus, in a matter of ten days, she would walk out of his life, possibly for good. Yes, a vacation fling could be very nice, but the reality was she already knew how easy it would be to fall for a man like Aidan. "And everyone knows how impaired my judgment is when it comes to men."

She waited a few streets over for the first bus of the day and made her way back to the Roker area. The waves crashed against the shore, almost daring her to cross to the island.

She glared at the water. "Just as soon as I get another boat." Glancing back at Dawson Tours, she set about securing another from the rental shop attached to the tour offices.

Twenty minutes later, she pushed the new boat into the water.

"Rachel, wait!"

Straightening, she glanced behind her. Aidan jogged down the steps from the street and hurried to her. Energy started to thrum through her veins, memories of his touch spilling from her brain. Already her body ached for him. Again. "What are you doing here?"

He stood before her, all muscle, with a flash of longing in his hazel eyes. But only for a moment. He shifted to the other side of the boat and whatever bit of desire she thought she saw in his expression disappeared. "I'm coming with you to the cottage."

"That's not necessary."

"I'm coming."

"Why?"

"If someone did do something to frighten you, I'm not letting you go there alone and unprotected."

"I work for one of the toughest companies in the world."

"Aye, but not as a bodyguard. You work in an office with computers. You can argue all you like, but I'll not let you go alone."

Butterflies stirred in her stomach, and she allowed a hint of a smile to cross her lips. "All right."

The silence while they rowed across to the island ate away at her with every stroke of the oars. He hadn't even looked at her since they boarded. Water lapped fiercely against the boat.

"I'm sorry I left so early this morning. I just wanted to get a head start on the day."

He did glance at her then, pinned her with a stare so cold a shiver zapped straight down to her toes. "And you couldn't wake me to tell me?"

"I'm sorry." She lowered her gaze and twiddled her thumbs. "I just…." *Have no idea what to say.*

Several more seconds drifted by while Aidan rowed with more force than she thought he needed. "Do you regret it?"

She jerked her head up and shook it. "Not at all."

"Are you sure?"

"I was afraid you would with the cottage and memories of your wife."

"I don't. Not a bit. I'm sure Gemma's told you about Brooke."

"A little." Most of Rachel's information had come from her own computer research when she'd first arrived and met him.

"I loved her. We had a good life for a while. Then we wanted different things." His voice strained with his words. "And then none of that mattered."

"Gemma said your wife wanted to come back to Sunderland, but you didn't."

"Aye, I was happy enough in London. I kept saying, yes, we'd come back, but I never looked into it until it was too late." His body remained rigid, the circular motion of his arms almost mechanical.

Reaching forward, she set her hand on his knee. His muscles twitched beneath her fingers, and his arms stilled. But only for a second.

"Why'd you stay?"

"Everything was in place shortly after she died. I'd been working at Dawson Tours. I'd started inquiries about the cottage. It seemed the right thing to do to honor Brooke."

"And now?"

"What do you mean?" His hazel eyes drifted up to her then.

"Are you happy?"

Aidan hesitated, glanced back over the water.

He thought for too long. The answer couldn't be yes, and her heart broke a bit for him.

"I'm happy enough." He shrugged. "I've got a good job, good friends, and a good home."

"I'm sorry for all you've gone through."

"But that's the past. You are in the here and now. For a while, anyway." When the boat arrived at the island, he pulled the oars inside, hopped onto the shore, and reached back for her. Setting his hands around her waist, he lifted her to shore. His fingers lingered. A glimmer of hunger danced in his eyes. "You're the one I took to bed last night. You're the one I want to spend time with while you're here."

Butterflies floated around her stomach. God, the man was delicious.

Taking his hand, she led him toward the cottage. "I bet you'll be surprised with how much I've accomplished so far."

She stopped short in front of the kitchen window. The curtain she'd put up the other day blew in the breeze. Shards of glass lay on the window ledge, the jagged edges almost daring her to enter. Aidan's chest pressed against her back, supporting her.

She glanced over her shoulder. "Guess it wasn't a ghost, huh?"

Maneuvering around her, he grabbed the doorknob. Just with the gentle touch of his fingers the door swung open.

Her insides curdled more with each step she took into the home. All her work was ruined. Dirt and trash littered the floor. The rocking chair her grandfather had made lay in pieces. In large letters, spray painted on the wall opposite the fireplace was a clear message:

Yank, Go Home

Rachel's knees buckled. "Aidan."

Instantly he braced his arm around her waist and kept her on her feet. "Aye, I see it."

"Why would someone do this?"

"I don't know." He cupped her elbows and steered her toward the door. "We're leaving and when we get back to shore, we'll call the police."

She nodded. "I so need my laptop. And a sausage roll."

An hour later, Rachel cradled her second cup of tea in a quaint little coffee shop at the foot of a hill and picked at the pastry on her plate. It wasn't a sausage roll, but it was almost as good. "Why'd you bring me out here?"

"You needed to get away or you'd not relax."

"How can I relax? Someone is trying to scare me into abandoning my quest." She set the empty cup on the saucer. "But it won't work."

"No. You're too determined."

"When we get back to the city, I'm going to complete a profile of this psycho."

"What will you do with this profile?"

"The same thing I do in my day job. Research, gather information, and hand it over to the people in charge."

Aidan nodded. "Good. I don't want you trying to catch him on your own."

Her cheeks heated, and she smiled. With every moment they spent together, Rachel wished for five more. It sounded ridiculous, but she couldn't help the way her heart reacted to him.

No, not her heart. Her *body*.

His cup clinked as he put it on the saucer. He crumbled his napkin and dropped it on the table. "Let's away." With a gleam in his eye and a smile on his handsome face, he grabbed her hand. "I've got something else that will help you relax."

He guided her outside, and once again the scent of flowers surrounded her. When they passed his car without slowing, she asked, "Where are you taking me?"

"Up there." He pointed to the columns on the top of the hill. It was a stone structure, fashioned much like a Greek temple.

She focused on climbing the hill and didn't speak until they had reached the top. Through huffs, she said, "It didn't look that high from the road." Her chest ached. Her calves, too.

She examined the monument and fought for the memory itching to get out. She'd been here with Nana and Granda, she was sure of it. But when?

"Look." He pointed behind her.

Whirling around, she lost another breath to the scene. Rolling green hills dotted with earth-toned semi-detached homes. Puffy white clouds touched the horizon. "It's beautiful."

"Aye." But that sneaky guy wasn't studying the scenery. His intense gaze stayed fixed on her.

A different kind of heat infused her cheeks. She was the plain sister, the computer nerd. Men like this never looked at her as if they wanted to ravish her.

Rachel glanced away before she said or did something stupid.

The floor of the monument stood a good three feet off the ground. She hopped up and got to her feet. "I remember this place."

"Aye?"

"Yeah. I came up with my grandparents one time. What's it called again?"

"Penshaw Monument."

With her arms spread wide, she twirled around. "I had to be about seven or eight. I ran around to each side so I could choose which was the best view."

"And what did you decide?" He raised one hand and squinted

against the sun behind her.

"This one." She pointed at him. "Definitely." Taking another peek at the typical English countryside, she listened to her heartbeat slow.

"Do you know the story of Penshaw Monument?"

"No." She sat on the edge of the stone and let her feet dangle.

Inching closer, he set one hand on each side of her. His scent wrapped around her. She shifted her gaze from his muscular chest to his face. Or more accurately, his mouth. A mouth begging to be kissed. For a few fanciful seconds, she wanted his lips pressed against hers, to feel the hard planes of his body crushing against her, to run her fingers over every patch of his hidden skin as she had through the night.

"It was built in 1844 in honor of the first Earl of Durham, but they ran out of money before they could finish it. In one of the columns are stairs to the top for people to climb. The secret staircase was closed in 1926 after four mates were playing and one of them fell to his death. They've only recently opened it back up to the public."

"How horrible for those boys." She glanced around her again and the breeze pulled at the tips of her hair. "Those poor friends must've felt so guilty."

Aidan leaned forward and kissed her.

"What was that for?"

He didn't answer with words. Instead, he grinned, maneuvered between her legs and pressed his hips against her.

She gasped. Already he was hard. For her. The knowledge that she, Miss Computer Geek, could arouse a man like this empowered her.

He said nothing, instead surging his tongue in and out of her mouth, sweeping it along her teeth. His hands drifted over her thighs.

Rachel's stomach muscles contracted. Swirls of heat zinged from his fingertips straight between her legs. He slid his hands under the hem of her shirt.

Electric impulses thrummed through her stomach and chest. His fingers were warm, solid, with a fleeting touch. How could she want him this much again?

She pulled her mouth away. "Aidan, we can't. Not here." And yet she shuffled closer to him, to savor the pressure growing between her legs. She arched her back as his hands moved up to cup her breasts. He rolled his thumbs over her nipples, which pebbled quickly.

"Your words say one thing and yet your body welcomes me."

"Anyone can see us." She kissed him.

"No one is here." Slipping his hands from her shirt, he grabbed her ass, and brought her closer to the edge of the rock.

"Right now, but at any moment they could come up the path." She held on to his shoulders.

"Aye, up the path, which means we'll see them long before they can see what we're about." Quickly, he unbuttoned her jeans, lifted her, and slid her pants just far enough off to give him access. With his mouth back on hers, his fingers glided inside her opening and his thumb teased her clit.

Already her body wept for him, for his touch, for the insanity of making love outside.

She gripped the button on his pants but stopped. "Please tell me you have a condom."

"Aye." He reached into his back pocket and pulled one out. "I've come prepared."

As he ripped the package open, she unzipped his pants and eased his cock free. She held him, gently stroked the length of him, and brushed her thumb over the tip.

A strained groan fell from his mouth, and he shoved her hands out of the way. "Get away," he ordered. Within seconds, he covered himself, and pushed inside her.

She wrapped her arms around him, leaned into him, and took his tongue into her mouth. Again and again he thrust into her, taking his time and creating a sweet torture. Rachel's breaths moved faster as Aidan made love to her. His hand slipped back under her shirt and squeezed one breast and then the other. Her nipples strained against the fabric of her bra until he slid his fingers under the material and toyed with the sensitive skin. She still wore most of her clothes, but the damn fine Englishman had her so over-stimulated she felt completely exposed. And the thrill of naughtiness consumed her.

He moved faster now. His heart beat as rapidly under her palms as her own. He kissed her once and lowered his head to take one nipple into his mouth. Rachel soared toward climax. Everything, at this very moment, was perfect. They were perfect together.

She glided through wave after wave of her rush until she fell like putty into him.

Aidan pushed on, faster and harder, as if her climax spurred him closer to his own. To watch him reach his release, to know she had done that to him, empowered her. Together they stayed—him standing, her half on the monument's floor and mostly on him—for several minutes.

"Tell me, lass. Are you quite relaxed now?" A cocky grin formed on his handsome face.

"A little too relaxed, actually."

He planted a kiss on her forehead and ran his hands over her back. How long had it been since she had felt so treasured?

Children's laughter traveled up the hill along with a playful bark.

Rachel's nerves tightened. "We have to go."

"Aye." He pulled himself free of her body.

Once her feet hit the ground, she reached down for her pants, and dressed. As Aidan finished zipping up his pants, too, she giggled. They'd just had sex. In public. And she'd loved it.

Now, if only the rest of her life could pan out as easily.

Aidan couldn't remember a better time at Penshaw Monument, and forever more, he would think on the sexy American lass whenever he passed here. Deep inside him muscles relaxed. Perhaps a brief affair was the perfect way for him to return to the land of the living. Too many had lectured him about getting on with his life. He'd not cared until three days ago when she'd stomped into his world and taken it by storm.

A storm he no longer feared.

Spending time with this woman soothed something inside him, allowed him to…feel. He'd closed himself off after Brooke's death, and he hadn't even realized it until now. Aye, this brief affair would be perfect. She was smart, sweet, and so gentle on his soul.

He reached out for her hand, and she gave it willingly. They had just finished zipping up their clothes when a mum, da, and two bairns reached the monument. He glanced at Rachel, sure her cheeks would flame at what they'd done.

Smiling, she turned away, and greeted the family. She looked beautiful with the faint breeze stirring her hair, her disheveled appearance, and the thoroughly satisfied look in her eyes.

He stood straighter. Aye, he'd done that to her. He'd been the one to bring her pleasure she hadn't expected on top of Penshaw Hill.

From his pocket, his phone rang. He pulled the mobile free and glanced at the number. His boss. "Hello, Craig."

"Aidan, I hate to do this to you, but Tommy's sick. I need you to take the afternoon tour to Durham."

He caught a glimpse of her out of the corner of his eye. Part of him demanded he tell Craig to bugger off. In his mind, he already had plans discovering other ways to make her shudder in his arms.

But reality shoved those thoughts aside. She was temporary. His job was his life.

He checked his watch. The tour would leave in under an hour. "Right. I'll be there in a bit." He exchanged goodbyes with his friend. "I'm sorry, but I've got to go."

"Really?" Disappointment crowded her bonnie features.

Perhaps he should call Craig back. "Aye. The regular guide is sick."

"Well, then, you have to do it."

"I'll take you back to the Hastings."

She shook her head. "I'll just go with you to the tour office and head over to the cottage."

"You'll not."

She stopped a few meters from the car's boot. "Excuse me?"

"You're not to go to the island alone."

"Aidan." She rolled her eyes. "The police have probably finished by now, and I've got tons of work to do before the weekend."

"It's not safe. Promise me you'll not go."

She opened her mouth as if ready to argue, and closed it again.

"I've got tomorrow off, and I'll help you with the work."

Her features softened. "All right." She started toward the passenger side. "I'll stay in town and do some investigating as to who might be trying to scare me off."

"Don't do anything dangerous." He set one hand on the doorframe and one on the top of the car.

"Relax. My specialty is computers, remember?" She smiled.

"Oh no, lass. You've plenty of other specialties as well." Already his body hungered for her. Again. Oh what he wouldn't give to have her mouth on his cock, to feel that talented tongue brushing the tip of him.

Rachel tossed her head back and laughed. "We better get going because if you keep looking at me like that, the afternoon tour won't have a guide at all."

଼

Rachel sat in the Thrush and Hound Pub with her laptop in front of her and her back to the wall. After four years working with the operatives of the International Protective Network, or IPN to its employees, and hearing tons of dangerous stories, she could no longer sit just anywhere. She needed to see all the exits and the whole room.

As she chewed on her thumbnail, she scanned the crowd. Her thoughts raced straight to the McAndrew brothers. Other than Aidan, they were the only people who showed any negative interest in her fixing up the cottage. She sipped on her pint and typed away on her computer.

Thanks to IPN's state-of-the-art databases and her expert hacking skills, she learned quite a bit about the boys. In all, Adam and David had been picked up by the police a handful of times for drunk and disorderly charges and vandalism. She could bring her concerns to the police, but they would ask where she got her information. Um, illegal computer hacking? She had no proof they were behind the cottage and boat sabotage and taking her suspicions to anyone in this town would be foolish.

She pulled her cell phone from her purse and called her go-to IPN guy, Ian MacKenzie. Once she explained her situation, she asked him to brainstorm with her about how to proceed. "I mean, I'm good with finding information and then turning it over to you guys. What to do next is a little out of my comfort zone."

"I'm coming down on the late train."

She rolled her eyes. "Ian, it's not necessary. I'm fine."

"I don't like you on your own while this is going on."

"I'm not. I promise. I've got an ally, and he's even making sure I'm safe."

Ian hesitated a moment. "A lad to do my job?"

Her grin grew wider. "No, he could never take your place."

"I only want you to be safe until you get back here, and I can do the job meself."

"I know."

"Speak with the police and keep me updated, or I'll be on the next train out of Edinburgh."

"Thanks, Ian. Hey, while I've got you on the phone, is it me or do the people in Sunderland sound an awful lot like the Scots?"

"Oh, lass, dinna say that to anyone there. Or here, for that matter."

"Why?"

"Do you not remember the history? The Scots and the English don't get along."

"I thought that feud was over."

"Feuds. Quite a few. Look up Culloden or the real William Wallace. Sadly, attitudes haven't changed much since those days."

"Thanks for the tip."

While taking another sip of her beer, she stuffed her phone back in her purse. She'd found out everything she could about the brothers here online. Logically, she needed to gather more intel about them but in some way so people didn't get suspicious. After a few more minutes, she snapped her fingers.

"Gemma."

The woman loved to talk, and surely Rachel could steer their conversation innocently toward the brothers.

Chapter Five

*W*hen Rachel called Heather Oaks Sheltered Accommodation Center at dinnertime, Nan didn't sound well. Of course, she told her not to return to Edinburgh early. The old granny insisted she'd be all right until the weekend, just three days away. They spoke for a good half hour about their plans for the cottage. She decided to keep the vandalism to herself for now. Nan shared more stories of her younger years and soon had Rachel laughing so hard tears fell from her eyes.

Yes, Nana would be all right until the weekend, and Rachel's worry all but disappeared.

On Thursday, bright and early, Aidan arrived at the Hastings Hotel ready to spend his only day off helping her fix up the cottage. The cottage he still wanted.

They worked together, laughed together, and shared silly details of each other's lives. After dinner, he escorted her to her hotel door. Her body hummed from his gentle kiss and begged for more, but he left her longing for him.

It was just as well. Too easily she was getting used to having him in her life. And although she'd be around for another week, she'd have her hands full with her grandmother and the rest of the repairs. She had to keep her priorities in order. Family, the cottage, and returning to work in Edinburgh. Aidan could not be added to that list. Her emotions, her hormones could have no bearing on her decisions.

The next morning, Rachel strolled along the streets of Sunderland's city center, determined to try the proclaimed "best Cornish pasties in all of Sunderland" before returning to the cottage for another round of repairs.

She spotted Gemma Barnes dressed in her Hastings Hotel uniform by the entrance to Champlain's Restaurant. "Morning."

The Englishwoman stopped and tossed her auburn curls over her shoulder. "Hiya! I'm just popping in for breakfast before work."

Rachel held the door and followed her friend to the line at the counter. The sweet scent of freshly baked pastries greeted her, and she couldn't help but inhale.

A few scattered tables remained empty, the rest occupied by hungry patrons. The line extended the length of the counter, allowing both of them plenty of time to drool over the rich array of breakfast items.

"I'm surprised to see you here, especially this early." Gemma pressed her palms against the glass partition protecting the baked goods and licked her lips.

"I've got a lot still to do." Her stomach growled. Everything looked delectable here. No wonder this place was always so busy!

"But you'll stay and have breakfast with me, aye?"

"I really shouldn't."

Gemma clucked her tongue. "Surely you can take time to eat and talk with me."

Jobs on her To-Do list scurried through her brain, but she did enjoy spending time with her new friend. She missed the camaraderie of a close female confidante. Plus, she could ask some questions about the McAndrew brothers.

Once they'd ordered and paid the cashier, they took over one of the small tables by the front window.

Gemma sipped her tea and jumped into the latest round of Sunderland gossip. The woman could talk the head off a wooden donkey. Rachel's brain spun with all the details until Aidan slipped through the door. An easy sigh escaped her lips, and right away butterflies flittered through her stomach.

When he'd finished at the counter, he ambled over to the edge of their table.

"A good morning to you, ladies." He glanced down at Rachel and smiled.

Her heart flip-flopped behind her ribs, and her skin warmed like the fire she'd made in the cottage the other night.

"What's brought you in here this early?" Gemma asked.

"I'm picking up some sack lunches for a tour."

"Would you like to join us?" Before the sentence finished falling from her mouth, her friend gave her the evil eye.

Uh-oh. She quickly turned back to Aidan.

"No," he said slowly. "I've got a tour."

Right. He'd already mentioned that. Duh.

"Aidan, your food's ready!" someone shouted from behind the counter.

Rachel ran her finger around the rim of her mug. "Have a good day."

"You as well, lass." Tossing a wave to her companion, he made his way through the crowd to the cashier.

"Have you taken one of their tours since you've been in Sunderland?"

"I don't have a lot of time here." Her gaze lingered on Aidan, who laughed with the man behind the counter.

"You really should think about it for next week. They're great fun, and he and Duncan are ever so smart."

"What about Craig?" Rachel asked.

She rolled her eyes. "Aye, even me daft brother knows a thing or two about tours."

Rachel broke off another piece of her sausage roll and popped it in her mouth. Going on a tour would give her a perfectly innocent excuse to spend a day with her hunky Sunderland laddie. But could she afford the time away from the cottage? Not to mention the time away from Nan.

She watched him leave the restaurant and head across the street. He walked with a purpose, tall and confident, yet still stoic and reserved.

Gemma leaned low to the table. "'Ere, do you fancy him, then?"

she whispered.

"What?" She jerked her head back to meet the gossip queen's gaze, which sparkled with the possibility. "No." The denial was instant, strong, and definitely a lie.

"You do." The woman pointed her finger at her and chuckled. "I can see the color on your cheeks."

She shook her head. "Wherever your thoughts are, bring them back. That's not someplace I want to go."

Gemma stared out the window and watched Aidan disappear from view. Or maybe she'd drifted to a distant memory. "He's a good man." Sadness claimed her voice. "He's gone through a lot and may seem a bit standoffish, but he's a good lad just the same."

A world of hurts lay wrapped up in those words and most probably in Aidan's soul as well. A world Rachel, the temporary foreigner, knew nothing about and had no business inspecting. Still, curiosity about his life tugged at her. A deep ache burned for him and all he must have gone through. Judging by the look on Gemma's face, the entire community must have gone through Brooke's death as well.

She drifted back from the haunting, and a bright smile lit up her face. "Have I told you I'm to be an aunt?" Without waiting for an answer, she rushed into the details of her impending aunthood, thanks to the oldest Barnes child and his wife, and kept Rachel busy for close to an hour.

By the time Gemma left and Rachel finished another cup of tea, clouds hovered low, hiding the top curve of the Sunderland Bridge in the horizon, and the sky had turned an ominous gray. Thunder rumbled in the distance. The rain still held off, but the weight of it hung in the air.

The McAndrew brothers shoved their way through the door before she could get out and her stomach twisted. David bumped into her arm, turned around, and stared at her.

"You're still here? I thought you'd be on your way back to Edinburgh by now."

"Why?" Before she could bite her tongue, the word flew from her mouth. "Thought your little pranks would scare me away?"

David crowded her into the corner by the door. The scent of alcohol wafted off him. His dark eyes bore into her with so much harsh emotion. "Don't accuse me of anything. Not without evidence."

Adam's panicked gaze toward his older brother was fleeting, but she caught it.

"You don't belong here. Aidan will get that cottage one way or another. Adam and I will help him see to it."

She swallowed the lump in her throat and straightened. Still, she remained too many inches shorter to beat back his intimidation. "Is that a threat, Mr. McAndrew?"

He leaned closer. "No, it's a fact."

Her heartbeat moved faster. She pressed her palms against the wall. She didn't inhale.

Adam grabbed his brother's arm. "Dave, let's away."

"Aye." David stood straight again and shook his brother's arm off. "I don't want to lose me appetite." He walked away.

"Watch how you go." Adam pressed his lips together and followed after his brother.

She released a heavy breath and willed her limbs to hold her up. Accusing the brothers had been foolish. She *knew* that. "This is totally why I spend my days behind a computer desk."

Suddenly spending the day alone on the island didn't hold the same appeal as it had when she first got up. She pushed the door open and stepped into the chill of the morning air. At this moment she wanted...Aidan.

Chapter Six

*A*idan pushed the door to the Dawson Tours office open for Rachel, and the bell jingled.

"That was a great tour today." She wandered to the wall of pamphlets and studied them. "I'll have to see about taking another trip with you."

The thought brought a smile to him. Stepping behind her, he circled his arms around her waist. "I never thought it possible."

"What?" So easily she set her hands on his, and relaxed against him. Too easily she fit in his world.

"I've given that tour dozens of times, and I can't remember the last time I had that much fun." He'd been quite surprised to see her this morning. In truth, he'd worried about her, especially after the stricken look she held, but soon after she'd paid for her tour spot, her shoulders had softened and that grand smile had taken over her bonnie face. She'd charmed the other tourists, young and old, and kept him company.

"I aim to please."

"That you have, lass." He spun her around to face him. Caressing her cheek, he reveled in the softness of her skin. "Rachel Grant, you're a marvel."

She chuckled as she slapped her palm against his chest. "To you, maybe."

"Aye, to me." He tugged her body against him. Aye, this would truly be his undoing. He needed to taste her, to experience her as much as he needed blood to pump through his body. Everything about her overloaded his senses and left his head spinning.

Slowly, gently, he bent his head and brushed his lips over hers.

Heaven. He took possession of her mouth, needing her more with each passing second. Her lips, warm and pliant, fell open to the command of his tongue, as though she were both uncertain and curious. He planned to give her no reason to hesitate in sharing the pleasure. Instead, he worked extra hard to be generous and to take his time, savoring as much the feel of her mouth on his as her curves crushed against the rest of him.

He stroked his tongue along the side of hers, taunting and teasing with a feather-light touch. Her tongue matched his stroke for stroke. As she slid her arms around him, a low, soft moan escaped from the back of her throat.

Desire, swift and pulsing, fired inside him, spurring him to take her, brand her, and make her his alone. His frenzied need took command. He braced his palms on the wall, one hand on each side of her head, and he dared to touch her with every inch of his body that he could.

A breath rolled up through her chest, and it moved through him, too, as though it were his own. Aye, she was a part of him...for another week.

Her hands slipped along his back. Cool fingers brushed over his skin at the nape of his neck. Now, it was his turn to shudder from her possessive contact. Gentle yes, but the pads of her fingers burned him with the power of her touch.

If one of them didn't stop this, he would surely come undone. But he'd definitely not be the one to end it. He was too weak. She made him too weak. Cursed woman.

When Aidan's mouth cruelly tore away from hers, Rachel whimpered. Until his lips closed over her earlobe, that is. A shiver rippled down her spine, eliciting another satisfied moan off her tongue.

Oh, yes! This was good. He was good. Every nerve ending begged to find out just how good he could be. His tongue toyed with her ear before his mouth moved along her jaw. His fingers teased the outer curve of her breast. She arched into his hand and as he tweaked one nipple, she lost all thought.

Liquid heat poured through her. Every part of her body shook from the sheer pleasure of his touch. Surely, she must have experienced this much bliss, this rapture somewhere in her twenty-six years. Then again, she'd never had a man like him making love to her skin. Rocking her thighs against his, she inched closer to his growing erection. She lifted one leg a bit to get nearer to him. Grabbing her leg, he pulled her against him.

The bell on the front door jingled. "Good God, can you two not get a room?" Craig Barnes asked.

She lowered her leg and jerked away from Aidan. Of course, he stared at her, all heat and hunger and absolutely no regret for her embarrassment. She pretended to read the tour pamphlets again until the heat in her cheeks dissipated. Crossing the room, he talked to Craig about their respective tours.

Crazy Train played from her coat pocket. She pulled her phone free. "Hey, Vicki."

"Where the hell are you?" her sister demanded. "And don't tell me Edinburgh because we know for a fact you're not there."

She stilled. *Uh-oh.* "I'm in Sunderland, in England. What's wrong?"

Vicki took an audible breath. "The retirement home said they called you this afternoon. When they couldn't reach you, they called Mom and Dad."

With a wave to her, Gemma's brother Craig hurried back out of the office. She wandered toward the counter.

"I went on a tour." On one stop she'd left her bag with Aidan's things. They must've called then. Why hadn't she checked her messages on the way back to Sunderland? "What happened?"

"Rach, Nan's gone."

"What?" She gripped the counter and tried to focus. "How can that be? I just talked to her yesterday, and she was okay."

"Pneumonia. They said she'd been sick for a few days, but through the night and this morning, she went downhill fast."

The breath in Rachel's lungs rushed out. *Nan. Gone forever.*

Her knees wobbled. She tightened her hold on the phone. Vicki kept talking, but all the words jumbled together in her ears. She recognized the words "I'm sorry" and "love you."

"You too. Look, Vicki, I need to call you back in a bit, okay? I can't do this right now."

"All right. Call me soon though. Or call Mom and Dad. They're worried about you."

They exchanged goodbyes and hung up. Tears flooded her eyes. No, she had to be strong for her grandmother.

"Rachel, are you all right?" Aidan said, breaking through the haze around her senses.

She understood his words, but her tongue refused to wrap around a reply.

He took a few slow steps toward her. His smile disappeared.

The hole in her heart closed up just a little. Yes, he would understand.

The phone slipped from her hand and crashed against the floor. Swatches of dark carpet threatened to rush up to meet her.

Aidan's arms wrapped around her instantly.

She sagged against him. Seconds later, he slid a chair beneath her. Silence crept over her shoulders and seeped into her ears.

Rachel slumped into the chair, the metal cold and impersonal after the warmth and strength of his body. Kneeling beside her, he cupped her cheek, his thumb stroking her skin. "What's happened?"

"She's dead."

"Who?"

"My grandmother."

"I'm sorry." He pulled his hand away and leaned back against the counter.

Her gaze followed him. She needed his touch. Craved it. Her eyes burned as they filled again. She squeezed them shut, but the tears gushed down her cheeks anyway. Swiping her fingers under her eyes did nothing to stop the flow.

"Don't worry about it. I'll manage." She blew out a breath.

"Aye, you're strong enough."

Her heart fractured again. What a poor attempt to soothe her.

After all they'd shared, didn't he get it? She needed his strength, his arms around her. *Please, Aidan.* Her body shook and it took everything she had to keep her hands in her lap. She gazed up at him.

He didn't move.

A sob wrenched through her. She was up and halfway to the door before he took hold of her arm. "Rachel."

His eyes reflected her own pain. For a moment, she clung to the hope that he would do something more to console her. But seconds of loud, tense silence spanned between them.

He dropped his hand to his side and said nothing. He couldn't console her.

Or wouldn't.

Tears again welled in her eyes, and without another word, she ran out the door.

CB

Aidan glanced up from his pile of papers and checked the clock at the far end of the Dawson Tours counter. There had been no sign of Rachel since she'd left him two hours ago. He scrubbed his hand over his face and stared out the door. Dull and dreary daylight still draped over the Roker Pier Lighthouse. A perfect match to his mood.

A right bugger, he'd been. When she'd needed understanding and compassion, he'd pushed her out the door. She, who'd reminded him life was still worth living. She, who'd brought her foolish yet admirable dreams and her quiet strength down from Edinburgh.

He allowed himself a slip of a smile. "Well, maybe not quiet."

The lass had never asked for anything, but when she needed help the most, he had failed her. He'd had friends and family to console him after Brooke's death. Rachel had no one.

Guilt could kill a man as easily as a blade.

He tossed his pen to the counter. The papers around him could wait. They would still be there tomorrow. Her grief would still be there tomorrow as well, but he might have the power to ease that a bit. *If* he went searching for her.

He locked up the office, grabbed a taxi, and rode to the town center. She wasn't in her hotel room. Standing at the foot of the Hastings Hotel steps, he swept his gaze the length of the street. "She can't have gone far," he whispered. He rolled his eyes. "Now she's got me talking to myself as well."

The last vestiges of daylight lingered over the far side of town. The streets were fairly empty, a tourist with a map here, a local walking with a purpose there. A pup hollered in the distance.

But no sign of his bonnie lass.

He could've kicked himself for letting her walk away earlier. No, for *sending* her away.

No matter. Those kinds of thoughts wouldn't help him. "Think, man. Where could she be?"

He marched up to Fawcett Street and studied the road, noting what each building might hold to attract a grief-stricken woman.

The answer stared him in the face. Or laughed, rather. His stomach knotted, and a bad taste filled his mouth. Where else did most people go for care of the soul?

The church.

Aidan remained rooted to the parcel of land just outside the Sunderland Museum. Gilchrist Church sat a good ways away opposite the Stadium of Light, posing as guardian to the usually busy street and to the hopes of some.

He was not one of them.

Duty and selfishness battled within him. He hadn't set foot inside a church since he buried Brooke. He certainly didn't have the strength to do it now.

A vision of Rachel's bonnie face swam before him, drained of color and wet with tears, a stark reminder of all that was important at this time.

Guilt carried him forward at a dead man's pace.

He wouldn't have to go inside. He could peek in and just make sure she was there. Surely upon seeing her so distraught, Father Gannon would have guided her through her grief. As long as she was in the capable hands of the good Father, Aidan could move on to one of the pubs.

He stopped outside the church doors at the bottom of the three stairs. As he stared at the ground, guilt settled heavy on his soul. If he set his foot on the stone, would the earth open and swallow him whole? He flexed his fingers at his sides. His shoulders tensed. No, his whole being tensed. Another pup howled from somewhere close by. The diesel engine of a bus chugged away from the corner. He took a quick glance behind him in hopes of seeing someone, anyone he might persuade to go inside.

"Of course not," he mumbled.

But this time it wasn't about him, his pain, or his guilt.

Taking a deep breath, he ascended the stairs and reached a trembling hand toward the church doors. So wooden, so tall, and so bloody heavy. The one he pushed open creaked as he stepped inside. A lone figure sat hunched over in the front of the church. Or perhaps she knelt there. He needn't go any farther to know it was Rachel. The long light hair and the purple shirt she'd been wearing earlier confirmed it.

Good. She was safe at least. He hadn't been spotted yet, so he could easily escape this, his own personal hell, and head to the Thrush and Hound.

Except he had a purpose here, didn't he? The reason he'd left the office still echoed in his mind. Aye, he'd found her, but his duty wouldn't be satisfied until he knew she was soothed.

Aidan hovered on the brink between two worlds. Sour thoughts vibrated through him. Flashes of Brooke's casket, the community, the hymns they'd sung to say goodbye. He slammed his eyes shut. *Breathe, lad.*

Brooke was gone. This was only a building of wood and stone. Would he let this woman suffer alone because his ghosts unnerved him?

He opened his eyes and stepped all the way inside the church. The door creaked and closed behind him, imprisoning him.

Rachel leaned back in her seat. All the way in the front pew.

He shuffled down the center aisle, his footsteps echoing off the stone floor. The scents of candle wax and incense assailed him, along with a requisite reverence he'd not been able to offer these past few years.

She sniffled on the heels of a sob, and another knife sliced through his heart. Gripping the pew, he stood before her. "Can I join you?"

She raised her puffy eyes to him. "I would like that, but don't feel you have to."

He forced the words from his lips. "I want to."

Her body relaxed even as a batch of fresh tears dripped down her cheeks. She scooted to the side to make room for him.

Stiffly, he took the seat. "Do you want to tell me about your gran?"

"Yes and no." She swiped the back of her fingers across her eyes. "She's always been the most important person to me, and now she's gone. I should've been there." She slumped forward.

Lifting his hand above her shoulder, he hesitated, but only for a moment. She needed comforting. He'd come to offer it.

"Calm yourself, lass, and tell me what happened." He set his hand on her back and moved it around in little circles.

"Pneumonia," she said after several long minutes of silence. "She slipped into a coma yesterday and died early this morning. The sheltered accommodation facility couldn't reach me so they called my parents, who now know I've been down here."

A soft tremor skittered along her spine under his fingers. "I'm so sorry." Shifting closer, he widened the circle of his arm against her back.

"My sister says they're really angry with me. I'm going to get an earful when they come over for the funeral." She sniffled some more. "And my parents are too distraught to deal with all the little details for that, so they want me to handle them from here."

All of him wanted to gather her into his arms and shield her. Who would be there to comfort Rachel?

She twisted her head away. "Why didn't I go back to Edinburgh when they first told me she was sick?"

"Because she wanted you here."

"But, I should've known better."

He cupped her cheek and turned her face toward his. "You have nothing to feel guilty about."

Just as her lower lip trembled, she closed her eyes. Tears bubbled free. The warm moisture dripped down her cheeks and ran along his thumb.

Knots unraveled inside him, but he didn't move his hand. "The doubts that linger on your heart would be there if you'd been by her bedside as well." He knew that all too well. "You did what *you* needed."

"Yeah, and I let everyone down in the process."

"How can you say that? Why are you here?"

She shrugged. "My family would say I had a lapse in good judgment."

"But what do you say?"

"I wanted to do something special for Nan because she's the most important person in my world."

"Do you think she knew that?"

"Yeah."

"Then does it matter what anyone else thinks?"

She hesitated. "No."

"Don't worry about your family. Believe in what you chose, and make your grandmother proud."

"I don't think I'm strong enough. Not without her." She lowered her head.

The hitching in her sobs all but ripped his heart in two. "You are the strongest woman I know."

She scoffed. "That's just a façade."

"You can do just about anything you set your mind to, so don't tell me you're not strong enough."

"But Aidan, I'm so lost. I don't even know what my next step should be."

"It's quite simple. You grieve, and then you take one step at a time."

"What if I can't even figure out where to put my feet first?"

He brushed his knuckles over her cheek and held out his palm. "Then you take my hand." What was he thinking? "And we find it together."

She narrowed those emerald eyes on him. "Being nice to me now won't get you the cottage."

Clenching his teeth, he counted to five. She was grief-stricken, he had to remember. "Will you forget the cottage, ye daft lass? I'm not so heartless as that."

She took in a deep breath and nodded.

The glimmer of hope drowning in her eyes held him still. "Let me be your strength tonight." Draping his arm across her back, he pulled her against him and tucked her head under his chin. She remained stiff, as though she doubted him, but only for a few minutes.

When she did relax, it nearly undid him. For a whole set of other reasons. Her curves molded against him, so soft and chilled and trusting. How could she be chilled? The temperature in his own body had sharply risen in the last few seconds. Her hair tickled the side of his jaw….

Aidan closed his eyes and thought of Sunderland in the dead of winter. Freezing air, a harsh wind to knock him clear off his feet into deep snow.

The feel of her pressed against him, a perfect fit in his arms, would not allow his thoughts to linger on any chill he'd conjured up, and his blood simmered just under his skin.

But he would put *his* needs aside for now and look after the lass. If nothing else, he owed her that.

Chapter Seven

Rachel had gone to Edinburgh four days ago, and Aidan missed her. A lot. It was good he had the overnight tour to Durham tomorrow. A bit of time away would do his brain good.

"Bloody hell." He jerked his backpack from his bedroom closet floor, tossed it to the foot of the bed, and stuffed clothes inside.

He bloody well missed her, which was not good at all. Their relationship was supposed to be casual, a fling, a brief affair. Then why had he let her get to him? With her sexy body, gentle heart, and eternal optimism, she'd slipped under his skin and secured her own place there. She'd be leaving before long, and he would go back to his own life. But these few days had proved he'd let her mean more to him than he'd originally planned.

Bugger.

He yanked a shirt and pair of pants off the hangers in his closet and shoved them in his backpack. When he'd zipped it closed, he glimpsed his wedding photo centered in between the windows.

He'd been twenty when he'd married and a widower by twenty-five. So much of his life had revolved around regret and pain. He reached out, his fingers touching the dark wooden frame. Would it be so wrong for him to pursue a chance at happiness? Gently, he pulled the wedding picture off the wall.

149

Ghosts had stripped away enough of his life.

The picture belonged in the closet. As he placed it on the top shelf, a loud thumping at the front door interrupted his thoughts. He wandered through the house to answer it. When he glimpsed Rachel standing outside, whatever doubts floated through his brain disappeared. She was a vision with her black slacks and her rust-colored shirt hugging her curves under her unbuttoned raincoat. Her golden curls hung around her shoulders, and a tinge of pink colored her cheeks.

Need tightened in his chest. His cock twitched. Instantly, he wanted her—to hold her, to strip her, to sink into her.

He opened the door and smiled. "This is a pleasant surprise. I thought you weren't coming home until tomorrow."

Silence mingled with the deathly glare spitting from her eyes.

He frowned. "What's wrong?"

She twirled the raincoat ties around her hand until her fingers began to change colors. "I have one question for you, and I want the truth."

"Always." He nodded and gripped the doorknob.

"Did you speak with the estate agent about the cottage the day after my grandmother died?"

His whole body froze. "Aye."

Instantly, tears gathered in the corners of Rachel's eyes. She nodded and turned around. She needed to get away before she bawled like a baby. Or punched him.

"Wait a bit." He grabbed her arm. "It's not what you think."

She stilled, but refused to look at him. "Of course it is. You went behind my back and did the one thing you knew would break my heart." She yanked her arm free and stomped down the stairs.

"Don't be so dramatic, you daft woman."

Curling her fingers into fists, she whipped around to face him. He stood there on the top step, his body tense as though he had the right to be offended. "Dramatic? How else am I supposed to be? I trusted you, believed you. In the end, you played with my emotions and used me to get what you wanted."

He shook his head. "You can't truly believe that."

She held her hands out to her sides. "What else am I supposed to believe?"

"How about listening to what I have to say? Yes, I spoke with the estate agent, but he called me. Because I'd been so interested in the past, he thought I'd want to know that it would soon be up for sale. I didn't call him."

She still said nothing, but her steel resolve began to crumble.

"You can have his phone number and ask him if you'd like, if you refuse to take my word."

"You have to see this through my eyes."

"Bugger, Rachel. After all we've been through." He closed the distance between them and grabbed her elbows. "After all the hours you spent in my arms, how can you think that of me?"

"You've always wanted the cottage."

"Aye, but I've always been honest with you about it. And when someone else tried to frighten you away, I was the one to help you."

"Good points," she mumbled.

"I want you happy and smiling and laughing. I've no intention of ever seeing you hurt." He raised his hands and cupped her cheeks. "That is more important to me than securing the cottage."

Her breath disappeared. Her skin tingled under his warm fingers, his palms callused and strong as a man's hands should be. Leaning closer, she touched his chest. He was right. Hurting her wasn't his MO.

He planted a kiss on her forehead. "Now, will you come inside, so I can properly welcome you back to Sunderland?"

She shouldn't. Letting her emotions and her hormones lead her choices could backfire. But she'd missed him these last few days, missed the feel of his arms around her, the feel of his lips on her skin, the sound of his sexy voice—until Vicki had planted the silly seed in her head that Aidan had already asked about the cottage.

But her body's need for him won out. She held his forearms. "And what will that welcome entail?"

With his mouth close to her ear, his warm breath tickled her skin. "I want to touch every inch of you. I want to taste your mouth, your breasts, between your legs." He cupped her bottom and braced her against his growing erection. "I want to use my tongue to torture you into orgasm after orgasm. Then, when you think you can't take anymore, I want to slide my cock between your legs and bring you home."

She shuddered with the images his words created, moisture already seeping into her panties. "Well, then." Rocking her hips against his, she shuddered again. "What are you waiting for?"

Laughing, he swept her into his arms, and carried her into the house. He took a shortcut into the bathroom to retrieve a few condoms. Once he entered the bedroom, he set her on her feet. Slowly, he stripped her out of her clothes. True to his word, he urged her onto the bed, braced his hands on her hips, and lowered his mouth to her clit. He sucked it into his mouth, circled it with his tongue, and in no time, Rachel arched off the mattress. Gripping the sheets, she closed her eyes. He licked her from her clitoris to her opening and slid his tongue inside.

She gasped. Her body trembled. The feel of his mouth on her, his tongue inside her made her heartbeat skyrocket, her vision blur.

His mouth returned to her clit, sucking it, grazing it with his teeth. At the same time, his fingers slid inside her.

Her body exploded in the pleasure he provided. She rode the wave of her release, cried out to him.

At once, he removed his hands and his mouth, and stood at the foot of the bed, watching her. His tongue drifted across his bottom lip like a hungry wolf.

Lust surged through her. When she had control over her limbs again, she propped herself up on her forearms. "How come I'm the only one naked here?"

He chuckled and held his arms out to his sides. "Come get me."

She scooted to the foot of the bed and set about unbuckling his belt. Her mouth watered with thoughts of tasting him. Aidan removed his shirt. As she pushed his pants and his underwear down his legs, her fingers shook. Carefully, she touched his cock, stroked him, cradled his balls, and brushed the pad of her thumb across the tip of him.

He sucked in a breath.

Releasing him, she glanced up. "Should I stop?" She'd never done this with anyone before, but it had never felt so right.

He shook his head. "No. Don't stop." His voice sounded guttural.

Again she stroked her fingers across him, faster this time and with more pressure. She planted a kiss on him then she slid her tongue around its soft, velvety tip.

"Bugger. Are you trying to kill me, lass?"

His reaction empowered her. Spurred on, she took him into her mouth, inch by inch. The moans escaping from him gave her a rush until he pulled himself out of her mouth. "You've got to stop now."

"Why?" She looked up at him, her stomach clenching. Had she done something wrong?

He reached for one of the condoms on the bed and tore the package open. "I need to be inside you." After covering himself, he claimed her mouth, kneed her legs apart and pushed his cock deep into her.

She inhaled sharply at the feel of him invading her body, claiming her body, sliding with precision farther into her. She swept her tongue into his mouth and wrapped her arms around him, brushing her fingers along his back. The sparse hairs of his chest tickled against her breasts.

Her heartbeat tripped behind her breast, and a soft whimper escaped from the back of her throat. Her bones threatened to melt from the heat and strength of his body's touch. This was perfect. *He* was perfect for her.

And Edinburgh was only two and a half hours away by train.

Hours later, Rachel rowed out to the cottage alone, gathered some of the dry wood from under the tarp in the middle of the living room, and placed it in the fireplace. She and Aidan had planned to spend the evening together later when they'd both finished some errands. Her most important errand was finding her sanity.

The wind howled outside. Tree branches clawed against the frame of the cottage.

Thuuummp.

A chill scurried down her spine.

Somehow over the last week and a half, she'd fallen in love with Aidan. This morning she'd been ready to do battle with him. This afternoon, she wanted a life with him. Sunderland had always been a special place in her heart, with its memories of Nan and the kindness of the townspeople, but it had taken this trip—and this particular man—to remind her. The biggest question was, would he want her in his life? Tonight, when he took her to dinner, she would broach the subject with him.

And the cottage. Nana's death negated her reason for being here, but now she couldn't imagine leaving for good. No, she had no intention of moving to Sunderland—Edinburgh held too much appeal. But she could cross the border on long weekends and holidays. She could learn more about the place that had held her grandmother's heart. Maybe too, she could make a compromise with her hunky Brit. He could use the cottage when she wasn't here. If he wanted. Another topic for them to discuss tonight. "Wow, tonight's turning out to be an extremely important evening."

Thump, craaack.

She crouched in front of the fireplace and struck a match. A few minutes later, flames licked the air in the fireplace, dispersing the odor of burning wood throughout the room.

Thump, thump, crack.

After replacing the matchbox on the mantel, she headed toward the bedroom for one of the clean blankets. A roaring wind and another crackling sound sliced through the air above her. Dust floated down from the ceiling.

Every nerve twisted in her body. She stopped, looked up, and lost her breath. Tree branches dangled through the cracks in the roof.

What the hell? Her heart slammed into her ribs as the cracks lengthened. More dust fell in, more ceiling pieces.

Run! But her body refused to follow orders, panic seizing her every limb. Leaves and branches closed the distance to her, and she screamed. The tree crashed through the rest of the ceiling and collapsed on top of her.

Chapter Eight

Aidan smelled smoke before he reached the island. Gray-black wisps curled up from the cottage into the dull afternoon sky. Bright orange flames licked the air, as though taunting him.

He'd been sitting in the office when he spotted her rowing out there. He'd warned her not to go without him. What had she been thinking? Fear clutched his heart. His gaze shifted around the shore. Her boat sat unattended.

"Rachel!" Why was she not running outside or even rowing back across the water?

When the boat slammed into the sand, he hopped out and raced up the path toward the home as if his heart depended on it. Once he reached the cottage, a curse forced its way through his lips. The oak tree had fallen completely, taking most of the south wall with it.

"Bugger!" Smoke billowed out of what was supposed to be a window. His heartbeat thumped against his ribs, in his ears. Where was she?

He scrambled through the front door. A wave of heat washed over him. Thick smoke invaded his senses and made him cough. His eyes watered against the bright flames already engulfing the couch, the bookcase, and charging swiftly toward....

"Rachel!" He caught sight of her rust-colored sweater trapped under part of the tree. She lay on the floor, sprawled out as peacefully as if she slept.

His body stilled. Numbed. Memories of Brooke lying helpless crashed into his mind. His heart wrenched. *Not again.*

But Brooke was gone. He'd loved her. He loved her still, but he was *in love* with Rachel. Totally. Completely. Differently.

He slid in by her side and pushed the tree limb. The rough bark chewed his palms. He pushed harder. His muscles screamed from the tension. The limb budged a bit. Smoke snaked its way down his throat. His coughing increased. Heat licked his back, threatened to singe the ends of his hair.

He would not lose her.

Gritting his teeth, he shoved again. The tree trunk lumbered off her legs. Aidan gathered her in his arms and carried her outside. Still, she hadn't stirred. He gently set her down on the ground at the outer edge of the clearing. Her breath rushed over the back of his fingers.

His bonnie foreigner was safe. He stood up and glanced back at the cottage. Her home wasn't. If he did nothing, the cottage would burn along with most of the trees on the island. His shoulders tensed. He should let the professionals deal with the fire, but they hadn't arrived yet. His gaze traveled back to the lass who held his heart. This cottage still meant something to her. For that alone, he had to try.

Aidan sprinted back toward the building.

The foul smell of burned wood and plastic invaded Rachel's senses before she opened her eyes. Cold seeped through her from the hard surface beneath her. Fear seized her nerves. Fire. She'd lit a fire when—

She scrambled to sit up. Her leg refused to move. White-hot pain shot up her calf. She sucked in a slow breath between clenched teeth, planted her palms on each side of her, and willed her eyes to focus.

The cottage loomed before her, flames crackling in the dreary sky, and wisps of smoke bleeding through the structure.

How had she gotten out?

She glanced around. She remained alone at the far end of the clearing. The smoke died down, the wisps disappearing on the wind. A siren of some kind wailed in the distance, the kind of sound that announced some deep heartache to the world.

Or maybe it was just her heart that was fractured. Nan's home, her own safe haven, destroyed. The irony was she'd been fighting the McAndrew brothers all this time, and yet….

"I'm the one who let it go up in smoke."

Wood smacked against wood as a shadow emerged from the front door. Aidan ran back to her, sputtering from the fumes no doubt. Her heart leapt. All her blood drained from her head and left her dizzy. If he hadn't come, she would've died.

She owed him her life.

"We've got to go." He scooped her into his strong arms and beat it down the path toward the shore.

Gazing over his shoulder, she watched her dreams disintegrate with each lick of flame reaching another section of the cottage. The scent of smoke lingered on him.

"My cottage," she whispered, tears rolling down her cheek and soaking into his coat.

"I couldn't save it." The regret in his voice formed knots inside her chest.

"Why'd you go back in?" He, of course, was much more important than the building.

"That cottage has a legacy. It means too much. I didn't want all the memories to slip away."

Rachel rested her head against his shoulder. He'd gone back in to save a memory. But was he speaking to her memory or his own? She closed her eyes and shielded her heart.

Voices shouted out in thick Sunderland accents. Metal and wood clanged together, and footfalls thundered against the earth. "'Ere, is she all right?" she heard Craig call out. A medley of commands traveled on the wind.

No, not at the moment. Her leg throbbed, her lungs burned, and her head felt as if it were going to explode.

"She's hurt her leg," Aidan answered.

He positioned her in his boat and rowed them away from the island. Members of the community, who had apparently rowed over on their own, poured bucket after bucket of water onto her burning home. She could still hear the snapping of flames, as eerily peaceful as if she'd been at a campfire roasting marshmallows. With every snap, another piece of her heart crashed into the water. Leaning her head back, she closed her eyes.

The rhythmic plop of the oars into the water and the gentle swell of the boat relaxed her. The stench of items burning gave way to fresh air. For a few minutes, she accepted the pull of tears and the pressure of sadness.

More voices punctured the air. Gemma's took the lead. "Is she all right?"

"She needs to go to the Accident and Emergency Department." When the boat hit the sand, he slipped his hands around her body and lifted her out.

She wanted to tell him to stop, to put her down. At the same time, her heart willed him to hold her forever.

"Craig and I brought the car." Gemma rushed toward the road.

Aidan followed her, his gaze traveling back every so often to the island. He settled her in the passenger seat of their friend's car.

"You should go back." Her heart splintered even as the words left her lips.

His mouth hung open, indecision marring his usually confident brow.

"The cottage needs you." She pushed his hands from her arm and thigh.

"What about you?" he asked, a hint of disappointment hanging on his words.

Her gaze drifted away from him. "Gemma will help me." She pressed her palm against his chest. One last reminder of how his body felt beneath her fingers.

"You need to go," she said with more authority than she actually felt. All she truly wished for was him to wrap her in his arms again and shelter her there while she sorted out all the details of her life. "Take care of the cottage."

"Listen to her. You can't help her now, but you can help the others." Her friend twisted the key in the ignition. Still more

Sunderland residents streamed toward the shore as a fireboat reached the island.

Taking the decision from him, Rachel reached for the handle and pulled her door shut.

CB

Aidan stood on the Roker shore and watched the last of the flames take down what was left of the cottage. Inside, helplessness curled around his chest, squeezing clean breath straight out of his lungs. Sharing the news with Rachel would break his heart.

Only a few firefighters remained, and most of the townspeople had returned to their pints or their duties. He crossed his arms and sighed.

"Aidan!" Someone called from behind him. He turned around to see Craig jumping down the last two stairs from the road and rushing toward him. "Where's your lass?"

"Your sister took her to hospital to have her leg checked hours ago. Why?"

"Your Adam's been arrested." He pulled his mobile from his pocket and dialed. "Officer Jackson said Adam confessed to cutting the tree that fell into the cottage when he went to question him. The lad said they didn't mean for her to get hurt. They only wanted to frighten her away. Someone said David was right upset somewhere in town, but so far they haven't been able to locate him."

His muscles tensed. David was the brother-in-law with the temper. He'd been against Rachel since the day she arrived, and he'd been quite vocal about it to anyone who would listen.

Craig held up his hand. "Gem, where are you?"

Please let her be safe.

Craig shook his head and pulled the phone away from his mouth. "She's just dropped her off at the Hastings."

"Bugger." He ran toward the stairs. David was just mad enough to do something stupid.

CB

Rachel hobbled out of her hotel bathroom. "I'm coming!" She hollered to be heard over the heavy thumping. With a cast on her leg, she could only move so fast.

"Open this door or I'll kick it in, you bloody bitch!"

She stood still in the center of the room, a few feet from the door. Blood drained from her head and sent the room spinning. Who the hell was that?

The thumping started again.

She glanced toward the phone on the nightstand. Should she dial the front desk or the emergency number 999? She scooted toward the bed.

The door crashed open. She screamed, fell backward onto the mattress, and looked up into the angry eyes of David McAndrew.

He stalked toward her. His giant fingers closed into fists. Spittle fell onto his chin as he spoke. "Why don't you go back where you've come from? You're ruining me family."

"I'm sorry you feel that way." Pushing herself up onto her unsteady cast and wobbly good foot, she swallowed the fear threatening to push lunch back up her throat.

"Because of you me brother's been arrested." He poked her between her breasts. "And they're looking for me."

"You two shouldn't have done anything illegal then the police wouldn't be after you."

"If you'd left us alone, left Aidan alone, and let him have the cottage, none of this would've happened. Why couldn't you leave well enough alone?" He raised his hand.

"No!" Rachel jerked back. She lifted her arm and closed her eyes.

But the blow never came.

"You'll not harm her." Aidan's voice held a deadly threat, but never had she heard such a sweeter sound.

She opened her eyes and released a breath. Her handsome Englishman stood toe-to-toe with his former brother-in-law. Tears pushed against the corners of her eyes and her limbs sagged in relief.

David shook his arm free. "But Adam's in jail, the cottage is—"

"Gone because of you, you daft lad."

David stood rigid, his face a mask of hatred. "Do you not care about your pledge to Brooke?"

"Dave, I care a great deal for the memories of your sister, but they'll not bring her back. Can you not understand? That part of my life's over. I've a right to move on."

McAndrew glared at them both. "I never thought you to be a traitor, but I suppose shagging the Yank changed your mind, eh?"

Aidan's fist flew into David's jaw. The young man stumbled backward and laughed. "Aye, I see how it is."

He came back swinging on his own. But her hero was stronger, faster. With a combination of punches, he knocked McAndrew to the floor.

Aidan turned to her. "Are you all right? Did he hurt you?"

She shook her head. "I'm okay."

"Are you sure?" He reached for her.

Footsteps rumbled in the hallway along with voices.

She pulled away just as Police Constable Jackson and another officer crossed into the room followed by the Barnes siblings.

"Rachel, Aidan, are you all right?" Gemma asked.

"Aye," he answered at the same time she said, "Yeah."

As soon as the officers yanked David to his feet, he began complaining and pleading his case. The officer she didn't know led him away. PC Jackson stayed behind just long enough to question Rachel and Aidan. As he walked out of the room and followed his colleague down the hall, she rubbed her arms. "Gemma, can you hang out with me for a while?"

"Me?" She glanced at each of the men and then back to Rachel. "Do you not want Aidan to stay?"

She kept her gaze on her friend. How could she answer without insulting him?

He took the choice from her. "Can you two wait outside a bit?"

"Aye," the siblings said in unison. They exited the room with Aidan closing the door behind them.

Tilting his head to one side, he stared at her.

She swallowed the lump creeping up her throat. "What's wrong?"

"You tell me." He crossed his arms.

Pegged. Damn. "I'm just really tired and achy." *And confused.*

Definitely confused. Damn him! He'd chosen the cottage and his memories over her, and yet her body still tingled for him. No matter how much she denied it, he resided in her heart, too. "It's been a tough afternoon."

"Because of the fire? David? Or something else?"

The hurt in his voice, the disappointment in his eyes made her feel like a jerk. But he was the one clinging to his memories. "I've been hurt before, and I know you care about me, but—"

"You care for a dog or a cause." He tossed his hands out in front of him. "I don't just *care* for you. I *love* you, ye daft woman!"

Her chest tightened. *But how much?* "What about your wife?"

"What about her?"

She tugged the hem of her sweater. "David talked about you promising to honor her."

"Aye, with the cottage." His voice quieted but still held a note of annoyance. "But that's in the past."

She rolled her eyes. "Come on, Aidan. Less than two weeks ago you were hell-bent on convincing me to go home. All along you've wanted that cottage."

He nodded. "And now I don't."

"How can I believe that? Before you carried me to the boat, you told me you'd gone in to save memories."

"Aye, *your* memories. I wanted to protect the connection between you and your gran."

Hmm. She hadn't thought of that possibility.

"Brooke will always have a place in my heart. I can't help that. But we were young, and we thought marriage was what we were supposed to do. Ours wasn't a perfect union. We weren't meant to be together. You're the one I want by my side…for as long as you'll have me."

Rachel chewed her bottom lip. "I so want to believe you, but I have to be sure. If you're wrapped up in memories of your wife, I can't compete with that. I don't want to settle. I deserve to be happy and loved for who I am."

Wait a minute. When had this trip stopped being about Nan's cottage and become about herself?

"In the last few days, I've been able to put my ghosts to rest. The question is, will you let your own ghosts interfere with all you could have?"

He obviously didn't understand. This wasn't about her ghosts.

Was it?

He fished for something in his pocket and pulled out a black, velvet box.

Rachel lost her breath.

He didn't open it but, instead, placed it on the bedside table. Without another word, he strode toward the door.

"Aidan, wait." She hobbled after him and cursed her broken leg. "Aidan!"

He kept going.

With a heavy sigh, she settled on the edge of the bed. Tears stung her eyes. She closed them. Could she trust him with her heart? "He already has it."

Gemma stomped into the room and crossed her arms. "Did you hit your head a bit too hard when that tree crashed down on top of you?"

"What do you mean?"

The hot-tempered Brit pinned her with a vicious glare—mean, like fire would spit from her redheaded curls at any second. "You have a chance so many of us would kill to have. How can you choose to throw away something so good for you so easily?" She tossed a brown envelope onto the bed and plopped into the chair by the window. "That came to the front desk for you."

She picked up the mail. The return address label read Heather Oaks. After opening it, she scanned the letter from the night receptionist. Something about her grandmother dictating this the day Rachel left for Sunderland. Glancing inside the large envelope, she spotted a smaller, white one. "It's from my grandmother."

Gemma sat forward but remained quiet.

As she tore the envelope open, her throat tightened. She stared at the piece of paper locked in her fingers. Nan's last words to her. If she folded it and put it away, that last conversation could be postponed. Indefinitely.

But her grandmother's last thoughts deserved to be read.

Butterflies flitted around in her stomach. Her fingers shook. The writing belonged to someone else, but the message was all Nana.

My sweet Rachel,

If I've not gone by the time you get this, I've no doubt it'll be soon. In doing the repairs to the cottage, I hope you take the time to fix it as you'd like. You see, the cottage and the land are yours, lass. Or rather, they will be once I've passed. I'll not trust my piece of heaven on earth to anyone else. Sunderland holds pleasant memories for me, memories of you as a little lassie sharing my happiness there. Perhaps now you'll find the sense of belonging you always seemed to be searching for. If anyone can see Sunderland for all it is and all it can be, it would be you.

You deserve to be happy. Hold no guilt in your heart for being there now, and let no one force that guilt upon you. You're living as you need to, and I admire that. Courage and strength flow through your veins. Never be afraid to seek out your own happiness and demand the love and respect you deserve. No one can fault ye for that, and if they do, then bugger them all!

Take care of yourself, lass, and know that I love you until the last breath leaves me, and even after, I'll love you still.

Nan

Tears seeped from the rims of her eyes. She stared at the letter. Then at the velvet box. Then back at the letter. So, what was it she wanted?

"What did she say?"

"The cottage is mine, and she wants me to be happy."

The way to do that flashed like a neon sign in her mind. She wanted a life with Aidan. She wanted to care for him, to cherish and love him for the next fifty or sixty years.

Adrenaline flooded her veins, alongside that fierce Grant strength. She reached over and clutched the ring box. With trembling fingers, she opened it and stared at the precious diamond with a Celtic band.

Gemma lurched closer and gasped. "Bloody hell! That's gorgeous!"

Rachel's heart squeezed. "Gem?"

"Aye?"

She couldn't help but smile. "You were right. I've been a fool. Help me find him so I can tell him I love him."

Her friend grinned, sprang up from the chair, and grabbed the crutches by the window. "It's about bloody time!"

ࡘ

The bell on the door announced another guest to the Thrush and Hound Pub, but Aidan didn't bother to turn from his seat at the bar. He sipped on his pint and tried to banish thoughts of Rachel and their heated exchange from his mind. A fiery woman, he'd chosen to love.

Perhaps he should walk away before he allowed any other part of him to love her. She already owned his heart. She'd claimed his body, too. He'd not surrender his soul as well.

"How can I get her to see what's important?" he whispered.

"Eh?" Craig asked and accepted his pint from Bradley.

"Nothing." He shook his head. Talking to himself had never been a problem before the lass arrived. That was something he would have to remedy. He closed his eyes and attempted to rub the headache from his temples. Love was complicated, but she couldn't just give up. He'd not let her walk away that easily. He'd lost love once, but he'd had little control over that. This time he could fight for what he wanted, what he knew to be right.

The bell on the front door jingled again.

That sodden sound grated on his nerves. "Bloody hell, Brad. How do you put up with that incessant noise?" Aidan gulped down the last of his beer, slid off the stool, and started for the door.

All his breath rushed from his lungs at once.

Rachel stood in the doorway, balancing her weight on crutches. Her green eyes sparkled with life again. She looked beautiful, her sweater revealing curves he still longed to explore. The solid black skirt almost completely hid her cast. When her gaze found his, anticipation danced across her face. His mouth watered. How he wanted her.

The evening crowd hushed. Gemma slipped inside the pub behind his lass.

He prayed his legs would keep him upright. "Hello."

She crutched her way to the middle of the room. Silverware clinked against dishes. Voices began again in whispers. Pub patrons pretended not to be listening to their exchange.

"I didn't want to come to Sunderland, but now I don't want to leave."

Did she want a response from him? Did he have one? No, his mind thought of nothing but taking her in his arms.

Worry lined her lovely brow, her soft lips. "Aidan, please give me another chance." Her voice crackled with emotion, whether unshed tears or secret fears he couldn't tell. She closed her eyes briefly, a silent acknowledgement of her vulnerability. He'd not say weakness because nothing about this woman was weak.

As he eased toward her, he kept his hands in his pockets so he didn't reach out to her. Not yet. "Are you sure?"

She nodded slowly. "Yes. You see, I was feeling kind of lost, like I didn't even know where I belonged. But a wise man once told me it's simple."

"Aye." He smiled. "You take one step at a time."

"And if I can't even figure out where to put my feet?" Glancing down at the cast on her leg, she grinned. "Or foot, in this case."

"Then you take my hand, and we find it together." She held his heart, owned it outright. Was she ready to surrender hers? He would cherish it forever, if she'd let him.

"So here's me, taking one step. You mean the world to me. I know it won't always be perfect, but I don't want to spend a day of my life without you in it." She leaned her weight on one crutch, lifted her fingers, and caressed his cheek.

The touch constricted his stomach. He was weak, so very weak. He framed the side of her face with one of his hands. "You, Rachel Grant, are my match in every way. You are the one I love. I want to wake up next to you every morning and make love to you every night. I want us to grow old together and watch our children grow strong and happy."

"And if we don't have forever?"

"I'd rather love you for as long as I can than watch you get on that train in a few days' time."

Tears shimmered in the corners of her eyes. She blinked them back. "You were never this optimistic before. What's changed you?"

"Do you not know?" Smiling, he brushed his thumb along her cheekbone. "It was you."

"I love you so much." The pain and doubts of the last few days slowly disappeared from her eyes, leaving those radiant emeralds overflowing with happiness, love, desire.

He slipped his arms around her waist. "So, you'll have me then? Faults and all?"

Reaching one hand to the back of his neck, she pulled his head down, and touched her forehead to his. "I'd be a fool to turn you away."

"Will you kiss the lass already?" someone shouted from behind her, someone that sounded a lot like Gemma Barnes.

Rachel's cheeks reddened, and she giggled.

He let out a chuckle of his own. "Aye, I can do that."

Anchoring her weight against him, he set his lips on hers. He kissed her thoroughly, with the promise of warm nights and lazy days of loving to come.

A collective cheer erupted through the pub. Voices returned, conversations continued, and drinks flowed, and Aidan knew he'd found his own paradise.

Chapter Nine

Seven Months Later

Rachel followed Aidan out the cottage front door and over to the ladder. He was so stubborn! "Will you turn around?"

"No, I'll not." He kept his back to her and climbed the rungs. A very nice backside it was, too, encased in those khaki pants he favored.

"Come on." She chuckled.

He glanced back at her with an unconvincing scowl. "I don't understand why you've brought that thing out here. I can't work with you, and that camera, watching me."

"I promise to tell you soon enough." She giggled as he huffed and returned to the Grant and Camden family crests he was nailing above the front door.

"Lass, we'll not have this place ready for the first tourists of the season if you can't stop playing about long enough to give me a hand."

"Trust me, my love." As she walked toward him, she focused the camera lens on his backside. "I'm working on a very important project."

He hopped off the ladder, swiped the camera from her with one hand, and tugged her to him with the other. The heat and strength of his muscles set off fireworks throughout her body.

"What might that be, Mrs. Camden?"

"I love the sound of that."

"It suits you." He pleased her with a kiss. "Now, what is it you want to share with me?"

"Yesterday before we came down here, I had a doctor's appointment." God love him, his smile disappeared in the space of a heartbeat. She pressed her palm over his heart, sensing the rhythm as it tapped against her fingers. "Don't look so scared, my love. This was a good visit."

He rolled his eyes. "There's no such thing as a good doctor's visit."

"Well, if you feel that way, I'll just keep the news to myself."

"You'll not." He dragged her closer.

"I will." Lifting her gaze toward the sky, she pretended to think hard on her next words. "Unless you can find some way to persuade me to share."

"Is that right?" he asked in between kisses on her eyes, her nose, and finally her lips.

With a wicked grin, she answered, "Aye."

A soft rumble of laughter rippled through his chest. "You may be the one who works for the IPN, but I'm confident I can find a way to make you talk." His hands slid along her back while his mouth came down on hers again. His tongue sought hers, stroked hers, enticed hers. Soft, warm, and entirely convincing.

Tree branches rustled in the distance. Voices converged on their island.

"'Ere, will you two stop?" Craig hollered from behind them, disgust yanking out his every word. "You'll drive away your first guests with that display."

Must not be getting any loving of his own. Poor guy!

He traipsed through the clearing and into the cottage with a box in his hands and Gemma at his heels carrying another box.

"Don't listen to him," Rachel said loud enough for Craig to hear. "He's only jealous. You can keep persuading."

"Aye, leave them be," Gemma ordered from inside the cottage.

"Bloody hell!" Craig came back to the doorway and bit into a crisp apple. His sister pushed him out the door.

"The fair-haired Leslie giving you the brush off, is she?" Aidan teased.

"You're so mean." She smacked his shoulder, but still she giggled. These days she had much to be happy about.

Gemma pursed her lips and tossed her brother an unsympathetic stare. "Aye, that's exactly what it is."

Craig stopped before them and glared at Aidan. "I wish a bolt of lightning would come crashing down on your arse!" With a severe bite into his apple, he started back to the water's edge. "'Ere, you'll stop snogging long enough to help us unload this boat, or I'll throw out your stores and row home."

Gemma smacked her brother. "Leave them alone. Can you not see they're in love?"

"More's the pity for it." He stomped off across the clearing.

"Take no notice of him." Her friend grinned as she started backpedaling. "You two come down when you're ready."

Aidan turned those dazzling eyes back to her with a hint of mischief floating in them. "Now, where were we?"

She fought to keep a straight expression. "The doctor says I've got some kind of bump that's apparently going to get bigger in the next few months."

His face fell a few inches. "Where?"

Smiling, she pressed his hand to her stomach. "Right here."

"Is it a tumor? Why are you smiling if you've got a mass growing in your stomach that will only get bigger—"

"Over the next few months." She bit her bottom lip until understanding dawned on his worried brow.

His hazel eyes widened and his mouth hung open. He glanced down at her stomach. "How many months?"

"Since it's already been about six weeks, I'd say we have another seven and a half months left."

"A bairn? We're to have a bairn?" Both his hands roamed over her stomach, as if attempting to feel the baby in there.

"Yep, and before we start renting this place out on a regular basis, I wanted to show our child where we first met and what brought us together."

He picked her up and swung her around. "That's grand!"

She giggled and hollered all on the same breath.

Immediately, he stopped and set her on her own feet. "I shouldn't do that, should I?" His brow creased, worry casting a shadow along his jaw. "I'm sorry. I'll not do that again. I'll not do anything to hurt you or the baby."

"You could never hurt us, Aidan." She traced the side of his face with her thumb. Her gentle, kind, compassionate Englishman. He would be a wonderful father. His patience and love knew no bounds.

"You're the love of my life, Rachel Camden." He bent his head and touched her lips again.

"'Ere! You two get a move on," Craig hollered from the shore.

She pulled back first and laughed. "We better go, or he *will* take off with our supplies." Linking her fingers with his, she led him toward the trees. "How long will they be here?"

His gaze swept over her once again and lingered on her stomach. "I'm not sure, why?"

Her body craved his intimate touch, the feel of his big, strong hands brushing over every inch of her skin. "I'd just like to celebrate with my husband." She captured his gaze. "In private," she added.

He stopped. Desire flared behind his eyes. "Can you still...you know, even with the bairn? It'll not hurt it?"

"We're safe."

"Gemma, Craig," he called into the woods. "Come back in a few hours!" With a wicked gleam in his darkening eyes, Aidan led her back to the cottage and loved her until the sun went down.

Simple Treasures

Chapter One

Colin Munro didn't know which knife to worry about more, the one pointed at his throat or the one at his crotch.

"You've got ten seconds to tell me who the hell you are, or I start slicing," the woman threatened.

He glanced into her stormy dark eyes. Joanna Grainger. The lass he'd been sent to keep safe.

Aye, but who would protect him?

"Take care where you move those blades." Of course, he wasn't terribly worried. If he needed to, he could easily disarm her. She stood about five foot six without the high heels she'd been wearing when she'd first entered her flat.

"I'm the one giving orders here." The steel at his neck pushed a bit closer to his Adam's apple.

"I don't think so." Colin smacked her arms, snatched the blades from her fingers with one hand, and pushed her back to the wall. The picture frame close to her head shook, but he hadn't shoved with nearly as much force as he could have. He pinned both her wrists to the wall above her head. "I'm Colin Munro, and I'm here to protect you."

"I don't remember asking anyone for help." She brought her knee up for a perfect shot to his groin, but he shifted in time to get his family jewels out of the way.

"You didn't, but Heather Winchester did." He imagined she could be quite bonnie when she wasn't scowling or threatening him.

The name of her university mate drew those big brown eyes wide for a moment. "Heather?" She dropped her leg, leaving her navy skirt sitting crooked on slim hips.

"Aye. Heather called Russell MacLeod of the International Protective Network this morning, explained you'd witnessed a crime, and she was worried about you. She thought you might need protection. They gave the job to me."

She narrowed her gaze on him. "Why should I believe you?"

"Because if I were here to kill you, you'd already be dead." Taking a step back, he tossed the blades to the coffee table. The sound of the metal scattering across the wood charged into the silence of the room. Her back, he noticed, stayed against the wall.

His chest tightened. No one deserved to live in fear.

"What did Heather tell you about me?"

Colin moved away, wandering into the living room, but kept her in the corner of his sights. He fingered the flimsy curtain covering the window. Her flat was on the fourth floor, with no fire escape and only the stairs at the front. No unmarked car sat in the street below. From what he could tell at the moment, no one spied on her. "She said you came back from Glenhalish on the early train today. During the ride, you witnessed a man being beaten, and you're frightened the attacker will come after you."

"Anything else?"

"You told security, and they called in the police, who apparently didn't believe you. They took your statement, probably patted you on the shoulder, and shoved you out the door."

"I know what I saw. I'm not crazy." She fisted her hands and tightened her jaw.

For her second sentence, he would have to reserve judgment. But he'd done his homework and checked up on her. Single, twenty-five—an American student on an exchange program. She'd been in the US military for four years and used their GI Bill to help finance her education once she received her honorable discharge. Serious, studious with a 3.2 grade point average in her university program. This woman wasn't the type to make up a story for attention. If anything, she seemed more determined to blend into the crowd.

She shivered and shook her head. "I should've stayed in Glenhalish through the rest of the week."

"Why'd you come back?"

"I'd made plans to be in Edinburgh for New Year's." She wrapped her arms around her midriff. A plain, white button-down shirt accentuated the curve of her breasts. "So much for celebrating."

"It'll be all right." Colin walked toward her and reached for her shoulder, intending to offer a bit of comfort.

Before he could touch her, she knocked his hand away. More strands of her brown hair loosened from the clip she wore atop her head. Every well-toned limb stiffened, and those dark-as-midnight eyes narrowed again.

"Lass, I know we've only just met, but I am on your side."

Her chin rose. "Do you have any proof you work for the International Protective Network?"

Bugger. No, he didn't because technically he wasn't an employee yet. He was the brand-new recruit of one of the world's best bodyguard agencies, and she was his special assignment. He reached into his coat pocket.

She shifted toward the blades.

"Easy." Slowly, he pulled his mobile phone free and held it out to her. "If you still doubt me, give Heather a ring."

She nodded. "I will, but with *my* phone." In a flash, she maneuvered around him and reached toward the coffee table. He doubted she even realized it, but her hand shook.

Colin grabbed her wrist gently. Something sparked beneath his skin and made his fingers tingle. Joanna sucked in a quick breath.

"Be careful you don't touch those blades again, aye?"

While she called her friend, he assessed the situation. Pressure fell on his shoulders with the lass. Part of him wondered if the owners were testing him, to see if he could be good enough for the International Protective Network. He'd been in Edinburgh for his final interview and had planned to head home to Thurso this afternoon when the owners had called him back. They'd offered him a position on the Edinburgh team *if* he could do one little favor for them.

Aye, he'd take care of Ms. Grainger to prove himself. He was used to having his abilities questioned. His own family hadn't thought he'd amount to much, and most of his mates from school were perfectly happy drinking and shagging up in Thurso.

A few minutes later, she hung up the phone and set it on the table.

"Everything all right?" he asked.

"Yeah." She crossed her arms and tapped one foot on the hardwood floor. Black stockings covered her perfectly formed calves. "Heather says I'm supposed to listen to you."

He matched her stance and smiled. "Well, for starters you're not to fight me again."

She had the decency to blush, although no words of apology left her sweet lips. "Deal."

He sat on the couch arm and braced his palms on his thighs. "Now, tell me again exactly what's happened from the moment you left Glenhalish."

Joanna pulled her hair clip off and ran her hand over her head. Thick strands with dark red highlights tumbled around her shoulders. She sat down on the far side of the couch. As she spoke, she sank her fingers in her hair and eased the gentle wave out of it. "I was going to the food car of the train when I saw them. As I reached and hit the button to go through their car, I looked through the window in the door."

"What did you see?"

"It all happened so fast. I mean, it had to be less than a minute. I'm sure I missed something."

"Do the best you can and tell me what you remember."

"One man was beating another. The victim lay in the aisle, and he didn't fight back. I thought I saw a knife or some other weapon. When the door opened, I didn't go in, but the attacker glanced up."

"Did you hear anything?" he asked.

"Just the door opening and then the attacker stopped. I backed up and ran for help, but I'm sure he saw me."

"How far away from the men were you?"

"Two, maybe three yards."

"Would you be able to ID him?"

178

"I don't know." She shook her head. "I don't think so."

"It doesn't matter. If he believes you can identify him, you are a threat."

"When I brought the ticket inspector back to the car, it was empty. They stopped the train, did a quick search, but found nothing."

"What about when you arrived in Edinburgh?"

"I got off at Waverley Station and talked to the police. You were right. They didn't believe me." A frown took over her face, as though a series of unpleasant thoughts traveled through her brain. "Wait. When did Heather call you?"

"IPN phoned me this morning." He'd been about to check out of his hotel when the call came in from his almost new bosses. They didn't have any other operatives available, and Ms. Grainger wasn't officially a client since this was a favor, but would he mind stepping in?

"So, have you been following me all day?"

He paused. Which answer would please her more? He went with the truth. "Aye."

Her shoulders relaxed, and she leaned back against the couch. "Good to know. I've been feeling like someone's been watching me since I got off the train."

Colin shook his head. "It wasn't me. You'd not know I trailed you."

She gripped the edge of the cushion. "Why? Because you're so good at your job?"

"Aye, I am." He held her gaze for a solid ten seconds.

She brushed strands of her hair away from her temple. "How long do I have you for?"

"Until you're one hundred percent safe."

"Promise?" she said with a quiet voice.

The tremor in her word struck a chord in his heart. Assisting a woman like Joanna, someone with truly nowhere else to turn for help, was why he wanted to join the IPN. "Aye, lass."

The clock on her mantel played *Auld Lang Syne*. They both glanced up. Eight o'clock.

He studied the room more thoroughly and took note of the Christmas decorations she'd scattered throughout. A nativity covered the metal desk in the corner by the window. A plastic wreath hung from the wall by the kitchen table. A sickly poinsettia stood next to the door with half its leaves on the floor.

"So what now?" Joanna asked.

"Go pack a bag." He pushed off the couch.

"What?"

"Until we know you're out of danger, you're staying with me."

Oh, hell no. "Wait a minute." Joanna held out both hands. "Who decided that?"

"I did."

She clenched her jaw. The man stood close to six feet with both arms behind his back and his feet braced apart. Perfectly chiseled jaw, chestnut-colored eyes, and buzz cut light brown hair. No emotion came off him, just cold, hard steel.

Yes, she was grateful to her friend for arranging a bodyguard, but leaving with Munro wasn't exactly her favorite choice either. "Don't I have a say in what happens?"

"No. Your flat is too exposed. I can protect you better on my own terms." Dark clothes covered his body, but the way he'd plucked her knives right from her fingers in the blink of an eye proved he was fit.

Her friend Heather swore Colin wouldn't have been hired by the International Protective Network if they didn't think he could do the job. But what if he wasn't an IPN operative at all, but a friend of the attacker just claiming to be a bodyguard?

She rubbed her temples. Panic was making her stupid. Uncle Sam had taught her to tie off her emotions and assess the situation logically. She only had to pull those lessons out of her brain's storage, dust them off, and she would be—

"Ms. Grainger, either you go pack a bag for yourself, or I'll go pack one for you."

She might not want to go anywhere with this man, but the bottom line was he was here to keep her safe. She'd accept his assistance…cautiously. No one had ever accused her of being stupid.

"Give me five minutes, and then we'll go."

He nodded once. "Fair enough."

Joanna walked to her bedroom, packed a small suitcase with a few days' items, and stared at her bookcase. On the top shelf, in front of her favorite novels, sat two decorative *sgian dubhs*, small knives with three-inch blades. She glanced toward the hallway to ensure Munro wasn't coming. Yes, he'd promised to keep her safe, but she refused to rely on him completely. And she knew he wouldn't let her take the blades she'd threatened him with. Grabbing the knives, she stuffed one in each coat pocket and wheeled her suitcase into the living room. "Ready."

"All right." Colin grabbed the handle of the suitcase.

"I can carry my own case," she said, but she released it anyway.

A hint of a smile crossed his lips. "Aye, I know, but you'll not."

The simple act of chivalry curled her toes.

Once she'd locked the door, she followed him down the stairs to the first floor. "Are you sure this is all necessary?" Crisp, cold air assaulted her as soon as they set foot on the sidewalk. A bus engine rumbled nearby. "I mean, wouldn't he have come after me when I got off the train?"

"If he thinks you're a threat, yes, it is necessary. He could be biding his time, waiting until the Hogmanay crowd, New Year's to you Americans, descends on Edinburgh so he can make it look like an accident."

Edinburgh's Hogmanay celebration drew upward of thirty thousand people from all over the world. She could easily be an "innocent victim" of the crowd if the attacker wanted. A shudder rippled down her spine.

Laughter and loud music drifted out of the pub on the corner of the road. A few cars were parked along the street. Snow from an earlier storm crunched under her boots. "Got any ideas on how we're going to find him?"

"*We* are not going to find him. The Edinburgh Police will hunt him down."

"But they don't even believe me."

"They will when I tell them to," he said with a straight face.

"You're pretty confident in your skills, aren't you?"

"Aye." He didn't look at her. "I do know where my talents lie."

Oh yes, she was sure he had many talents, and many opportunities to hone his craft. From what she knew of his business, the International Protective Network recruited only the best of the best. "How long have you worked for IPN?"

"Long enough."

"What does that mean?"

He ignored her and kept walking.

Her stomach knotted. "Hey." She hurried to catch up to him in the middle of the sidewalk and grabbed his arm. "How long?"

He looked her in the eye. "You're my first client." Without waiting for a response, he started walking again.

Joanna stared straight ahead and followed him into the deserted street. This was not good. Not. Good. At. All.

"The car's just there." He pointed to the lone vehicle across the street and up one block.

Tires squealed behind her.

She turned toward the sound.

"Move!"

Headlights blinded her. She froze.

Her heart galloped against her ribs.

A vehicle barreled toward her.

Chapter Two

*W*hy wasn't she moving? "Joanna!"

Colin dropped the suitcase, grabbed her around the waist, and yanked her to the sidewalk. He cushioned her in his arms as they tumbled to the pavement. The car's engine revved as it sped past them. Streetlights and colored bulbs blurred together against the darkness. Silence once again settled on the street.

Joanna raised her head. Her softness curved around his body and ignited an unwelcome surge of lust.

"Are you all right?" He loosened his grip but still held her while her limbs shook.

She flattened her hands on his chest and stared at them. "Someone just tried to run me over."

His cock grew harder with each move she made. Like a wee laddie with his first lover.

"Aye." His gruff voice caught her attention.

As her eyes grew wide, she stilled.

He gritted his teeth. *Damn. After the near rundown, how did she pick up on the bit of lust in my voice?*

"Sorry." She shifted onto the pavement, but not without accidentally shoving an elbow into his ribs. Her skirt gathered high around her thighs. One shoe dangled off her toes, the other lost somewhere in the road. With her hands and knees on the snow-packed sidewalk, she peered into the empty street. "They wanted me dead."

No sense in acknowledging her deduction. Colin climbed to his feet. "Here." He cupped her elbows and brought her to stand before him. With a quick scan of her body, he asked, "You're not hurt?"

She shook her head. "I'm okay."

But she clearly wasn't. While he uprighted her suitcase, she didn't move. As he chased down her purse, she continued to watch the road, her gaze bouncing from one end to the other.

"Let's get you out of here, and I'll call it in." He ushered her to his car and opened the passenger door for her.

"Do you think they'll come back?" She slid into the seat and looked up to him.

"No."

"Good." She drummed her fingers on her thighs.

Colin opened his mouth to add he didn't think they were finished, but he grabbed the words before they set loose. She understood she was a target. He needn't drill it into her.

He tucked the belt of her coat onto her lap. "Watch yourself."

Once she'd pulled in both feet, he shut the door and rounded the hood.

Joanna held up her shaking hands. Usually she was the calm, sensible, strong one of her friends. But then again, she wasn't usually the victim.

Well, not anymore. Once, in battle, was enough. After all the aggravation that one event had caused, she vowed she would never be a victim a second time.

Clasping her hands together, she breathed on them. Despite the weather being warmer than the last few days, a chill still ran rampant over her spine. In the space of twelve hours, she'd become a Hogmanay tourist with a big-ass bull's-eye on her back.

Colin's large body slid behind the steering wheel. He, of course, didn't look worried at all.

She'd spent four years in the military, had been injured downrange. One man would not bring her down. She pursed her lips and blew out a slow breath. She'd be smart. And logical. And she absolutely wouldn't think of the sculpted muscle she'd grazed while lying on top of her temporary bodyguard. Or the glorious pressure between her legs.

Closing her eyes, she willed her brain to stay on task. Colin had been sent to keep her safe, not satisfy her as a woman. His penis growing hard had been a physical response only.

With a heavy sigh, she reopened her eyes. "You didn't happen to get the license plate number, did you?"

"No." He glanced over his shoulder and pulled the car into the road. "I was a bit occupied."

Saving her sorry ass. No, he hadn't said as much, but he didn't need to.

Joanna held her tongue during the ride through the streets of Edinburgh's New Town and stared out the side window. Truthfully, she was a little worried she might get hysterical if she spoke again. Between her failure to protect herself and her unwanted reaction to Colin's body, she questioned her sanity.

Colin tugged his cell phone from his coat pocket and made a call. His end of the conversation consisted of short, quipped phrases, and inside of three minutes, he hung up. Less than ten minutes later, he eased the car into an underground garage of one of the most expensive hotels in all of Edinburgh. They bypassed the front desk and rode the elevator up to the top floor. Soft yellow light guided their path down the carpeted hallway.

Inside the room, an overnight bag sat on the floor by the television, and a garment bag hung in the closet. In the center, there was only one bed. Granted it was queen-size, but still…one bed.

Behind her, the door snapped shut, and she jumped.

Damn it. This fearful reaction had to stop. She'd been strong, independent, and efficient before. Surely she could reclaim those traits, couldn't she?

He dropped her suitcase by the bed. "I'll take the floor."

"You don't have to."

A wisp of a smile tugged his mouth and, for the first time, revealed a pair of dimples. "I'll not have you sleeping down there."

Her belly curled with his chivalrous intention. "I meant we could share it. We're both adults." She could certainly keep her hands to herself. Yes, she found him handsome, but sex, even with a hot

Scotsman, wasn't even on her radar at the moment. Staying alive until they caught the son of a bitch who had tried to run her down remained her priority.

His gaze held hers, almost as though he challenged her to deny something had shifted between them.

"Or not." She crossed her arms and wandered toward the window. Outside, the festival lights sparkled over the city center. "So, now what?"

He grabbed her sweater at the elbow and tugged her away from the window. "We wait. I've got a few calls in to find out what our options are."

Right. Because he was a new IPN operative. He'd never guarded anyone before. "Didn't they go over this in your training?"

His fingers danced over the buttons on his phone as he texted someone.

"Colin?"

He didn't look up. "It's complicated."

Knots crushed together in her stomach. "What's complicated? It's a yes or no answer." She fiddled with the hilts of her sgian dubhs in her pockets.

Still he said nothing.

The knots tightened. She marched across the room and stood toe to toe with him. "Hey." She yanked the phone from his hand. "If you expect me to trust you, I deserve the whole truth."

Silence stuck between them for so long she wondered if he'd actually tell her anything.

"I haven't finished the hiring process yet."

"What?" She didn't even deserve a real bodyguard? "Perfect." She stalked to the door, but paused, her hand choking the knob. What choice did she have but to stay? The reality was she needed an ally. This man, operative or not, was her only option, and he had already saved her life.

Colin needed to get control of the situation. His first day on the job was not supposed to fall apart. He'd be sacked before he even earned a pound note. His nerves clenched. His feet itched to run across the room so he could grab her and set himself between her and the door. But he stayed rooted to the floor where he stood. "Joanna, you're not to go."

Please.

She whirled on him. "So, technically you don't work for the International Protective Network?"

"I was here in town for my last interview and to complete some paperwork. I've been offered a job, but with the holidays the human resources department hasn't yet cleared me." He'd not share the news her safety was his final test.

"They couldn't give me a real bodyguard?" she grumbled.

He gritted his teeth. "I'm just as good as anyone they already have on their payroll." How many times would he have to prove his competence?

His phone rang.

She jerked and mumbled a curse word.

"It's my mobile."

While he spoke to the IPN technical analyst who was hunting down the car from the attempted hit and run, he kept an eye on Joanna. She sat on the edge of the bed by the nightstand and removed her jewelry. Still with her coat on.

When his conversation ended, and he'd slid his phone into his pocket, he returned to her side. "Joanna. I may be new to IPN, but I'm not incompetent." He'd convince her and the staff at the agency.

She turned to him, moisture crowding the corners of her eyes.

His heartstrings tugged. "Trust me and I promise I'll not let you down." Because failure was not an option.

α

The scent of strong coffee dragged Joanna out of sleep. She stretched in the bed and glanced across the room. Faint streaks of sunlight mingled with the receding darkness.

Colin sat by the window, a manila folder on the table next to him, a newspaper on his lap, and a mug in his hand. He wore the same sweats and T-shirt he'd slept in, and his feet were bare. The blankets he'd slept on were folded neatly and piled on the empty chair across from him.

"Good morning," he said without looking up.

She pushed herself upright. "Is it?" She yawned. "Are you sure?"

He cracked a small smile, and again those dimples came through. They gave him a boyish charm so far removed from his adult persona they could've been two different people. Perhaps they were. While sipping his drink, he kept his focus on *The Scotsman* newspaper.

She pulled her knees up and wrapped her arms around them. Yesterday, she'd been so panicked with the train episode and the aftermath she hadn't really taken a serious look at her guardian. He was handsome, for sure, but he was quiet, mysterious. His work probably required those qualities, but was he the same way in his private life? When he grinned, a spark of mischief swirled to life in his eyes, and even she, someone who no longer searched for trouble, was tempted to follow him.

But they weren't lovers, weren't even friends. She was only a job for him. Still, would it kill him to be a bit more…approachable?

"There's coffee if you want it, or tea." He twisted his wrist and glanced at his watch. "We have an appointment later this morning at the police station."

"What for?"

"They want another word with you about the train incident, and they want to talk to both of us about the car last night."

"So, you corroborate my story, and everyone believes me now? Doesn't matter I was a soldier. Because I'm a woman, I can't possibly know what I'm talking about? No, they think I'm an idiot who's going to freak out at the first sign of danger." Her injury downrange had definitely made her gun-shy about following her instincts, but she refused to let one action and its consequences shape her future. After tossing off the covers, she stomped over to the kettle and poured her first cup of caffeine for the day. Tea always calmed her.

"Well, you were a bit troubled by the events of yesterday." He didn't even look up.

She resisted the urge to throw her cup at his head. "There's a difference between freaking out and being troubled. I'm out of practice. For three years I've been a college student whose biggest challenge has been studying for exams in a foreign country."

Still, he didn't take his attention off the newspaper. "All right."

She stared at him for several seconds more. "That's it?"

The papers rattled in his hand, and he met her gaze. "What?"

She set the teacup on the counter by the bathroom door. "Did you believe me when I first told you about the beating?"

"Whether I believed you or not was irrelevant. Protecting you became my duty, and I'm honor-bound to see it through." With no emotion whatsoever, he returned to the fascinating articles of *The Scotsman*.

She planted her hands on her hips and bit her tongue. So, he hadn't believed her. He didn't consider her a partner. He wouldn't listen to her suggestions.

A hundred colorful metaphors sprang to the surface of her brain, but she'd keep quiet. Whining would get her nowhere. Today, she'd call on her soldier training and her sharp mind, and contribute to the investigation into the missing victim. Whether the men wanted her assistance or not.

She stepped into the bathroom. In record time she was out, dressed, and ready to battle the day. Standing at the counter, she poured her second cup of tea.

"I'll be out in a few minutes." Colin squeezed past her and propped one hand on the doorframe. "Don't open the door to the room, and don't sit by the window." A smattering of freckles covered the bridge of his nose, and light brown hair dusted his chin and cheeks. Shards of heat bolted throughout her belly.

"Nobody can see in the window. We're on the top floor," she countered.

His jaw clenched. "Joanna, stay away from the window."

"Why?"

"Because I told you to, and I know what's best."

She opened her mouth to argue she deserved to hear his reasoning, but he shut the door. Damn, the man was insufferable! She clenched the teacup. "Five...four...three...."

The shower turned on. For a brief moment, Joanna's thoughts drifted to his big, hard body under the spray of water—

"No." She clamped her mind's vision closed and wandered back to the bed. She wouldn't dream of seeing all of him, didn't want to see all of him. Nope. Not ever. He was annoying and bossy and coldhearted and definitely not her type.

Besides, her thoughts needed to be on the victim she'd encountered on the train and the man behind the wheel of the car last night. Her safety remained priority number one.

She grabbed the TV remote from the bedside table, scooted against the headboard, and pressed the Power button. After flipping to her regular morning show, she set the remote down and sipped her tea. The news was in full swing, with discussions about the number of tourists expected for Hogmanay and all the precautions the city was taking to keep everyone safe.

She tossed a glance toward the bathroom, where the water continued to gush. She had her own guard. Yes, a brand new one. One who didn't even have a badge yet and who thought he was indestructible.

But he had saved her life the night before. As she ran her hand across her stomach, she could almost feel Colin's strong arms around her, pulling her from the car's path. She, a decorated soldier, had frozen in the headlights. If he hadn't grabbed her, hadn't accepted the assignment from the MacLeods, she would be lying in the morgue today with a toe tag.

A shudder raced down her spine. But she was alive, and today she could help solve a crime.

"Have you seen this man? Local authorities are searching for Mark Rawlings, a visiting university professor who disappeared over the weekend. He was last seen early Boxing Day."

Boxing Day. December twenty-sixth. The day before the train ride.

The announcer spoke on, but the words jumbled together in Joanna's ears. Her heartbeat thumped against her ribs. The teacup rattled on its saucer.

Staring at her from the television screen was a picture of the victim on the train.

"Colin!" Joanna's heart pounded faster. She set the saucer on the bedside table and scrambled to the foot of the bed, as if sitting closer to the television would give her more insight. Listening to the announcer list details and stats of the missing man, she prayed she remembered them correctly.

When the water turned off in the bathroom, she jumped up, hurried to the door, and knocked. "Hey, we've got something!"

No response.

Too keyed up to sit, she paced across the room. Finally, she'd be able to do something for the missing man. She had more proof she wasn't crazy. Soon, she could enjoy the holiday as she'd planned.

The bathroom door flew open. "What is it?"

When she pivoted by the round table, she jolted to a stop. Her jaw dropped. Colin stood in the hallway with only a white towel wrapped around his trim waist. She'd expected him to be fit since he was a professional bodyguard, or soon to be, but all the visions in her head could not compare to the real sight. Not quite a six-pack of his abs, but damn close. A thin layer of hair coated his chest, with the majority of it under his belly button and leading to—

"Joanna."

She blinked her way back to the present. "On TV. It's the victim from the train. He's missing." As she scrambled across the mattress to grab the remote, he walked toward the foot of the bed. She focused on switching the channel to another news show.

He propped his hands on his hips—which loosened the towel.

Heat spiraled through her, connecting the ache behind her breasts to the clenching between her thighs.

She yanked her gaze from him. The missing professor. The beating she witnessed. Someone trying to run her over. Hello? Where were her priorities?

As he listened to the broadcast on a different station, she resumed her pacing. Her mind slid into overdrive, and her nerves threatened to rip to shreds. When the segment about the professor ended, she asked, "So now what?"

"We need to get to the police as soon as possible. You may be the only witness to the man's disappearance."

"I remember a few details, but most of it was a blur." But the attacker had gotten a perfect view of her. Knots formed in her stomach all over again. "I mean Professor Rawlings lay on the floor. People held him down and hit him."

"People?" Colin's head shot up from the screen. "Your earlier statements said one man."

"I only saw the one, but it all happened so fast." Could there have been more than one man attacking him? "I assessed the situation and got the hell out of there." She rubbed her thumbs against her temples. She could handle reexamining the details of the night once she locked her emotions in a box in the back of her mind. But doubts crowded her brain, thoughts of the weak woman everyone assumed she was. "I don't know." At the moment, all she wanted was Colin to wrap his arms around her like last night and assure her everything would be all right.

He stood still, away from her. "You'll be surprised with how much you do remember. Give it a chance." His voice remained calm, professional. Icy.

Yeah, because nobody was after *him.*

"Now, do you remember where the train was when you found the lads?" he asked with absolutely no emotion.

She pivoted to face him. He stood with his arms folded across his massive chest and a day's worth of stubble on his chin. "Do you have no heart at all?"

"What do you mean?"

"A man is missing, possibly dead, and another is trying to kill me. I know you don't really know me enough to be worried for me, but can you at least look a little broken up over the injustice of the guy's disappearance?" All of these points allowed for panic, or at least sorrow. *Something.*

He sighed deeply. "I know you're upset, lass, but try to calm down."

"Don't patronize me."

"I'm not. I'm simply saying—"

"You are." She pointed at him as she passed him yet again.

He remained silent for several seconds. In the background, someone on the TV gushed about the weather forecast.

"Joanna, which stop were you around when you caught sight of the men?"

"I don't know. It could've been anywhere. I can't even pronounce half the names in Scotland, never mind remembering one when I was sc...." *scared.*

He was right, damn coldhearted Scotsman. If she planned to assist with the investigation, she needed to calm down. She hugged herself, pivoted, and crossed the room again. "Why didn't I pay better attention?"

Colin stepped into her path. Heat and the clean scent of his skin wrapped around her. He hesitated for a moment before reaching over and cupping her shoulders. "Relax. You don't have to be specific."

The pressure of his fingers loosened the knots of tension inside her. She stared at his chest, at the muscles of his arms, and borrowed confidence from him. She was *not* helpless. Duh, she'd been in the military for four years. She'd been wounded on a mission. One man stalking her shouldn't scare her so deeply.

But downrange no one had come specifically for her.

"Let's start at the beginning. Was it the train from Glenhalish to Glasgow or from Glasgow to Edinburgh?"

"The first one."

"Good." He smiled, but neither dimple came through his cheeks. "Now, how far away from the Glenhalish station were you when you wanted a tea?"

Shaking her head, she answered, "I don't know."

"Think back. Was it your last chance to get a cup?"

"What does it matter?"

"If they'd announced it was your last chance to get food, you were closer to Glasgow. You can do this, Joanna. You only need to think logically."

With the unwavering pressure of his hands, stress coasted down her back and out her heels. She nodded, closed her eyes, and drifted back to the train ride.

Colin held onto her, gliding his fingertips up and down her sleeves.

In her mind, she could hear the rumble of the wheels on the track. The old couple sitting next to her gave off the scents of lilies and joint ointment. She'd been getting the tea for the woman because her knees had been bothering her, and Joanna had offered to run the errand.

She sprang her eyes open. "The snack cart had already come

through, but they hadn't announced last call yet."

"Good." His smile grew a bit wider. "Your information will assist the police." As though suddenly aware of his gentle caress, he jerked away.

"How will it help?"

"Doesn't matter." He shook his head. "Are you sure—"

"It matters to me." She folded her arms. He'd drifted into the land of humanity for a brief time, but now he'd gone right back to the secretive, steel-hearted professional. "What are you thinking?"

He waited, stared at her, sighed. "They usually make that last call announcement about an hour before arrival at the final station. So the train had to be a good ways away from Glasgow. If we can pinpoint where it happened, the police will be able to ask more questions of people who might actually be able to help find the professor instead of questioning blindly. Lass, are you absolutely certain he was still alive when you arrived at the car door?"

Joanna's stomach dropped clear to the floor. It had never occurred to her the man might've been killed while on the train. "I thought so." She reached back into her memory, seeing all those limbs, all the blood and bruises. "But no, I'm not sure."

"All right." He walked toward the bathroom. "Let me finish getting dressed and we'll go."

She closed her eyes, pushed all visions of Colin aside, and allowed the rush of shivers to run through her body. Had she witnessed a murder?

Colin closed the bathroom door and gripped the edge of the counter. What the hell was he doing? He needed to remain focused on his duty as a bodyguard. The lass was his client. He had no reason to touch her, no matter how much he wanted to do so, unless she was in immediate physical danger.

But her accusation he had no heart had struck a chord within him. To prove her wrong, he'd attempted to comfort her with a gentle massage. In truth, it had taken all his strength not to wrap her in his arms, to feel her soft skin pressing against his chest. He wanted to rub away the shiver he'd seen in her shoulders and to kiss away the fear she'd tried so hard to deny claimed her.

What was that about? Anyone in her situation was allowed to be frightened, but he had her covered. He wouldn't let her down, yet she questioned him at every turn, demanded answers, and argued with him whenever she didn't get the answers she thought she deserved. The woman was maddening.

He scrubbed his fingers over his morning stubble. Perhaps he could be a bit more cooperative without sacrificing his professionalism. He'd choose his words wisely and comfort her with them when he could. If his efforts resolved the issues between them, they would be worth it.

But he couldn't touch her. Absolutely not; otherwise, she'd surely strip away the tenuous hold he had on his brain functions.

He shaved, dressed quickly, and drove Joanna to the police station, where they spent two hours discussing the events of the past twenty-four. Joanna studied the pages of mug books, trying to find the man she'd caught a glimpse of on the train, and Colin worked to keep his mind on the case and off the individual woman. The police had nothing new to share, but the detective promised to contact them if he found any other details. Once the police were satisfied with their eyewitness accounts, Colin drove back to the Balamorran Hotel.

In the lobby, he steered her toward the restaurant. A few minutes waiting for their to-go meal wouldn't hurt. He'd keep his back to the wall and scan their surroundings.

"We're eating in here?" she asked with a lilt of hope in her voice.

For that reaction alone, he considered her subtle request. But her happiness wasn't his responsibility. Her safety was.

He grabbed a take-out menu and handed it to her. "No, we'll take it up to the room." He glanced over her shoulder to study the menu, but he still caught sight of the disappointment lengthening her bonnie features. A hard punch to the gut would've affected him less.

"Why? We can get a spot away from the windows and near an exit. We won't even have to stay for dessert."

"We're not staying," he snapped. "Now, choose your meal, so I can put our order in."

If looks could kill, he'd surely have one of her sgian dubh blades planted between his eyes. Aye, she'd thought herself clever for hiding the knives in her coat pockets, but he'd found them before she woke up and stashed them in his overnight bag. A bodyguard shouldn't have to worry about the client gutting him.

She glared at him, opened her mouth, but pressed her lips back together before any words spilled out.

Once they'd placed their orders, Joanna folded her arms and glanced out the window overlooking the center of town. Already the sky held a hint of darkness. Colored lights sparkled on the Ferris wheel by the Scott Monument and along the Princes Street Gardens where celebrations for the New Year's holiday had already begun.

Joanna sighed. "I came back from Glenhalish because I wanted to experience Hogmanay. I hadn't planned on experiencing it quite like this."

The shimmer of innocent enthusiasm in her eyes disappeared, and in its place, moisture sparkled.

Damn. What had happened to his plan to be more cooperative? "Joanna." He tugged on her elbow. "I haven't had a chance to evaluate the safety of the restaurant."

"We're in a hotel with a doorman in a fancy, traditional uniform out front. I'm probably safer here than anywhere else in Edinburgh."

He nodded. "Aye, I know, but I like to check it out for myself first. That's why we're eating upstairs."

"Then you could've just said that, Colin, instead of biting my head off."

"Forgive me. I'm not used to explaining my thoughts or having my directions questioned."

"Where did you work before? A communist country?"

The hostess called his name.

Joanna slapped her hand on his arm. "Well, you better get used to it because as long as we're together, I will want to know the reasons behind every decision you make concerning me." Without waiting for his response, she sauntered over to the hostess podium and picked up their dinner. The bag crinkled beneath her fingers while the two women chatted about something.

He raised his gaze to the ceiling and willed his headache to go away. Protecting this stubborn American lass was turning out to be quite a test. If all his IPN clients behaved as she did, perhaps this wasn't the job he wanted.

Across the lobby, a bagpiper played his own version of *Scotland the Brave* in front of the bar. A handful of tourists stood listening.

Colin closed the distance between him and the women, grabbed the plastic bag of food from Joanna's hand, and tugged her away.

She jerked to a halt and yanked her arm free. "What are you doing?"

"Taking you back to the room."

Around them, hotel guests slowed, stared, eavesdropped.

"Then you talk to me. Don't drag me behind you—"

"You're not behind me." Again he reached for her, but she backed away.

She shook her head. "That's not the point. When people work together, they talk to each other instead of ordering each other around."

"We're not partners." He touched her back and pushed her forward.

Of course the lass dug in her heels. "You have no soul, do you?" she said loud enough for the passersby to hear. Some even gasped, and from across the lobby, one of the hotel employees rounded the desk and started in their direction.

He leaned down to speak into her ear. "Joanna, you've got all the lobby watching us. If you don't want me tossing you over my shoulder and carrying you away, you'll walk with me now."

"You wouldn't dare." She glared at him. Her continued defiance sparked anger in his gut, and he met her stare head-on. A moment later, she blinked. Her feet shuffled toward the elevator, and he maneuvered her inside it before the hotel employee reached them.

"I can't believe how rude you are."

"Your protection is my top concern, nothing else." He jabbed the top floor button, and the elevator doors closed. "If you refuse to do as I ask, I am allowed to do whatever is necessary to see to your safety. This is my job."

"We may not be partners, but I'm not going to blindly follow your lead. I'm not an idiot, and I won't let you treat me like one."

If she only knew what he truly thought of her, of how often he wanted to touch her, to take her in his arms and promise to keep her mind off the madman targeting her. If she only knew how much restraint he'd used to keep from crawling into the bed last night just to lie next to her.

She accused him of having no soul? If she only knew how torn and tattered it had already become.

She rambled on and on.

"For the love of Hogmanay!" He dropped the dinner bag to the floor, maneuvered her against the back wall of the elevator, and set his mouth on hers. He invaded the space between them, pressing his body to hers. Her scent made him dizzy, her soft curves stoked the raw fire under his skin, and her lips, so soft and pliable, threatened to make him beg for more. Her breasts crushed against his chest and made his cock grow harder. For a moment, he wanted to be inside her, to bring her to screaming his name. If sounds needed to come out of her mouth, better they were shouts of ecstasy than insinuations of his ineptitude.

She'd accused him of having no soul? Aye, perhaps not, but she, the devil lass, made him wish for one, if only to prove her wrong.

ೞ

Sparks flashed from the pads of Colin's fingers and ignited a shudder along Joanna's spine. His big body surrounded her, his hand hovering at her waistline, not touching anywhere else. Maybe in the back of his mind he thought about the knife blades from her apartment.

She shoved at the solidness of his chest. "What are you doing?" Deep inside her, an alarm rang, but its caution had nothing to do with her safety and everything to do with the wild desires threatening to invade her brain.

"Trying to shut you up."

Joanna reached one hand behind his neck and guided his mouth back to hers. All at once, she lost herself in the feel of him. The taste of coffee and dark mystery rolled together on his tongue.

His lips moved from hers to trail along her jaw line. Tiny kisses landed against her skin, each igniting a new fire within her.

His touch stoked her desires and nothing about those was sweet and innocent. She closed her eyes and relished the sensation of …him.

Even through her clothes she could feel the outline of his erection against her belly and damn if it didn't make her want more. She adjusted her legs to allow him deeper, to enjoy the pleasure of him bumping against her clitoris. Need pulsed between her thighs.

She'd accused him of being too aloof, but he proved her wrong. At this moment, *she* was his focus, and he was doing a great job tending to her current needs. Yep, he might only focus on one thing at a time, but maybe that philosophy wasn't so wrong.

But even with the precious nudge of his body, all these feelings he weaseled out of her weren't real. Couldn't be. She'd only known him roughly twenty-four hours, and as soon as she was gone, he would forget about her. Plus, they were due to the situation, weren't they? With a madman after her, danger around any corner, she couldn't think straight and logically. Her fear was to blame. Wasn't it?

Or was it because she'd gone so long without a man's caress?

Gently, he rocked his hips against hers. A soft moan escaped her lips. He slid his tongue inside her mouth, taunting and teasing hers. His fingers edged under her sweater. The glorious pressure of him growing harder fueled her confidence.

A bell rang and something swooshed behind him. A discussion came to an abrupt halt.

The elevator!

She pulled back as much as she could. Colin didn't cooperate. Instead, he stared at her, grinning, with one knee between her legs. Moisture seeped into her panties. Every limb threatened to collapse like jelly.

Someone cleared his throat. "Excuse us." Feet shuffled inside the box, but the conversation did not resume.

"Of course." Colin casually smiled to the other people, picked up the dinner bag, and moved to Joanna's side.

The elevator doors closed.

She didn't dare look anywhere except at the numbers on the panel. Still, she was aware of a woman staring at them. Heat flashed into her cheeks. Part of her wanted to turn her face against his coat, so no one could see her. Part of her refused to give any of them, including Colin, the satisfaction of knowing how easily he'd affected her. Damn it, she was a grown woman, not a high school virgin copping her first feel.

Hundreds of thoughts floated through her head, but the most important question continuously popping up was who presented more of a danger to her…the mysterious man from the train or Colin Munro?

Chapter Three

*J*oanna bolted upright. Darkness wrapped her in its hideous embrace. And silence reigned. Her heart raced. She flattened her hands on the mattress beneath her.

Mattress. Bed. Colin's hotel room.

Rustling sounds came from the floor. The bedside lamp flickered on. Colin propped himself up, one knee bent and an arm dangling over it. He squinted against the brightness. "Are you all right?"

"I'm sorry. I didn't mean to wake you." She brushed her fingers under her eyes.

"Don't be daft, lass."

"I had a bad dream." She smoothed her hair back off her face. Moisture beaded at her temples.

"Here we call it a nightmare." He smiled, and at once she relaxed her shoulders.

"Americans do, too." After another deep breath, she said, "I'll be all right." Once her heart rate slowed to normal. With her forearm, she wiped perspiration from her forehead.

He stood, padded into the bathroom, and ran the faucet. When he returned, he sat beside her, tucked his finger under her chin, and pressed the cloth to her cheek. The cool moisture soothed her burning skin.

She reached up and covered his hand with hers. "I can do that."

"I know." He brushed her fingers away. "But you'll not."

After a few seconds, he moved the wet towel across her forehead and to her other cheek.

When he reached her neck, she sighed and closed her eyes for a few valuable seconds.

"Thank you."

His gentle caress reminded her how much she'd missed simple comfort…from anyone.

"You're welcome." The cloth soon disappeared. "Now, will you tell me what you dreamed about?"

"Mark Rawlings. I dreamed I was back in the train car and he was bleeding out on the floor. The guy with him faded into the background, but I could see the man's hands and lips moving. I couldn't hear anything, though. Then somebody jabbed me with something, and my blood drained out of my body, but there was nothing I could do. The guy standing stayed in front of me. There was another voice, but the words were garbled."

"Did you see anyone else?"

"No, but at the end I wasn't paying attention. I was losing consciousness." She tilted her head to one side and into her palm. "Colin, what am I going to do if we don't find the professor's attacker soon?"

"*We'll* take it one day at a time." Strong, confident, able to leap tall buildings and all…even in the middle of the night.

"I'm sorry about snapping at you earlier." The truth was she didn't know him and he was helping her.

"Which time?"

"All of them." She chuckled.

"It's a normal reaction. Dinna worry about it."

"Yeah, but I have no right to take it out on you. I mean, you're only doing a job, and I don't need to make it more difficult by being obnoxious—"

"For the love of Hogmanay, will you keep quiet, lass?" The overdramatic huff and the roll of his soft, amber eyes took the sting out of his words. "And just accept the help."

"Thank you." Her insides curled. With each passing moment, she found something else to like about the man, some other action or comment which sliced through her misguided initial opinion of him. Maybe he had good reasons for being indifferent to the world around him.

But he wasn't as impartial to her as he tried to be.

As her nerves from the nightmare settled into the comfort of having him next to her, she pulled her gaze from his. And stared at the little dip at the base of his throat, at the width of his shoulders, at the corded muscles running down his arms.

Her belly fluttered with desire. She hugged her pillow to keep from reaching out to him.

"You won't believe me, but I used to be a lot stronger." Shrapnel from a roadside bomb had shattered her faith in her own instincts, and one man's reaction on the home front had stripped away the rest of her confidence in others.

Colin brushed his thumb over her cheek. "You're still strong. You're standing up for a man you don't know to see justice done despite the threat to your own life. What's more courageous than that?"

"I'm only brave because you're next to me, even though you're not a full IPN operative yet."

"And who was it who held blades when she thought the strange man in her flat had come to kill her?" He smiled.

"I know hearts and flowers aren't your thing, so thank you for these words." She patted his chest. He was making an effort for her, and she tucked the bit of kindness next to her heart.

Aye, kissing her in the elevator hadn't been *his thing* either, but he'd done it anyway. Och, the lass would ruin him for sure.

The sheet dropped from around her chest, and the flimsy material barely covering her breasts left his mouth watering. Aye, he remembered his place—pseudo bodyguard, potential agent in a world-renowned organization—but a red-blooded man could only resist a woman for so long.

He trailed his fingers along her jaw line, her neck.

Her sharp intake of breath coiled his stomach muscles. As did her fingertips slipping under his T-shirt and over his abs. Slowly, he leaned his head down and pressed his lips to hers. She was his sweet peppermint candy, overwhelming and addictive. He pushed his tongue against the seam of her lips, relentless until she surrendered to him, granting him entry. He circled her tongue, teased the roof of her mouth, and when she groaned, his cock ached. All at once, he wanted to strip her naked and sink into her body.

Her arms circled his neck, and she pulled him down with her as she leaned back to the mattress. She explored him with her gentle touch, which only made him ache more.

Colin shoved the bed covers out of the way, slid his hand under her nightdress, and set it on the back of her thigh. She leaned along the length of him. His own body cried out at the pressure. He grew considerably harder. Damn, the lass was like the finest Scotch, and he held an empty glass. She cradled his erection between her thighs, and the naughty lass rocked against him.

He squeezed her arse, stroked it, and snuck his fingers inside her panties and between her legs. Already she was wet for him. He listened to her heavy breaths, her fight to keep from making too much noise.

Colin loved a challenge. He fully intended to make her cry out in pleasure. He kissed her properly, moved down her chin and onto her neckline. His mouth watered with thoughts of nibbling on her breasts, on the tight buds he caressed through the material. While running one finger over and over her clit, he slid another one lower, lower and into her opening.

Joanna gasped and arched off the bed. She cradled his head with one hand while the other drifted along his back.

Colin so needed to be inside her, to feel his own release surrounded by this alluring woman who would risk her own life for a stranger. He removed his hand from her body, shifted on top of her, and gripped the edges of her nightdress.

But she pulled the material away. "Do you have a condom?"

When Colin stepped into the bathroom, Joanna blew out a deep breath. Making love with him was so very wrong, but already oh so good. How long had it been since she'd had sex? *If* they actually went through with it. He still wore his pajamas, and she refused to remove her nightgown. As her heart thundered, her thoughts strayed to the scar across the side of her breast, her reminder even women soldiers could be injured on missions.

She slapped her forehead. Having sex with Colin was a bad idea. But if he was only temporary in her life, why not make the rest of the evening work in her favor? Physical satisfaction and the intimate contact she'd deleted from her life could both be restored with one act.

The bathroom door flew open.

Joanna's jaw dropped. Colin stood in the hallway, completely naked. The visions she'd had in her head about how delicious the rest of him looked under that towel he'd worn this morning couldn't compare with the real thing.

"Are you ready, lass?" He ripped open a condom wrapper.

"Uh-huh." Oh was she. As long as she could keep him from touching her breasts, they could both have a very fulfilling night.

Once he'd covered himself, Colin crawled back onto the bed, stripped off her panties, and settled between her legs. He scooped his arms underneath her and slowly pushed inside her, inch by inch. His mouth claimed hers, his teeth tugging her lip. He trailed kisses along her jaw all the way down to the neckline of her nightdress.

She closed her eyes and gave in to the rhythm he set. His strong body caressed her, cherished her, and Joanna lost herself in the sensations of their joining. "Thank you, Colin. Thank you, thank you, thank you." Until now, she hadn't known how much she had missed intimacy.

She brought his face back to hers and kissed him with everything she possessed. She matched the pace of their lovemaking with her tongue as it slid in and out of his mouth, teasing his tongue and making him work for it. His hands slipped under her nightgown.

Joanna stiffened, but quickly took charge. Grabbing his hands, she guided them to her breasts but *on top* of the nightgown. He cupped them, rubbed her nipples into even harder buds through the material. When he moved one hand over her stomach, she intercepted it, guiding him to her clit. He took the hint and teased the tiny nub.

Deep inside her, tension rose as she charged toward her release until she stood on the edge of a precipice, ready to fall over. Colin increased his speed, pushing inside her over and over, faster and faster.

Her world exploded. The room swished in and out of focus. Warm tingles coursed through her body and settled in between her legs. Her breasts ached, longed for the completion of his lips on her skin, but she refused to entertain the idea.

Once again, Colin scooped her against him and thrust still harder and faster. His rock-hard body stiffened, and he grunted through his own release.

Afterward, he rolled to one side so as not to crush her with his weight. He splayed his big hand across her stomach, the heat of his caress soothing. Until he inched under her nightgown again.

Joanna grabbed his wrist.

He held still.

"Please don't," she said. *And please don't ask.*

"Why?"

A different kind of heat traveled up her neck. "Just...don't."

He studied her for several seconds before he tucked a flyaway strand of hair behind her ear and smiled. "Only when you want me to."

In a perfect world, that would be now. She would be able to tell him the story behind the scar maiming her skin, and he wouldn't care. He would be able to have sex with her, all of her, and she'd be able to feel like a whole woman again.

But they definitely weren't in a perfect world, and Colin Munro wouldn't get the chance to crush the confidence she'd managed to rebuild in the last three years.

⑳

Colin woke up several hours later with Joanna in his arms. Her arse pushed snugly against his cock. His very hard cock.

What was with her decision to keep him from her breasts? He loved them, and hers were just the right size—a perfect fit in his palm. His mouth watered even now with the thought of circling her nipple with his thumb and taking the bud into his mouth. He longed to brush his tongue over it, to feel it grow hard, to tug gently on it with his teeth.

But she'd ruined that possibility, and now a new day dawned.

He slid out from under the covers. Joanna didn't even stir. He tiptoed into the bathroom and closed the door. And what about his job? The one he didn't have for sure yet? Och, if the MacLeods or anyone else at IPN found out he'd slept with the client, he'd never finish the hiring process. It had been a stupid decision all around. It wouldn't matter he'd done it to comfort the lass.

Bugger.

Once he'd showered, shaved, and dressed, he stared at the bathroom door and rolled his shoulders. His goal today was resisting her at all costs. His future, what was left of it, depended on it.

Aye, but how easy would it be to stay away from her when he was stuck in a hotel room with her until further notice?

"Bloody hell."

With as much strength as he could gather, he opened the door and stepped into the room. Like a flash of lightning, Joanna rushed by him.

"Morning," she said before she closed the bathroom door.

He stared after her. "Morning to you," he muttered, although he knew she couldn't hear him. Truthfully, he was a bit relieved he had more time to gather his courage. Business. Focus. One step at a time, one main goal.

After arranging for room service to bring up breakfast, he called IPN's technical analyst. "Rachel, it's Colin. Have you got anything for us on Professor Rawlings?"

"Nothing to suggest someone tried to kill him." In the background, her fingers clicked across a keyboard. "He's a psychology professor spending a year at Chillum University in Glasgow. He pays all his bills on time, pays his child support regularly, has written articles for psychology journals around the world. He's here for the year teaching a few classes and working on a book he's wanting to publish."

"So nothing to help us."

"Afraid not. He's well liked by students and colleagues. When I called the school to get more information, they all gushed about him." Her fingers tapped over more keys. "The guy is too good to be true."

Aye, exactly why there must be something to explain why he'd been attacked and gone missing.

"He also volunteers his time to counsel students on campus."

Colin straightened in the chair. "Maybe someone went after him because they didn't like his advice. Can you look a bit more into that for us? I know the school's not likely to give you much information, so just do what you can."

She chuckled. "Because we haven't worked together long, I'm going to forgive you for your lack of faith. *When* I get something, I'll send it to your phone."

"Thanks."

"How's your girl?"

"She's not my lass." He gritted his teeth instantly. She couldn't possibly know he'd broken rule number one of a business like the IPN. *Don't be daft and give it away.*

"Okay, the woman you're guarding. Whatever. How is she?"

"She's grand." Short and to the point. Exactly as his answers should be before he had to kick his own arse.

After they promised to call back if anything new came up, Colin hit the End button.

As the water shut off in the bathroom, someone knocked on the door and announced, "Room service."

While he poured them both a cup of tea, she reentered the room. Today, she wore a jean skirt reaching just above her knees. Black stockings caressed her calves and feet. A deep orange sweater revealed the shape of those taunting breasts, and damn it if his mouth didn't water again.

He worked hard to ignore her. While she ate, he refused to watch her mouth. When she tucked her legs under her and read parts of the newspaper, he didn't ask what was so interesting. As she paced, the room growing smaller with each hour they were trapped in it, he kept his head down and focused on the flyer someone had tucked under one of the breakfast plates. It announced a party in the hotel that evening.

She fished through her suitcase, pulled out a booklet, and sat across from him. The scent of her perfume drifted over the table and tickled his nose. "Today, I had planned to start attending Hogmanay events." Wistfully she stared out the window.

"Why is this holiday so important to you?" He'd grown up only hours from Scotland's capital city and had never thought to attend the events. Yet this lass from another country had come to cherish his culture.

She put him to shame.

"I don't know." She swiped her hair off her shoulders. "Until I came to Scotland, the only time I'd ever left the United States was with the military. And during those trips, it wasn't like I had time to go sightseeing."

"True enough." His own passport held more stamps than he could count, but he'd not been a tourist on many of them. Police trainings, Royal Navy events.

"When I'd see news clips of the Hogmanay celebration, it looked like so much fun in such an old and historic city. I mean, Edinburgh is hundreds of years older than Boston and New York. To think I could stand on the same street to ring in the New Year like someone from the Medieval times did just sounded like fun. I promised myself I'd come here someday, and as soon as I had the opportunity, I signed up for the exchange program."

"Had you planned your activities for the whole three days?"

"Some. There are events I definitely wanted to see, like the torchlight procession and the party in the garden on New Year's, but I also wanted to leave some time open in case some of my friends came around." Gazing at her lap, she ran her palm over the booklet's cover. "And all because I wanted to get a cup of tea for someone else, I might not be able to do anything."

"I'm sorry, lass."

She rolled her eyes, jumped out of the chair, and paced again. "Listen to me. How selfish can I get? A good man was attacked and is now missing."

Colin itched to rise and shake some sense into her. He gripped the arms of his chair instead. "You were getting tea for someone who couldn't get it, you've given the police all the details you can remember from the train instead of walking away and hiding, and you're giving up something you've wanted for years so another man can get justice. Those are not the acts of a selfish woman."

No, but sleeping with the lass was definitely the act of a selfish Scotsman. He told himself he'd done it to comfort her, but truthfully, he wanted her. Plain and simple.

When she reached his side of the room again, she stopped in front of him and smiled. "Thank you. I needed to hear that."

Sadness touched her eyes, and he was almost sure she didn't believe him. How could she not? She was a remarkable woman, despite driving him mad and—

A sharp knock rattled the door.

Adrenaline flooded his veins. He leaped to his feet.

Joanna tensed, jerked 'round.

He grabbed her arm, brought his finger to his mouth to signal her quiet, and tugged her toward the door. Before he glanced out of the peephole, he shoved her into the bathroom. Almost instantly, his shoulders relaxed when he recognized the visitor. "It's the policeman we spoke with yesterday."

He opened the door. "Morning, Inspector."

The man strode into the room and peeled off his gloves. "Morning to you both."

He and Joanna followed behind the man. Inspector Cameron, if Colin remembered correctly.

"I'm glad to see you're staying in. The city's quickly becoming a madhouse with the tourists."

"Do you have some news for us?" Colin took a seat on the corner of the bed. Joanna chewed on her thumbnail.

"It's about your lad from the train." He nodded to Joanna. "The missing professor."

"Did you find him?" she asked, her eyes sparkling with hope.

"Aye."

"Good." She clasped her hands together, as if in prayer. "Now maybe he can explain what's going on."

"Not so good. He's dead."

All the color drained from her bonnie face. Colin rose to catch her, but she retreated and slumped into one of the chairs. "How long?" she asked. "Was he dead on the train?"

"We'll not get the coroner's report for a bit."

Colin pulled his gaze from Joanna. "What can you tell us?"

"Locals on a walk found him alongside the tracks in Corlallan. The other lad must have tossed him off after you saw them. That's why there was no body when you brought the ticket inspector back to the car. The professor had been severely beaten, which probably killed him." Inspector Cameron turned his focus to Colin. "Thanks to the computer lass at your IPN, we've narrowed down our suspect list."

Damn, Rachel's good.

"We've got a search for the top lads on the list."

"Anything else, Inspector?" he asked.

"Not at the moment, but I'll give you a ring when I have something." Cameron turned to Joanna. "Dinna worry, lass. It'll not be long before we solve the case, and in the meantime, you're in good hands, aye?"

"Thank you, Inspector," she said, but she didn't lift her head.

Colin walked the man out, closed the door, and locked it.

She shifted to the bed and crushed a pillow to her chest. When he approached her, he could see her fingers changing color. Her tender heart was filled with all sorts of fears and worries most probably.

Something sliced deep within his gut. He, of all people, wanted to wrap his arms around her, to shelter her, to remind her she wasn't alone.

But he shouldn't. She was his client, not his lover. Okay, not his *permanent* lover.

"It's all right, lass. I'll get you through it." But would his words be enough to soothe her?

As if asking the very question, she caught his gaze and held it with a trace of vulnerability souring her bonnie face. And just as quickly, the expression disappeared, replaced with a hint of hopelessness that seeped right through his skin and invaded his core.

He sat back in the chair and picked up another part of the newspaper. The constant urge to comfort her physically threatened his focus, and anything making him weak needed to be treated like the ailment it was. Swiftly and decisively.

Aye, his words would have to be enough because he would slice his right arm off before he touched her again.

⚘

Joanna crumbled the newspaper in her hands and tossed it to the edge of the bed. Outside, darkness had seeped over the sky, and the lights of the evening festivities shone brightly. As she ran her fingers through her hair, she said, "I'm going stir-crazy in here! Can't we go anywhere? I mean, I'd settle for a walk through the hotel."

He chuckled.

She scooted to the edge of the bed. "I'm not trying to be difficult, Colin, but how about it? We've been in here for almost twenty-four hours. I'll do whatever you want."

Flashes of her in his arms the night before, of her arching her back and squeezing her legs around him, flooded his brain, and instantly his cock twitched.

"We can walk from here to the elevator and back. Or we can take it to another floor and walk up the stairs."

Again, memories surged into his mind of their explosive kisses in the elevator and her reaction when they'd been caught. His body ached for her, for the feel of her soft skin brushing against him, for her sweet, sultry mouth taking him captive.

He cleared his throat and grabbed the flyer he'd read earlier about the hotel Hogmanay party. Aye, perhaps getting out of this box would benefit them both. "I've got just the plan."

Both her eyebrows rose. "Oh?"

"Come." Leaning toward her, he reached for her hand.

When they entered the conference room, bagpipe music greeted them along with a waitress holding a tray of fancy drinks. "Do you want one?" he asked her.

"No thanks." Her gaze shot up to the streamers, balloons, and New Year's banners dangling from the ceiling.

"Do you not drink?"

"I do, but…." Like a bairn in a sweets factory, she stared with her jaw hanging open and a smile toying with her lips, as though too afraid to believe the scene was real. "I want to be sharp until this lunatic is caught."

He clenched his teeth. Did she not trust him yet? "I can do my job, you know."

"Yes, but technically you don't have the job yet."

Aye, and she had the power to take it away from him before he even had a chance to prove his worth. One word about them sleeping together to her friend Heather or to anyone at IPN headquarters and he'd be done for.

But tattling didn't fit with what he knew of the lass. No, if he lost his opportunity to join IPN, it would be his fault and his alone.

"And whether you want my assistance or not," she said, finality ringing in her words, "I intend to be part of the solution to the good professor's murder."

He'd rather she leave the investigating to the police and her safety to him, but at least she was a smart woman. Too often as a soldier and as a policeman up north, he'd been forced to deal with victims who didn't have a clue. Still, if he didn't keep a good eye on her, Joanna might be too smart for her own good.

He escorted her through the party, strolling by the buffet table and the band.

"Colin, is it really all right for us to be here? I mean, for one thing, we're not dressed for the occasion. People are staring at us like we've crashed the party."

"Dinna worry about what they think. And yes, the party's for anyone in the hotel. I already checked when I studied the floor plan."

"So, we're safe here?" She leaned closer to him. Her warm breath rushed over his ear and sent a shiver down his back.

"We're in an inside room with no windows. There are security guards stationed throughout the area. The lad is wanted. He'll most likely not take the chance to be seen." He scooped up one piece of black bun cake for her and a second for himself. "For now, enjoy your first Hogmanay experience."

"Thank you." With a genuine smile finally touching her eyes, she accepted the treat. Her fingers brushed against his and sent a spark along his arm and straight to his groin.

A slow Celtic melody began playing on uilleann pipes. A sea of fancy gowns, kilts, and suits overtook the dance floor. For the first time since he'd met her, Joanna beamed, and strands of gold shone in her eyes.

Aye, the lass's glow rivaled the sun, and warmth rolled through him.

She swayed side to side in time with the music.

He slid his hand in hers and clasped her fingers. "Come."

"Where are we going?"

He tugged her toward the other couples and chuckled. "You ask too many questions."

Desire flashed through her eyes and yanked the memory from him of how he'd silenced her in the elevator yesterday.

When they reached the floor, she wrapped her arms around him and rested her head on his shoulder. He pulled her close. The feel of her curves nearly undid him, but he'd give her the holiday fun she needed. The lass asked for so little and she was doing so much. Her now-familiar scent of flowers and sunshine tickled his nostrils and tightened his groin some more. His own family wasn't sure he'd make the Edinburgh IPN team, and yet a woman he'd met only a short while ago trusted him with her life, and for her faith alone, he would spin her around the dance floor.

Something settled in the center of his gut, but he wouldn't question it. For now, he was just a lad holding a beautiful lass and enjoying her gentle touch during a party.

"This is nice. Thank you." She smiled. "Pretending to be normal, even for a few minutes, is exactly what I need."

"Oh, lass." He chuckled again. "You are anything but normal." She was so much more.

All the color drained from her face.

Bugger.

"What's that supposed to mean?"

He'd not meant the words the way they sounded. "You're more complicated than most of the women I know."

Her jaw dropped.

She'd taken it as an insult. He'd meant it as a compliment.

She stepped back, whirled around, and rushed toward the door.

"Joanna, wait." He grasped her arm and held her next to him. "Complicated is a good thing."

She held a hand up. "You should quit while you're behind." After yanking her arm free, the crowd swallowed her up.

Closing his fists, he stalked between couples and Father Time impersonators. With each step he took and no sign of Joanna, his chest tightened.

Quickening his pace, he pushed through the double doors into the hotel lobby. There, hopping through the narrowing gap of the closing elevator doors was Joanna.

Chapter Four

*W*hen Colin stepped off the elevator alone, he expected to see her in the hallway. But she wasn't there. He ran down the hall. Pulling his key card from his pocket, he said, "Joanna, let me in." How had she gotten inside? He'd pocketed both key cards from the front desk the day he arrived, and yet he only found one. His client must have slipped one out while he was in the shower. Or sleeping.

Inside, she stood in mid conversation on her mobile. "I understand there's a holiday and most of the agents are away, but there must be someone who can take over."

Bloody hell! "Joanna, who are you talking to?" He released the door and locked it behind him.

"And technically he's not even an employee yet, so I think I deserve an actual bodyguard—"

For the love of Hogmanay! How did she have the IPN number? With her words, she'd surely ruin his chances of making the team. "Give me that." He ripped the phone from her grasp.

"Hey!" She reached for the mobile with one hand and smacked him on the shoulder with the other.

"Who am I speaking with?" he asked as he hurried away from her and slipped into the bathroom.

A woman chuckled. "Rachel."

Colin closed his eyes and leaned his forehead on the door. She must've hit redial when he was in the shower earlier and taken down the number. More proof she didn't trust him. "What did she tell you?"

"You're being a jerk." The smile in her words took out their censure. "What did you do?"

He rubbed his temple. "I said some things, and she twisted them in her mind." And refused to let him explain.

"Look, I don't know you, but I'm going to give you some advice. Don't try to explain your case tonight. Leave her alone until morning when you're both calmer."

"I am calm." He clenched his teeth.

"And I can hear it in your voice. Trust me. Give it some time."

"Thanks. And uh, there's no need to mention this call to anyone, aye?"

"Of course not. I'm not on company time at the moment, so your secret is safe with me."

"Thanks, Rachel." He hung up, took a deep breath, and walked out of the bathroom.

Joanna stood by the bed, pulled off her jewelry, and slammed each piece onto the bedside table. Tears touched her eyes, but she swiped them away as quickly as they fell. Colin's words had been so hurtful. She wasn't normal. Yeah, but did he have to say it in the conference room of the Balamorran where anyone could hear him?

And complicated? Yes, but he had no idea why. And clearly he had no desire to find out.

Sleeping with him last night had been a colossal mistake.

"Joanna." His voice remained clipped, as if he had a reason to be angry.

"I don't want to talk to you."

"You don't have a choice."

She was strong enough to face him, wasn't she? Folding her arms, she tapped one foot on the carpet. "What?"

"What did you tell Rachel?"

Another slice through her heart. He didn't even care about how he'd hurt her. Instead, his precious assignment remained his top priority.

Powell, her boyfriend until she'd returned home to recover from her injury, had slept with her and, hours later, proposed to another woman. His perfect match, fewer complications he'd told Joanna. He'd thought she understood.

She'd believed Colin might be different.

"What did you say to her?"

"I asked for a real bodyguard."

"I *am* a real one." He clenched his fingers but kept his hands by his sides. "And I know what I'm doing."

Yeah, breaking her heart.

His fingers relaxed, and he shrugged. "Most of the time."

"Everyone's busy." She glared at him up and down. "Apparently I'm stuck with you."

"You didn't tell her about…last night?"

"That you slept with your client? No, I'm not that petty." Tugging the bedspread off, she added, "I only told her you were rude, obnoxious, cold, and heartless." She stripped off the extra pillow and tossed both items onto the floor.

Colin released a heavy sigh, his breath brushing over her cheek. His hands covered her shoulders and, damn it, another swirl of lust charged through her. She closed her eyes and tried to block out his touch. This had nothing to do with her heart. Her body craved only the physical comfort he'd offered.

"Will you let me explain about what I said downstairs?"

"No."

"You're making a bigger deal out of this than you need to."

"I don't think I am."

"Dinna be so emotional."

"Emotional?" As her eyes flew back open, she clenched her teeth. Where the hell had she left her sgian dubhs? "Well, I'd rather be too emotional than have no feelings at all like you." She jerked to the side, away from him.

"Joanna." He grasped her elbow. "Please listen."

Part of her wanted to haul off and belt him. The other part wished for him to make amends. Without glancing at him, she waited for his words.

"You're the last person I'd want to hurt."

Right, because she could potentially ruin his career before it even began. "I already told you I'm not a tattletale. Let's just pretend it never happened, focus on keeping me in one piece, and then we'll go our separate ways."

"Will you stop talking about the job? This is about you."

Again, tears fell, and a vicious ache pounded through her head. She massaged her temples. "It's late. I'm tired. I want to go to sleep."

Tugging away from his grasp, she grabbed her nightgown and walked into the bathroom on unsteady legs. Colin Munro had given her a lesson. If she couldn't have a man want her for the woman she was, she'd rather be alone. Even though she was complicated, didn't she still deserve to be loved?

∛

The next morning, Joanna curled her feet under her bottom and settled into one of the no-longer-comfortable chairs. She kept a book in her lap, an anthology of holiday romances, but she'd been on the same page for the last five minutes.

Why? Because her brain kept returning to their arguments last night. Had she cut Colin off too soon? Maybe if she'd listened to him instead of going to bed, their morning wouldn't be as awkward as it had been. There might be a perfectly reasonable explanation why he'd insulted her.

His phone rang.

She glanced over to the bed where he lay stretched out on his back with his eyes closed.

He conversed with someone using his curt phrases, his free arm still across his forehead.

To be fair, he had kept her safe so far. He could handle the job he hoped to seal in a few days' time. From here on out, she would force herself to treat him like a professional, even when the fears and longing closed in around her head. She'd learned to lock her emotions in a steel box in the back of her brain long ago. Surely she could remember how it was done.

Colin tucked his phone into his pocket, slid off the bed, and grabbed their coats. "We have to go."

His urgency revved her nerves. "What's up?"

"We have an appointment downtown."

She set her feet on the floor. Her heart skipped a couple of beats—because of the news, *definitely* not because Colin looked so scrumptious in those jeans and navy blue chambray shirt.

Damn it, what kind of woman was she to still be interested in a man who'd tossed insults at her? She slipped on her boots, so she wouldn't have to look at him. After grabbing her purse, she met him by the door.

When she walked toward the garage, he tugged her arm. "We're taking the bus."

"Is it safe enough?" But he wouldn't have suggested it if there was still danger.

Colin said nothing else to her as he pulled out money.

"I can pay my own way." She slipped her hand into her purse.

"I know, but you'll not."

The bus arrived within minutes. He paid for both of them and walked to the back. She sat next to him.

"What's going on, Colin? Is everything all right?"

"Oh, aye. Dinna worry."

But she did. "What aren't you telling me?" she finally asked when he'd kept quiet too long.

"Nothing." He kept his gaze straight ahead, his face devoid of emotion.

"Hey." She pressed her fingers against his forearm. "I'm not a little girl. I can handle whatever you share with me."

"Aye, you're strong enough to handle anything." He smiled and brushed his knuckle along the side of her face. "Even a daft arse who doesn't know how to give a lass a compliment."

She swiped his hand away even as her belly churned with butterflies. "Don't try to distract me. Tell me what's going on."

"I will." Both dimples came out and made her knees melt. "Just not yet. Have a bit of faith, will you?"

They exited the bus near the Scottish National Gallery, walked along the path in Princes Street Gardens. Children laughed, music played, city workers brushed snow from last night off of the benches. He hooked his arm through hers and guided her to a row of wooden stalls with various foods, arts, and crafts for sale. He stopped at the first concession stand, ordered something, paid, and turned to her with a Styrofoam cup in each hand. He held one out to her. "Here."

She accepted the cup with deep red liquid inside and steam swirling up around her nose. "What is it?"

"Mulled wine."

Her eyebrows went up. Several of her friends had talked about how much they liked the drink, but she'd never had any.

"It's a favorite around here during the holidays. Try it." He sipped his own.

She touched the cup to her lips and drank just enough for a taste of the sweet, warm liquid. "Not bad." After taking a few full sips, she asked, "Colin, what are we doing here?"

His smile brought back those dimples she was beginning to love. "Inspector Cameron called to tell us the professor's killer has been arrested."

Joanna's heart leaped. "You mean it's over?"

"Aye. They picked the lad up earlier today. He's not talking yet, but at least he'll no longer be a threat to you."

She jumped into his arms, wrapped her legs around him, and sloshed mulled wine over the side of her cup. But she didn't care. "Thank you!"

Colin circled her waist with one arm. "Oh, I had nothing to do with it, but if this is my reward, I'll change my story and tell you I took the lad down myself."

She stiffened and dropped her feet back to the ground. She was supposed to be angry with him, but how could she be when she would now be able to enjoy every aspect of the Hogmanay holiday? "Sorry."

He chuckled. "Don't you dare apologize. I'm a man. When a beautiful woman throws herself at me, I'm quite happy."

He'd called her beautiful. Trying to make up for his insults the night before, no doubt.

But wait. If she was no longer in danger, why was he still with her?

And here of all places?

Laughter pierced the air. Bagpipes played from the street corner by Waverley station.

"Joanna, I'm sorry about yesterday. I didn't mean to insult you. I only meant to point out how different you are, but in a good way." The cold air turned the tip of his nose pink. He stuffed his hand into his pocket.

"It's okay."

"No, it's not." He shook his head. "I don't usually have a problem speaking my mind or with the consequences, but with you I keep catching my tongue. You are so different from the lasses I know and come into contact with on a daily basis."

She grinned. "Another compliment?"

"Aye." He ran the pad of his thumb down the side of her face. "You are very real and genuine and because of that I find you so refreshing. You spend your life seeing the positive around you, while I've fought tooth and nail for everything I want."

She leaned her head into the warmth of his palm. "Let's face it, Colin, we live in two different worlds. You can't drag me kicking and screaming into yours, and we can't combine them."

He leaned closer, his cheek grazing hers. "Ah lass, I'd rather have you screaming for another reason altogether." He nibbled on the outer shell of her ear.

A shudder rumbled down her spine, and a vision of them making love again crowded her brain. Right away, her body wept for his touch. She turned her head and kissed him long and hard, her tongue playing with his in ways she'd been envisioning all day.

Colin chuckled and raised his eyebrows. "Are you saying yes, then?"

"Yes."

"Oooh."

"But first, we're going to play with our clothes on." She took his hand and tugged him to the Ferris wheel.

They wandered around Princes Street, rode on the Ferris wheel, glanced at the stalls selling items, and even slid across the skating rink. Once the stream of sunlight faded away, Colin took her home.

When they stepped into the hotel room, he pulled her into his arms, close to him until her thighs cradled his erection. And damn if she didn't want him, all of him. Again. As he pushed his tongue into her mouth, he peeled away her coat and raised her skirt. She rocked against him and wrapped one ankle around his leg. Colin cupped her bottom and lifted her. He slid his fingers inside her panties.

"Good God, woman. You're soaked through."

"Don't blame me. It's all your fault." With a nervous giggle, she set her feet down and pulled away from him. "Wait there."

"I don't think I can."

"I promise it will be worth it."

"I have no doubt."

Joanna grabbed her suitcase, rolled it into the bathroom, and pulled out her best bra and panties. Black lace. It was a beautiful set. It better be for the amount of money she'd spent on it. But she'd needed the confidence boost after her injury, and ever since it had become like her security blanket, serving as a reminder she was still strong and deserved the best in life. When the shrapnel had cut into her, leaving her with a six-inch scar across one side of her left breast, it had stolen more than her skin and blood. It had marred her perception of her own femininity. Her ex had insisted the scar had nothing to do with his decision to leave her in the dust, but how could she ever be sure?

She'd had the bra for months now and had never worn it for a man. Had never wanted to until now.

But was she ready? If Colin rejected her, she wasn't sure she'd recover again.

She brushed her thumb across the lace. Could she wear it and not have him take it off?

With shaking knuckles, she stripped and changed. In the end, it wouldn't matter. After tonight, she would go back to her flat, and he'd finish his new-employee training. He would go about saving the world, and she'd go back to shaping her own.

She opened the door and stood there for his view in her matching lace underwear.

He stood buck-naked by the bed. Well, except for the condom he wore. With hungry eyes, he looked her over. "Oh, lass, you are so absolutely beautiful."

"You're not so bad yourself."

He held out his hand. "Come to me, please, and let me love you the proper way."

"Actually, I have something else in mind."

She strutted over to him, gaining courage with each passing second he stared at her. Before him, she shivered. This man made her knees weak with a simple touch. She turned around and pulled his hands to her breasts. His cock settled against her bottom. As he stroked her nipples, she leaned her bottom against him harder.

The warmth and texture of his roughened palms over her sensitive skin made her sigh. She'd missed intimacy, craved it. Craved him. Her body said yes, but her brain refused to surrender completely. He backed up and sat on the bed with her on his lap. He brushed her hair to the side and kissed her shoulder. One of his hands remained teasing her nipple into a hardened bud. The other slipped beneath her panties and stroked her clitoris. Expertly, Colin planted butterfly kisses along her shoulder and neck while he caressed, rubbed, and pinched her into a frenzy of need.

Joanna reached for the back of his neck and rubbed his head. The coarseness of his buzz cut against her palm soothed her. His touch was magical, made her forget she was a broken woman. His desire for her boosted her confidence. She shifted in his lap. He helped pull her panties off moments before she slid down onto the hardened length of his penis.

He groaned and nipped at the skin between her shoulder and neck. His fingers rubbed faster, which stirred her to move faster. Each time she eased down, she took a bit more of him into her body. He grazed his knuckles over her clit while the other hand slid under her bra.

Right near her scar.

She reached for his wrist, but too late. He'd skimmed the raised skin. He stilled. She closed her eyes and let go. At the moment, she needed her breasts to be in his palm more than anything.

He traced along her scar and passed it to touch her nipple. Ahh, perfect. She moved faster until she could barely remember her name. Every muscle in her body threatened to crumble, which would be okay because Colin would be there to catch her.

They crested the wave of release together, and he got his wish—Joanna called out his name as she rode through her orgasm. She collapsed against him even as he still shuddered with his own release. As soon as he was physically able, he cradled her in his arms. With her ear against his chest, she could hear the rapid beating of his strong heart.

A short while later, he pulled himself free of her body. As he discarded the condom, she lay down on the mattress.

"Is there something you want to tell me?" Standing next to the bed, he stared down at her.

She looked up at the ceiling. "About?"

He crawled onto the bed, covered her with his body again, and stroked the scar. "How this came about."

"No." She met his gaze, challenging him should he push the issue.

He nodded once. "All right." Shifting his weight so as not to crush her, he kissed her nipple through the lace bra. His warm lips closed over the bud.

Heaven help her, his devotion was exactly what she needed. "That's it?"

"Aye. I don't need the details to have my way with you." He brushed his tongue over the bud once, twice, and the third time he took it, material and all, into his mouth.

Joanna's back arched off the bed, and she gripped the sheets on either side of her. With one innocent phrase, her sexy, powerful Scot had knocked a huge dent in her biggest fears. Maybe she wasn't as broken as she'd first thought.

Colin brushed his fingers over the scar trailing out from under her bra. They were making progress. At least she hadn't shoved his hand away and bolted upright. Perhaps she'd accepted he would not be distracted by a faint mark. "You're a brave woman, Joanna Grainger."

"Why? Because I'm physically flawed?"

"Aye." He leaned down and kissed one end of the white line. Keeping his hands on her hips, he moved his lips to the next section of the mark. "You would make a fierce Highland warrior lass."

"I'm still not ready to talk about it." She swept her hand over her abdomen, as though gearing up to push him away should he breach her defenses.

The worry in her eyes steered his next words. "No matter. You'll tell me if and when you want to." He kissed along the rest of her scar. "For now, I'm going to do my best to get you to stop talking and start shouting my name again."

She lazily tossed both her arms above her head. "Give it your best shot, Scotsman."

He winked and kissed from her blemish down toward her clit for another round of lovemaking. Her pelvis trembled against the mattress, and the moans threading through her mouth kept getting louder.

"Let it go, love. I want to hear you." He grazed his teeth over her tight nub. With his tongue, he circled it, teased her.

Her heavy breathing and moans stirred him on. He moved down, down until he thrust his tongue inside her.

"Oh, Colin, please…."

"Yes, love? Tell me what you want."

"I, ah…I…." Tremors erupted through her body.

He chuckled at her struggle to form coherent thoughts. "Do you want this?" He again swiped his tongue over her swollen clit. "Or this?" He slid two fingers inside her and moved them around, mimicking what his cock had done earlier. "Or both?"

When he applied pressure in both places, she finally screamed out his name. And Colin held her until the waves of her orgasm finished shuddering through her.

A short while later, he lay with Joanna's head on his chest and one of her legs wrapped over his thighs. Her fingernails drew designs lightly along his abdomen. She still wore the lacy bra. He'd not tried to take it from her for fear of upsetting her. Aye, he admitted, because she wouldn't have continued to make love to him, and somehow, over the last few days, he'd gone from wanting her to needing her.

What the devil had he gotten into with her?

From the counter of the bathroom, his watch alarm triggered.

She lifted her head, errant strands of hair framing her bonnie face. "What's the alarm for?" As she moved, her body shifted on top of him. Her thighs cradled his cock, almost hardening it again, and both her palms pressed against his chest.

With a smile, he answered, "We have somewhere to be." Gently, he rolled her off him and climbed out of the bed. He couldn't wait to see her reaction to his evening plans.

She grabbed his wrist and pulled him back toward her. "Where?"

"Somewhere special." He brought her hand to his mouth and kissed her knuckles. "Now get up and get dressed. We leave in five minutes."

Quickly, she gathered her clothes and covered her beautiful body from his view. No matter. He knew the luscious curves and intimate tastes of almost every inch of her skin.

She yanked her hair into a knot at the back of her head. "But where are we going?"

Colin slid an arm around her waist and tugged her toward him. She laughed and braced her hands on his chest. He loved the feel of her against him, her curves, soft skin, the scent of her perfume. "You ask too many questions, lass."

"I'm not really good with surprises."

"The torchlight procession begins in two hours, but we want to get there early to make sure we get torches."

Her brilliant eyes lit up. "Really?"

"Aye." He leaned his head down and kissed her. Greed took over the moment she opened her mouth, and he sought her tongue, circling it with his own. Cupping her bottom, he pulled her closer.

Joanna shoved him away. "Colin, you said we needed to get going."

"Aye, I know, but now I'm not sure I want to anymore." He nuzzled her neck, nipped her earlobe.

"Tell you what. If you give me what I want out at the torchlight procession, I promise to give you what you want when we come back."

He stilled. "Aye?"

His cock grew harder with all the images flying through his head. Of Joanna beneath him as he slid inside her body, of Joanna above him rocking slowly to accept him deeper, of Joanna on the bed and him taking her from behind.

"Yes." She kissed him and pulled out of his arms. "Now let's go!"

They reached the Royal Mile with plenty of time to spare and proceeded through the line to collect their torches quickly. Already thousands of tourists gathered. They stood on the cobblestone road near the front of the procession. In the distance, bagpipers tuned their instruments.

"How many people come for the march?" she asked.

"The city expects over seven thousand torchbearers this year."

Excitement buzzed through the crowd, which only made her giddier. Her dark brown eyes sparkled, while the chill of the winter evening deposited more color into her cheeks. "I remember seeing pictures of Hogmanay on the news as a kid. When I was in high school, I promised myself I'd get here at some point."

"And here you are."

From the very front of the line, a sea of fire approached. The family before them turned around and lit their torches. Flames crackled as they lit the next ones in turn.

Colin's heart expanded. Aye, he hadn't thought it possible, but standing with such an amazing woman and seeing the world through her eyes, opened his own to all he'd been shutting out.

The skirl of the bagpipes commenced in the crisp, night air, signaling the start of the procession. Thankfully, there had been no more snow.

Joanna closed her eyes and smiled.

"What is it, lass? Are you all right?" He wrapped one arm around her shoulders and pulled her against his side.

"This is magical."

"Aye, it is." With a gentle squeeze, he kissed her temple.

The processioners marched through the city, down by the Winter Wonderland Festival, and along Princes Street. When they climbed the path to the top of Calton Hill, several torches had gone out, including Colin's, but more fire flickered in the distance. The Viking ship burned, its flames reaching higher with each second.

"There's nowhere else I want to be." He kissed her nose.

It was as though the lass had released something in him that allowed him to be...happy. Who would've thought he, Colin Munro, would come out here on such a cold night to march with thousands of others with a lighted torch? Earlier today, when Inspector Cameron shared the news of the arrest, Colin had thought to be on the road back to Thurso. But he'd canceled his plans because walking to Calton Hill to watch a boat burn meant so much to her.

Joanna gazed all around them with the sweetest smile and childlike awe. "Awesome!" She looped their arms, plopped a sweet kiss on his cheek. "Thank you for bringing me."

"You're welcome." His stomach knotted while at the same time something else let go in his chest. Music continued to play as the last of the crowd settled into place before the fireworks started. He pointed in the distance. "Do you see what's burning over there?"

"Wow. Is that the Viking ship?"

"Aye. The whole event is a smaller version of Up Helly Aa, a procession held in the Shetlands as a way to break up the long, cold winter. It usually signifies the end of the Yule season. In the beginning, men would drag flaming tar barrels through the city streets and raise hell. Eventually, they moved over to carrying torches instead. At the end of the march and the singing, people toss their torches into a boat, watch it burn, and spend hours singing, dancing, and drinking."

"I'd read about it but never dreamed I'd actually see it." A gust of wind blew out her torch, and she tossed it into a nearby garbage bin.

"The one in the Shetlands is the largest fire festival in the world."

After the announcer spoke, fireworks shot up into the sky. Joanna jumped with the first crackle, but Colin said nothing to joke with her. She'd been vulnerable enough. He wouldn't draw attention to her reaction.

The crowd dispersed slowly once the fireworks display ended. Joanna faced him. "What a wonderful experience, to feel like a part of something so huge, to share the experience with strangers who would walk beside you. To take over the streets of Edinburgh and to look back at a sea of flames reaching from the Royal Mile, down the Mound, along Princes Street, and all the way up here. With you." She sighed deeply. "It was perfect."

She leaned forward.

Something flashed between the columns of the National Monument, over her head.

Not a torchlight.

Every muscle tensed. "Get down!"

Chapter Five

Colin shoved Joanna to the ground and collapsed over her.

Something cracked in the air.

Someone screamed.

The weight of him crushed her into the muddy snow. Moisture seeped into her clothes. Her heart thumped louder, heavier into her ribs. Still Colin remained on top of her.

He wasn't moving. Had he been hurt? For her?

More screams. Another person hollered, "Help, police!"

Still, he didn't move.

"Colin?" Her stomach clenched. *Please let him answer.*

The pressure released above her. "It's all right, lass."

"No, it's not." She sucked in a deep breath. Her heartbeat didn't slow.

Colin knelt beside her and kept his hand on her back. To keep her down or to comfort her, she didn't know. Maybe both.

Whistles blew; more yelling pierced the air. Many feet soon crowded around them. Voices with varying Scottish accents argued, among them Colin's. He rose to his feet and continued the argument. But none of the words made any sense. She listened only to the rush of blood in her ears, to the harsh breaths soaring in and out of her lungs. Her limbs shook as she scrambled to all fours. The danger was supposed to be over. She wasn't supposed to be a target anymore.

Colin's hand returned to her back. "Joanna, you can get up now."

She shook her head. No, her arms and legs would definitely not hold her yet. Tears stung her eyes, but she ordered them to retreat. Damn it, she'd been in the military, had shot at people who'd shot at her. Why was this event so frightening?

He knelt beside her. "Hey." Tucking his fingers under her chin, he forced her to look up at him. "It's safe to get up."

But she didn't. She kept her hands on the ground, sunk deep into the frigid snow. "I thought he was in jail."

"He is. We've just checked."

Anger shoved against the panic inside her brain. "What the hell is going on?"

He pinched her chin. "I don't know yet, but I will find out." He sealed the promise with a kiss.

Joanna wrapped her arms around him, held him tight. His strength enveloped her, calmed her, seeped into her skin.

Two policemen stood nearby, one of them speaking into a walkie-talkie. Once she stood, Colin gathered her close and guided her toward the path back down Calton Hill. "They're bringing a police car to the foot of the hill for us."

Inside the car, with the flashing red-and-blue lights, Joanna leaned against Colin again. She closed her eyes and wished the whole night was over. She wished she was back in his arms, back in bed with him. But most of all, she wished to be completely safe again.

⌇

Back in their hotel room, Joanna collapsed onto the bed. She hadn't even removed her coat. The ceiling spun out of control. She peeled her gloves off and shoved the heels of her hands against her eyes. None of this made sense.

Colin's voice, terse and demanding, drifted to her ears loud and soft depending on where he was in the room. He'd left a message for Rachel at IPN, and now he spoke with the police.

Until he slammed his phone down on the table.

Her heart spiked again. With her forearms bracing her, she pushed herself up. He stood tense with both hands on the table. Should she poke the lion?

"There were two men on the train with the professor," he said a few minutes later.

"How do you know?" She stripped off her coat and scooted to the foot of the bed.

"CCTV has a photo of David Stewart, the man they arrested today, getting on the train with another lad, Ronnie Latham."

Running her fingers through her hair, she wracked her brain for the memories she'd been shoving away. "How could I have not known?"

Colin folded his arms across his chest and shrugged. "I think on some level you did."

"What makes you say that?"

"At one point, you mentioned hearing a second voice. In your dream the other night, you mentioned several arms. In the darkness, you witnessed something."

"Why didn't I trust myself?" Three years ago she'd been sharp, decisive, a professional soldier. How had she lost so much of her talent so soon? "If I had realized it sooner—"

"Don't torment yourself. If you'd realized it sooner, Rawlings would still be dead and you would've still been hunted."

She lowered her head. "We could've died tonight."

He crouched before her and took her hands in his. "But we didn't. You survived."

"Because you were there."

"I don't plan on going anywhere yet." He brought her knuckles to his lips and kissed them. "But with or without me, you are strong enough to face the crisis."

She shook her head. "I'm not sure I believe you." Her courage lay buried deep within her, tucked in a far corner of her soul with layers of dust and debris. It had been missing for so long, she doubted she could yank it free for anyone.

"You are. I know it. You know it."

Oh, he was so very good for her ego. How could she have thought him cold and uncaring? Sure, his people skills were a bit unconventional, but he'd been on her side in every sense that mattered since day one. "Thank you for the vote of confidence."

As if struck by her thoughts, he released her, stood, and walked away from her.

Colin needed to get a grip. He'd almost failed tonight. In some way, he had failed. Because he'd been so wrapped up in the lass, he hadn't noticed the potential danger until it was almost too late. Indeed, his heart still pumped furiously against his ribs.

"Colin." She approached him from behind and stroked his shoulder blades. Her gentle touch sent a soothing rumble through his back. "What's on your mind?"

"It's nothing."

"I don't have to be a genius to know you're all wound up." She massaged more of the tension from his shoulders. "Talk to me. You said yourself I'm strong enough."

"On Calton Hill, I wanted to pop back up and run after the coward who shot at you from the dark, but I couldn't. I had to stay with the job I'd been given. Protecting you."

"And you did."

"Aye, but I'm used to fighting, to bringing people to justice. Standing around while other people hunt for the criminal doesn't feel right." He stared out the window, lost between thoughts of what he'd hoped for when he accepted the assignment and the reality he'd encountered since.

"What else?" She caressed the side of his face.

"I don't know what I want anymore."

"Sometimes that's the perfect place to be." She smoothed her thumb along his cheek, a small smile on her lips.

At the moment, the best place to be was here with Joanna. Borrowing her words, he said, "Thank you."

Leaning forward, he kissed her slowly, sweetly, while he worked to strip her down to her panties and bra. He pulled his own sweater over his head.

She skimmed her hands along his chest and fidgeted with his pants button and zipper. He stepped out of his trousers. Already he'd grown hard with thoughts of taking her again. But he wanted the whole woman. "Will you let me love you, Joanna? All of you?"

The worry in her gaze nearly broke his heart. She nipped her bottom lip, reached behind her, and unfastened her bra. Colin tugged the straps off her shoulders. Along her left breast lay the rest of the pinkish white scar.

This was why she'd been reluctant to strip naked for him when they'd made love before. *This* was what she hadn't wanted him to see. But why? He reached out and gently grazed his fingertips over the marred skin. "Will you tell me about it?"

"There's not much to tell. I was in Iraq, and I was wounded. Shrapnel from a roadside bomb sliced into my lung."

He glanced up at her. His own warrior lass. "I'm sorry."

"I'm not." Her chin shot up. "I'm proud I worked to protect my country."

Shame filled him. Truthfully, he hadn't spent more than a few minutes considering why she'd balked at his touching her breasts. He'd wanted her body, and when she'd freely given herself to him over and over again, he'd greedily taken all he could get without a thought to her wants and needs.

I'm sorry for being so daft. But the words didn't leave his mouth because they were only words. In order to do her justice, he would show her how much he cared for her and about all the complications, which made her the exact woman he wanted to be with.

Tonight. Be with *tonight*.

"Without a doubt, you are a brave and bonnie lass. Have you any idea how much I've longed to have my lips here?" Finally, he had what he wanted, his mouth on her nipple. He gave the same attention to her other breast before he took them both in his hands.

Her knees buckled.

Colin wrapped an arm around her waist, leaned back on the bed, and brought her with him. The weight of her toned limbs sent him straight to Heaven. She straddled him and leaned over with her hair falling forward. He ran his fingers in her strands and brought her mouth back to his. She moved over him until he was rock hard and her juices seeped through her panties. She drifted over his body, swirling her hips against his, taunting him through the flimsy fabric of her undergarment.

"Lass, if you don't take those off I'll be forced to rip them from your bottom." He reached over to the bedside table and fumbled for a condom.

The wicked woman wiggled against him. "Go for it, Special Agent."

Groaning, he gripped the material and ripped through it. She lifted just long enough for him to peel it off her.

"Quite impressive, Mr. Munro." She laughed and tossed her hair over one shoulder. "What other talents do you have?" Slowly, slowly she rolled the condom over him.

"I think it's time you showed me more of your talents." With his hands on her hips, he thrust his cock deep inside her. His heart thumped like crazy.

"Oh, yeesssss." Quickly, she became the leader, rocking over him, riding him slowly at first and increasing her speed in increments. He nearly jolted out of his skin.

Again he clamped his lips on her breast, the damaged one.

"Thank you for making me strong again."

He circled the nipple with his tongue and then grazed his teeth over the tight bud. With each noise she uttered, he vowed to compel her to produce several more. He moved his mouth from her nipple, tracing his tongue across the soft, velvety flesh until he came in contact with her scar. He gave gentle kisses to the whitened skin. "Oh, no, lass. I only reminded you your strength was there all along. Now keep quiet and make me come."

"Yes, sir."

And soon, the lass fulfilled his wish.

ↄ෫

Colin propped his head in his palm and listened to the soft swish of Joanna's breaths as she slept. The lass had stood up to his uncompromising ways and forced him to have a look at the world through her eyes. He thought he'd been living— his focus on his career, keeping his emotions to himself so no one could use them against him. Logical, methodical, and uncluttered. Until a wee American had threatened him. Until she'd accepted him, all of him. Until she'd blessed him with a simple gift.

He collapsed back on the bed and dropped his forearm over his eyes. Was he strong enough to accept her gift without losing the dreams he'd chased for so long?

Last night had been about giving her comfort, but he had received just as much. She'd given of herself generously to revitalize him as well when he hadn't even realized he needed it.

But reality would come upon them soon enough. She was still his client, and he was expected to keep her safe while the police chased the lad who'd tried to kill her. No matter how much he loved having her in his arms, being inside her, and making her tremble from his touch, he needed to stay focused on the job.

He only hoped he could be as strong and brave as she when the time came to let her go.

Chapter Six

"*A*bsolutely not!" Colin slammed his fist on the table in the interrogation room. Releasing Joanna when they had caught the other criminal was one thing, but allowing her to slip away from him for a bloody daft idea was entirely different.

Inspector Cameron remained quiet. Joanna jumped.

Immediately, guilt seeped into him, but what they'd suggested was absurd. "You're mad." He pointed to the inspector first before he turned to her. "And you're mad to go along with it."

She raised her stubborn chin. "Actually, it was my idea."

"What?"

The inspector looked up from the circles he'd been drawing on his notepad. "It's true. At first, I reacted like you. But hear what she has to say."

Colin's brain spun. She had come up with the insane idea to draw the shooter out? "And when did you think of your brilliant plan?"

"Last night." Her cheeks held a tinge of red.

He chewed on his tongue to keep the accusation from spilling from his lips. So, while she made love to him, she'd plotted how she would jump straight into danger and deny him the chance to secure his dream job. "When did you share your plan with Inspector Cameron?"

"I called him while you were in the shower."

He pinned her with a stare. At least she had enough sense to fidget in her seat. "The man's not daft. He'll not fall for it."

"I've worked out some of the details. We're going to have the news announce David Stewart has been arrested and confessed," Cameron explained.

"No!" With each word from either of their mouths, Colin's control slipped further away.

A right bodyguard he'd be. His charge had joined forces with the local police to make him look incompetent.

"Munro, if you'd only calm down." Cameron rubbed his forehead and drew another circle on his notebook.

Too much adrenaline coursed through his veins. "I'll not calm down, thank you very much. I'm not putting Joanna in danger."

She crossed her arms. "Let me save the two of you the trouble of continuing your argument. It's my decision."

Colin closed his fists to keep from strangling her. "No, it's not. It's my job to keep you safe, and I intend to do it properly. Tossing you out in the open to give this madman another shot at you is not the way to keep you safe."

Joanna unfolded her arms and rose. Standing tall and proud and strong, she set her hand on his chest.

Could she feel the frantic thundering of his heart?

"If we don't try to capture him, he wins. I may still be alive, but I won't be living when I need to look over my shoulder all the time. And if he goes into hiding, how long will you be around for me?"

Forever, if she'd let him. To protect her from anyone who threatened to bring her unhappiness.

What the devil? Her determination combined with her oh-so-familiar scent wrapped 'round him and squeezed common sense out of his head. Forever? Bloody hell, he'd gone mad as well. She'd taken him there.

"Colin, the inspector and I are following through with our plan with or without your consent, but I'd rather have you on board." She leaned closer to him. "I know we have our differences, but please be there with me. Be there *for* me."

He brushed his thumb down the side of her cheek. "Of course I'm going to be there. I'll not walk away when you need me most."

"All right. Let's get busy," Cameron said.

For the next hour, Colin listened to how the Edinburgh police planned to paint a giant bull's-eye on his lass's back. Aye, he'd said it. His lass.

Because for once, he'd opened his eyes. For once, someone else was more important than his precious career.

ભ

When they returned to the hotel room, Joanna began pacing almost immediately. He glanced at his watch. Ten in the morning. Only four hours before he would have to leave her here, under Cameron's care, while he snuck into her flat.

As he stripped off his coat, the knots in his gut tightened. With each pivot she took, a bit more of his body tensed.

"You should try to relax," he offered because he'd promised to be supportive.

"Not until the lunatic is in custody, and I'm hopefully still in one piece."

In the police station, she'd held confidence like a battle weapon. Here, her courage unraveled with each step. "Suddenly, I'm not feeling as strong as I'd thought I'd be."

"I'm calling Cameron." He pulled his phone from his pocket.

"No, don't." She rushed forward and grabbed his mobile. Her fingertips brushed against his skin, a spark tracing up his arm. "I can do it. It's just scary, that's all."

"And don't forget daft."

"But it has to be done." After she ran her hands through her hair, she held them out, palms facing him. "At the rate we're going, we won't have to pretend I'm arguing with you."

He tugged her into his arms and tucked her head under his chin. "Joanna, I don't want to fight with you. I'm worried."

"You and me both." She trailed her knuckles up and down his spine. "Whatever our differences are, can we call a truce for now? Going through with Inspector Cameron's directions, I really need to feel you've got my back completely."

"Aye, lass. You have it." He planted a kiss on her forehead. "This time, I will be your partner." Although, he didn't have to enjoy it.

"Good, because I'm really having a hard time believing someone's goal is to see me dead." She trembled a wee bit.

"But keeping you in one piece is mine." He smoothed his fingers through her soft, brown waves.

Shifting her hips to cradle his growing erection, she planted her lips on his chin. "Is that your only objective?" Under his sweater, she raked her nails over his abs.

With each moment, she made him harder. With each passing second, his heart swelled even more. "Well, no." He ran his hands down her back and into the back pockets of her jeans. He squeezed her bottom and pulled her tight against him. "It doesn't have to be."

"What other objective do you have?" She nipped his chin.

"To drive you as mad as you're driving me."

"How do I make you crazy?" she asked with a wicked gleam in her eyes.

"Your touch, your scent, your mind, your curves." No longer could he wait to possess her again. He groaned, lowered his head, and kissed her. He controlled her, poked his tongue into her mouth, along her teeth.

Her hands drifted down his chest until they hit his pants. Deftly she unbuttoned and unzipped them and set his cock free. "And how do you plan to make me crazy, my sexy Scotsman?"

"Dinna worry, lass. I've got plenty of tricks for you." Colin shifted them toward the dresser where his shaving kit sat. While he grabbed a condom package, ripped it open, and prayed he'd get it on quick enough, she stepped out of her jeans. Never had he wanted a woman so badly. He needed to be inside her, needed her body caressing his, making him surrender to her.

With the condom in place, he lifted her, rested her bottom on the desk, and slid inside her. Sighing, she wrapped her legs around him and joined his rhythm of their lovemaking. Slowly, he thrust in and out, a little farther each time, savoring every moment with his remarkable woman. "I love to be inside you."

She nibbled on his earlobe. "Me too."

Oh yes, she loved everything about this man. His touch had nursed her bruised ego, his actions had expanded her heart, and his body had brought her intense climaxes like she'd never known. Who knew sex could be magical every time?

He inched his big, warm hands under her sweater and sneaked them up her sides. His thumbs brushed against the tips of her breasts.

Through her shudder, she pulled her top over her head and tossed it away.

One of his hands continued teasing her nipple, and she leaned into his palm. Oh, she needed his touch. Wanted it. Intended to enjoy every single moment.

He moved his mouth over her skin, down to her shoulders. With his teeth, he lowered her bra straps down one arm at a time. She reached behind her and unsnapped it. Colin pulled it off from the front and gazed at her, scars and all.

Out of habit, she brought her arms in front of her.

"No." He tugged her wrists out of the way. Colin, God love him, clearly had other plans. "You'll not hide any part of your beautiful body from me."

He traced her scar, his mouth clasped on her nipple once again. Faster and faster he pushed into her, and Joanna gripped his shoulders as he took her on an amazing ride. She tossed her head back, arched into him, and surrendered to the power of his loving.

Right away Joanna lost herself in the feel of his lips, the sensations driving through her. Pressure built in her belly, between her legs, behind her breasts. His arms wrapped around her, pulled her close. When her release exploded through every inch of her skin, and she cried out his name, her limbs slackened against him, her body totally at his disposal. Whatever else he wanted to do to her, Joanna Grainger would not have the sense or strength to stop him. Nor did she want to.

He pushed on, toward his own completion, cradling her against him and loving her with everything he had. Watching him succumb to the tremors of his own release made her want him even more. She'd elicited his response. With fear, indecision, scars and all, she still possessed the power to make a man melt...for her.

CB

After Colin discarded the condom, he grabbed another and set it on the bedside table. He glanced at the clock. Two more hours and he'd walk away to let her jump into danger. She and the inspector both knew he objected, but they would move forward with their daft plan anyway. He remained a lad staring into a sweetshop with chains on the doors.

At least he could arm her. He rummaged through his knapsack and pulled free her two sgian dubh knives. Truthfully, they looked more decorative than useful, but he'd buy her a hundred more if one of these stopped someone from harming her. He set them on the table by her purse.

Joanna lay on her belly, feigning sleep. He knew because her breathing changed when she was truly sleeping. He crawled back into bed, kissed her along her spine, and pushed her hair to one shoulder. "Oh, lass, you have no idea what you do for me, or what you do *to* me."

A sly smile twisted her lips as her hand brushed behind her and gripped his cock. "I have a pretty good idea of what I do to you." Her soft, gentle fingers stroked him hard again.

He grunted. Two could play that game. He cupped her bottom and drove his digits inside her. Already, she was wet for him. "I see we're good for each other, aye?"

Her wicked grin grew wider. "Absolutely."

With his free hand, he grabbed the condom, ripped the package open with his teeth, and covered himself. While kissing her shoulder blade, he covered her body, his hard planes against her soft curves, pushed her legs apart, and slid inside her from behind. Their last session of lovemaking had been fast and frenzied. Now, he intended to take his time, to cherish her, to imprint everything about her into his very soul.

Aye, he had one. It had only taken a brazen American lass to remind him.

CB

Joanna stepped out of the taxi in front of her flat. With her head and heart pounding, she glanced in the back seat where Inspector Cameron sat.

"Dinna worry, lassie. You'll be all right. Now make it look like you're angry with Munro. Just think of something daft he's done over the last few days."

She smiled and a bit of tension rolled off her shoulders. "Shouldn't be too hard." Her sexy Scotsman was a good man, but he could definitely be a royal pain in the ass, too.

The inspector shook his head. "No, lass. Look angry. You've got to make this believable. If Ronnie Latham believes you're on your own, he's more likely to come for you."

"Right." After a quick, deep breath, she said, "Here it goes."

She stood up straight and yelled at him as though he was Colin and he'd offended her with some stupid decision. When she finished, she slammed the taxi door as hard as she could and bounded up the stairs to her apartment.

With shaking fingers, she shoved the key in the lock, sprang it free, and slipped inside. She pushed the door closed and rested her forehead on it. "Colin?" she whispered.

"Aye, I'm here." His voice was a soothing balm for her worried heart. Of course, she'd rather have him with her, to wrap his strong arms around her, but his words over an earpiece would have to do for now. "You did a brilliant job."

"I was so scared."

"I know, love."

"Where are you?"

"Close by. I promise."

"I wish you were here."

"I know, but soon enough I will be, and then I'll be able to have my way with you again."

A throat cleared. "You two do know I can hear you, aye?" Cameron said.

Colin answered aye at the same time she said yes.

"And anyways, you shouldn't be talking to each other at all. He's got to think she's completely on her own. If he arrives and she's talking to herself, he might know what we're about."

"Right," she whispered.

"Lass, just know we're with you at all times," the policeman said.

The line went silent.

Joanna closed her eyes, mouthed the words to a childhood prayer, and pushed off the door. As casually as she could, she set her pocketbook down and hung up her coat. Like the men had coached her to do, she circled the apartment and checked the locks on the windows. Cameron had assured her they'd gone through the place before she returned, but for her own peace of mind, she glanced in each closet, under her bed, and behind the shower curtain to make sure she was alone.

With shaking limbs, an elevated heart rate, and knots in her stomach, she grabbed the remote and pretended no one was trying to kill her.

Ѹ

Colin pinched the bridge of his nose and breathed deeply. Being stuffed into the attic room, waiting for a man to attack Joanna, would surely drain the life out of him. Two hours had already passed, and he had a cramp in his calf. So badly he wanted to hear her voice, but he couldn't risk starting a conversation. Every once in a while he would toss her a word of encouragement, but she kept quiet. Cameron also gave them updates of what was happening around the building. Of course, there was no sign of the lad they were after. And truthfully, Colin wasn't sure if that was necessarily a bad thing. Aye, he wanted her safe, but the plan still punched his gut. If the lad did choose tonight to try to kill her, too many things could go wrong.

No, his lass was strong. She could hold her own. With a smile, he risked telling her, "Lass, I hope you've got those blades handy." If she could threaten to cut off Latham's parts, she could protect herself until he could jump down from the attic and finish the job.

Yes, she was quiet and praised the simple things in life, but *she* wasn't simple. No, he'd been right to call her complicated, and if she would let him, he'd love the chance to unravel her puzzles for the rest of his life.

In his stomach, nausea struck. To spend all his remaining years with her? Aye, he loved spending time with her, loved watching her get excited about mulled wine or a Ferris wheel ride, loved claiming her body. But to offer her forever?

Aye, because he loved her.

Bloody hell.

ᚖ

Joanna made herself dinner, washed the dishes, and stared at the television. The local news shared updates of Hogmanay events around the city. She settled on the couch with the lights off and a blanket over her as if she planned to ring in the New Year alone. The sgian dubhs Colin had returned to her this afternoon remained under her pillow, close enough for a quick grasp.

The clock rang with its "Auld Lang Syne" tune.

Joanna jumped. She planted her hand on her chest to calm her heart. With each passing moment, she had less confidence their plan would work.

Thump-thump.

She grasped the back of the couch and twisted to look down the hallway. Had the sound come from one of the other rooms? Every nerve begged her to call out to Colin, but he'd warned her against it. She nibbled her top lip. She could do nothing to give away his presence—even though she wasn't quite sure where he was.

"Easy, lass." His voice soothed her frayed nerves.

"It's only fireworks, people getting ready for midnight," Cameron added.

After another half hour, she got up to get some popcorn, although the thought of eating anything roiled her stomach. Her hands shook as she poured the popcorn into a large bowl.

Gripping the sides of the dish, she closed her eyes and blew out a slow breath. She would be all right. She could handle her part of the job, and Colin had her back.

As she returned to the couch, she tossed a glance toward the door.

Shadows shifted under it and stopped.

She gasped and froze.

"What is it, lass?" Colin asked.

"I think he's here," she said barely above a whisper. Mentally, she gauged the distances—four feet from the couch, twelve from the door.

"Cameron, do you see anything?"

"A couple entered the building a few minutes ago, but no one else."

Her stomach knotted. The door handle twisted. Still, she couldn't move.

A loud commercial drew her attention for a split second.

Her heart rate increased.

The shadows under the door shifted, grew smaller.

Maybe it wasn't him?

The door to her flat burst open and slammed against the wall. The bowl crashed to the floor. All her air rushed out of her lungs as a bulky man dressed in all black charged toward her. He shoved her to the couch. His thick fingers gripped her throat.

"You have been nothing but trouble since the train ride," he hissed into her ear. "But that ends tonight."

No, no, no! Joanna dug her hands under the pillow, grabbed the knives, and plunged one into his arm. Gritting her teeth, she jammed the second one into his thigh.

Chapter Seven

*H*er intruder roared like a lion on fire. A string of swears, some in English and some in what sounded like Gaelic, flew from his mouth.

"Colin!" Joanna scrambled toward the opposite end of the couch.

The man grabbed her ankle and yanked her back toward him.

"Let go!" She kicked and kicked until he no longer pulled. His fingers remained around her calf, but with little pressure.

"You'll let her go, and I'll let you live." The threat was pure steel, but Colin's voice had never sounded so sweet.

The intruder released her, his fingers trailing along her skin like icy sludge.

Joanna flipped over and scooted away. Every inch of her body shook fiercely.

Latham stood in Colin's custody, presumably something poking against his back, while her blades stuck out of his limbs. He pinned her with a vicious glare. Pure hatred oozed off his ratty head.

"Step away from the lass."

The man limped backward until he was at the end of the coffee table. He smiled at her, and his fingers wriggled as if he was getting ready to pick something up.

But there was nothing usable around him. Except—

Her heart stuttered. She lurched toward him. "Colin, the blades!"

In slow motion, Ronnie Latham twisted and shoved one arm in

Colin's face. With his other hand, he pulled the blade from his thigh.

"No!" she screamed.

Colin ducked in time and threw a punch under the man's jaw. The blade soared from his grip. He fell backward and crashed onto her coffee table. Colin stepped on the man's leg injury. The thug hollered and swore some more.

Her man's chest rose and fell with his heavy breaths. "You're done now."

Police officers charged through the doorway with Cameron in the lead. "Bloody hell!"

"It's all right, Inspector. Mr. Latham is ready to go into custody." Colin got off the man's leg. "He'll be needing a trip to the accident and emergency room, though."

As soon as the uniformed officers took Latham into custody, Colin rushed to her and wrapped her in his arms. "Are you all right, lass?"

She set her head on his shoulder and hugged him tight. "I am now. Thank you."

"No, thank you for being brave enough to see justice done even when I doubted you."

Heartbeats thundered against her chest, but she couldn't be sure if they were hers or his. It didn't matter. She was safe and exactly where she wanted to be. Forever.

☙

Joanna stared out the hotel window and sighed. Bright lights and thousands of people flooded the streets of Edinburgh as a few snowflakes drifted toward the ground. She'd purchased a ticket to the party down in the center of it all, but at the moment, she couldn't imagine a better place to be than right where she was.

Behind her, Colin poured two glasses of champagne. Buck naked.

She nipped her bottom lip and smiled. He really was gorgeous, and she was so very lucky to have him in her life.

With no shame whatsoever, he strutted across the room and handed one flute to her.

"Thank you." When she tilted her head toward him, her hair fell forward.

He swept the strands back over her shoulder. "I'll do anything for you. You know that, aye?"

"Those words are so good to hear, but all I need is your love."

"You have it, lass. For as long as you want it." He kissed her temple.

"And you have mine." She brushed her lips across his chin.

Glancing out the window, she gripped the sheet wrapped around her and sighed. In a few more minutes, a new year would begin, one she fully intended to enjoy in every way possible and with the perfect man for her standing by her side.

He wrapped his free arm around her belly and pulled her back against him. "Are you disappointed you're not down there in the crowd?"

"Absolutely not." She grinned. "Besides, there's always next year."

Outside, music erupted, fireworks shot into the sky over Edinburgh Castle, and the crowds cheered.

She shifted out of his hold and turned to face him. "Happy New Year, my love."

"Happy Hogmanay." He leaned down and swept his mouth over hers.

She sipped her champagne, readjusted the sheet slipping from her breasts, and set her glass on the table. "So, I was thinking." She grabbed his glass as well, placing it by hers. "Tomorrow, well, today now, we could go back to my apartment and hang out there."

"I can get to work fixing your door." He tugged lightly on the sheet.

"Oh, I had other plans." She ran her fingernail down the center of his chest.

His eyebrows shot up. "Aye?"

"We've christened pretty much every surface in your hotel room. What do you say we start the New Year off right and begin christening every surface in my place?"

"Your suggestion sounds grand. But...." He grabbed the edge of her sheet and peeled it off her one inch at a time. "We haven't finished in here yet."

"What are you talking about?" She scanned the room, visions of their nights and days of loving flooding her brain. The bed, the chair, the desk, the shower—

He yanked the sheet off her body. On the heels of a yelp, she laughed. "Colin!"

"Hush, lass, and let me have my way with you." He turned her to face the window, moved her right near it, and crowded her backside.

Instantly, her arms shifted to cover her most intimate parts. Heat traveled up her neck even though she knew no one could see into their room from below.

Colin tugged her arms away and settled both against the window. The chill of the winter evening seeped through the glass and into every inch of her.

"Go on and watch your fireworks show. You get what you want, and I'll take what I want."

He wrapped one arm around her midriff and slid his fingers between her legs. He brushed his mouth over her shoulder and gently nipped at her skin. Desire flushed through her. With her hands braced on the window, she eased back against his cock. She needed him inside her now. Again.

He lifted her off the floor, shifted her bottom, and slid his cock inside her. As the fireworks continued, rocketing through the air and high into the night sky, her man had his way with her, and soon, the fireworks outside couldn't hold a candle to the ones bursting in her heart.

Chapter Eight

Colin fidgeted with his tie as he raced up the stairs in the International Protective Network Headquarters. He thought he'd gotten up in plenty of time to make his appointment with the MacLeods, but Joanna had tugged him back to bed and....

Bugger.

He shoved the door open into the waiting area of IPN and immediately halted. Three women stared at him, one behind the front desk, one sitting with a magazine in a chair, and one standing next to the counter.

The one closest to him pursed her lips. "I'd like to keep that door, lad, if you don't mind." Her reddish, chin-length hair framed her face. Though she could be no more than five feet tall, she pierced him with an evil eye sending shivers down *his* back.

"Sorry." He held the handle and gently eased the door closed. Soft music filtered through hidden speakers, and the room smelled like...sugar biscuits?

"Mr. Munro, I presume?" The mean-looking woman approached him with her arms still crossed.

"Aye. I'm sorry I'm a bit late. I...got distracted." *To put it mildly.*

"It's all right. Your instructions were to arrive anytime before ten thirty." She twisted her wrist and pointed to her watch. "And as you see, it's ten twenty-eight."

The other two women in the room snickered and returned to their respective papers.

"I'm Bernadette Langford, head of Human Resources." She held out her hand, and he shook it. "It's so good to finally meet you. Please, follow me."

Much like a lad walking to the head teacher's office, he followed her down the hallway while his stomach knotted. Colin flexed his fingers at his sides. Technically, he'd done nothing wrong.

Well, unless they counted falling in love with the client a problem.

Ms. Langford led him to the conference room he'd used during his last visit. "Please, have a seat." She closed the door behind her and sat where a manila folder lay open, displaying several pictures of Joanna, him, and the newspaper clippings of the professor's death.

She rested her forearms on the table. "Now, first we'd like to thank you for taking the assignment on such short notice. We didn't have any other operatives available, but we were all confident you could handle the job."

"Thank you."

"I don't know if you're aware of all the details, but Mr. Latham and Mr. Stewart have confessed to killing Professor Rawlings."

"Did they say why they did it?"

"Stewart was a student of the professor's who had fallen in with the wrong crowd on campus. The professor was trying to get the lad out of a life of drug use, and Mr. Latham was trying to convince the lad to work for him selling drugs to the new students."

"Such a waste."

"I agree." She sifted through the newspaper clippings before she looked back at Colin. "So, how was the whole experience for you?"

He swallowed back the lump threatening to choke him. *Besides the fact I broke the very first rule of any good bodyguard?* No, those words would remain behind his tongue. "To be honest, it was a bit difficult."

"Oh?" Her eyebrows shot up. "How so?"

"I found it hard to sit back and let the police handle the investigating and the chasing. I realize keeping Joanna, Ms. Grainger, safe was my top priority, but at times I wanted to beat the man responsible for making her hurt."

She pinched her chin and nodded. "I see."

Had he said too much? Did he sound like a vigilante? He drummed his fingers on the chair arm.

"But you were able to stay with Ms. Grainger at all times and see to her safety? That wasn't a problem for you?"

"No, ma'am."

"Please, call me Bennie." She smiled and patted his hand. "Now, was there anything else about the experience you would like to share with me?"

He froze. Did she already know he'd bedded the bonnie lass and branded her as his own? Was she giving him a chance to admit his mistake? Although, loving Joanna was no mistake, but damn.

"No, there's nothing else."

"Well." Once she closed the folder and picked it up, she tapped it on the table. "We here at IPN are very impressed with your work. You appear to be just the type of operative we need. You're focused, determined, dedicated, and you don't let your emotions get in the way of your assignment. Therefore, Mr. Munro...." Standing, she held out her hand. "Welcome to the International Protective Network. I'm pleased to say you are our newest operative."

"Thanks very much." As he shook her hand, his shoulders relaxed, and he sighed. He'd done it. He'd made the team he'd come to Edinburgh to make, and the most important thing to him right now? Getting back to Joanna's flat to share the news with her. Like a giddy lad about to meet his favorite football star, Colin grinned.

"You're to report here next Monday at eight o'clock."

"Thank you, and I'll be on time."

She reached for the door and pulled it open. "Yes, I'm sure Ms. Grainger will see to it."

His stomach dropped like a lead weight.

"Don't look quite so shocked. We know a lot more than you think."

"And yet you still hired me?"

"Yes. We're not heartless, and you are human, and because we don't expect you to fall in love with every client." She gave him a wicked grin of her own and winked. "I don't think Ms. Grainger would allow it anyway."

Still, he didn't move.

With a hearty laugh, she shoved him through the doorway. "Go home, love your lady, and be ready to protect someone else's lady or gentleman next week."

ଔ

Joanna tugged her coat tighter around her as she hiked up the sidewalk toward the restaurant where she and Colin had agreed to meet once he had checked in with the IPN officials. A gust of cold air toyed with her hair, whipping loose strands around her head. Her breath curled up into the air. From somewhere along the road, bagpipe music clashed with the sound of vehicles.

She glanced up the street toward the high-rise that carried Colin's future. Oh, she hoped their union didn't cost him the job he so desperately wanted.

The lobby door flew open, and Colin stepped onto the sidewalk.

Inside, her heart warmed. How lucky she was to have this man in her life. She stopped in front of him. "So? What did they say?"

The grin on his handsome face widened. "I officially start a week from yesterday." A fleeting strand of gold glimmered in his eyes. Joanna beamed. She curled and uncurled her gloved fingers. "You have no idea how much I want to wrap my arms around you and kiss you right now, but I don't want anyone to see."

Colin wrapped his arm around her waist and tugged her to him. "They already know about us."

She slid her hands inside his coat as he leaned his head down and captured her lips with his own. His unique scent tickled her nose, and his tongue swept through her mouth.

"And they still hired you, even after you admitted to seducing the client?"

"Well, you weren't technically a client. Assisting you was a favor to your friend Heather and her lad, Malcolm. And technically I wasn't the one doing the seducing at first."

"What?" She playfully slapped his chest. "Who pushed who up against the elevator wall for that first kiss?"

His laughter rumbled under her fingers. "True enough."

The memory of the hunger rushing through her when he'd taken control of her that day stirred her desire. They had spent countless hours making love and sharing dreams since. How could she want him again so soon?

"So, where do we go from here?" she asked.

He nipped on her bottom lip. "I'd like to take you home and have my way with you, but I think we should have some food to sustain us first." As he chuckled, he brushed her hair off her shoulder.

With one gloved hand, she caressed the back of his head. "I'm serious. Next week you'll start work here in the city, and I'll be prepping for another semester at the university. We won't have that much time to be together."

"We'll make the time. I've only just found you. I'm not about to lose you now."

Butterflies flitted through her belly. "Really?"

"Aye." He kissed her. "I love you, Joanna. I want to make a life with you, however we can."

"I love you, too, my sexy Scotsman." She pressed more kisses on his mouth. "So, what do you say we head to the restaurant and start planning our future together?"

A wicked gleam whirled in his eyes. "I have a better idea." In a flash, he crouched down, and tossed her over his shoulder.

"Ah, Colin!" She laughed and playfully thumped him on the back. "What are you doing?"

He patted her bottom and walked toward the apartment. "I'm taking my lass home."

"What about lunch?"

"Food is overrated."

~ABOUT THE AUTHOR~

Alexa Bourne is a teacher by day and a romantic suspense writer by nights, weekends, and all school holidays. She also teaches online classes for writers throughout the year. She is thrilled to be writing for Decadent Publishing and to have the chance to share her love of Great Britain with readers everywhere.

When she's not concocting sinister plots and steamy love scenes or traveling and exploring new cultures, Alexa spends her time reading, watching brainless TV and thinking about exercising.

She loves to hear from readers. To find her, visit www.alexabourne.com or www.alexabourne.blogspot.com or follow her on Twitter @AlexaBourne.